To Ethel Lynch and Phyllis Lynch, my faithful secretaries,
without whose assistance my books would not
have been made ready for publication.

Lucinda of Perryville

A NOVEL
First Edition

L. Walker Arnold

ARNOLD
PUBLICATIONS
Nicholasville, KY 40356

Lucinda of Perryville

© 1993 By L. Walker Arnold
Published by Arnold Publications

First Edition, October, 1993

Cover Art by Dan W. McMillan

Library of Congress Card Number: 93-072731
ISBN: 0-9629688-3-8

Printed in the United States of America

Arnold Publications
2440 Bethel Road
Nicholasville, KY 40356

Phone (606) 858-3538

Chapter 1

*O*n Sunday morning, April 14, 1861, Lucinda Perry and her younger brother, David, were the only members of their family to attend worship service at Bethel Church. She could have ridden the family mare, Katy, to church, and he could have ridden his own black mare, Charcoal, but they had chosen to walk to church this morning. As a consequence, they arrived at church after the service had started. When they entered, David went to sit by his sweetheart, Verna Taylor, and Lucinda took her usual place in a pew with some other unattached young ladies.

As Lucinda sat down she noticed that they were unusually subdued. She glanced around at the older people and saw that they appeared rather grim. Greatly puzzled she gave attention to the singing of the choir and noticed that most of the choir members were not singing, and some of them were openly weeping. Only when the pastor, Rev. John Western, arose to preach did she learn the reason for the strange behavior of the congregation.

"People, the war has started," he announced, and he opened the large pulpit Bible with such force that the hardcover thumped on the pulpit.

During the rest of the service he talked more about the start of the war than he did about the gospel. In a rambling talk, he did his best not to take sides or to lay blame, though he did say it was reported that the South had fired the first shot.

The older people listened in worried silence, and the younger people listened quietly, appearing scarcely to believe that the war had started. Yet they were tense and worried.

When the service ended, Lucinda arose, white-faced and anxious, and left the church with the other young people. Outside she asked how Brother Western had learned that the war had started. A half-dozen eager, young voices answered her question. She turned then, as if to go, but she lingered, waiting for David and Verna to come from the church.

"I'll see you all later," she told her friends when David and Verna came out. Then, knowing that David would walk Verna home, she hurried down the steps and across the churchyard to the Mackville Pike and started running toward home. When she reached the lane that led to the farmhouse where she lived with her parents and her two brothers, she paused momentarily for breath, then hurried on. She was now facing the cold April wind, and it cut through her thin spring coat, chilling her to the bone. The wind brought tears to her eyes, but she kept on running, for she could not wait to get home and tell her family what had happened.

In minutes she came in sight of the large two-story farmhouse where she lived. The long front porch and large, white columns that reached to the high balcony that ran the length of the porch made the house appear massive, but she only thought of it as home.

When she reached the front gate, she swung it open and raced on without closing it. She ran across the big front yard, puffed up the front steps, bounded across the porch, pushed open the front door and stumbled into the house.

"Mama!—Papa!—The—war has—started!" she shouted.

"Shut the door, Cindy. That cold wind will freeze us all to death," her mother called as she hurried toward the dining room with a platter of fried ham in her hand.

"Where'd you get that idea, Cindy?" her father asked, rising from his chair in the parlor by the fireplace where a few embers were smoldering on the hearth.

"At church, that's where. That's all Brother Western talked about this morning. He didn't even preach a regular sermon."

"That's all people have been talking about for months," countered her older brother, Tad. "What makes the preacher think the war has started?"

"It come out in the *Louisville Journal*, that's what. A man who come from Perryville this morning told Brother Western that he saw it in the paper."

"Just more talk," Tad insisted.

"Just you wait, Tad. David will be here before long, and he'll tell you that he heard the news same as I did."

"When was this war supposed to have started?" Tad taunted to tease her.

"Last Friday, that's when. The preacher said that last Friday Southern troops fired on some place in South Carolina. . . . Fort Sumter, he called it."

"It's hard to believe," her mother commented as if in a dream.

"If the war really has started, this will go down as the darkest year in the history of our country," her father said solemnly.

"If the war has started, I reckon I'll have to enlist," Tad said. "Kentucky is a neutral state, but it's in the South; and them Yankees ain't got no cause to come down here and tell us how to run our business."

"Tad, don't say you're going to enlist. I don't want you or David either one in the war," Mrs. Perry reproved sharply.

"Trouble is, Tad, if I know you and David, you'll be

fightin' on different sides. . . . you for the South and him for the North. Like as not you'll be shootin' at each other before the war's over," his father told him.

"I'd sure join up if I was a man," Lucinda asserted, smiling perversely.

"Then it's a good thing you're not a man," her mother scolded.

"Which side would you join up for, Cindy?" Tad teased.

"Oh, I don't know. I reckon I'd just wait and see which side was winning, then I'd join up with that side."

"I reckon you wouldn't. You'd join with the South, same as I would," Tad said, looking at her closely.

"Dinner's on the table, and David ain't here. Didn't he start home when you did, Cindy?" her mother asked.

"Mama, you know he had to walk that Verna Taylor home from church before he'd come."

"Then the rest of you come on before dinner gets cold."

"I'm ready to eat, Nancy," Lewis Perry said, looking at his wife. "I worked up an appetite this mornin', gettin' them stray calves back in the pasture and mendin' the fence."

"Then you herd the strays in this family to the dinner table, Lewis. They'll stand there talking half the afternoon if you don't," she told her husband.

"Come on, younguns, let's eat. David can catch up when he gets here," Lewis said to Lucinda and Tad, and with his long arms he motioned them into the big dining room.

"Is there anything I can do, Mama?" Lucinda asked.

"You can pour the coffee. I've got everything else on the table."

"All right, Mama." Lucinda started skipping to the kitchen, humming to herself as if she had forgotten the war.

"That girl! I don't know where she gets all her energy," her mother exclaimed, shaking her head.

"She's been like that ever since the day she was born," Lewis Perry declared.

"I know this much, she ain't been still since she learned to walk," her mother agreed.

"And she ain't never stopped talking since she said her first word," Tad put in.

"Are you all talking about me?" Lucinda asked as she came skipping back with the coffeepot.

"Slow down, Cindy. You'll scald somebody with that hot coffee," Tad cautioned.

"I thought I'd freeze on the way to church this morning," Lucinda said as she started pouring the coffee. "Walking out the lane and up the pike to the church, the wind nearly cut me in two."

"Didn't you get cold on the way home?" Tad asked.

"A little bit, but I was too excited about the war to care. Besides I ran all the way."

At that moment the front door opened and David came in and paused to remove his coat. "Did Lucinda tell you all about the war?" he asked as he entered the dining room.

"You know she did, David. That redhead ain't never kept nothin' to herself in her whole life," Tad answered, turning to his brother and pulling back a chair for him.

"My hair's not red; it's gold," Lucinda countered, turning her blue eyes on her brother in mock anger.

"It's the reddest gold I've ever seen," Tad bantered.

Lucinda made a face at him, then started pouring coffee for David.

"I declare, I never get used to David being taller than Tad. I notice it every time I see them standing together," Nancy commented.

"He growed a lot while he was up East last year going to school," Lucinda observed.

"I wonder how come you're so small when both of your brothers are such big strappin' men. I declare you're not a smidgen over five feet tall," Lewis said, looking Lucinda up and down.

"I am too, Papa. I'm five feet and two inches tall—in my stocking feet."

"Cindy's small and dainty like a girl should be," Nancy defended.

"I reckon I won't be going back to medical school this fall since the war's started," David said, changing the subject.

"If you enlist, maybe you can get in the medical corps. The training you've already had ought to make you of some help," Lewis suggested.

"I hope I can. The medical corps would give me a lot of experience."

"Let's forget the war, so we can enjoy our dinner. Papa, will you say grace?" Nancy asked, turning to her husband.

Lewis Perry bowed his head and prayed briefly, almost inaudible. "Pass the biscuits," he said aloud when he ended his prayer.

"I worked hard on this dinner while Lewis and Tad were working outside and Cindy and David were gone to church. Now I want all of you to forget this war talk and eat," Nancy said firmly.

"All right, Mama, but I just want to say this first. I don't see why . . ."

"Lucinda, you heard your mama," Lewis cut in with a voice that sounded like a rasp.

Lucinda looked hurt. Her lower lip almost dropped in a pout, but she shrugged and started eating.

"I like having my family around the table for Sunday dinner. Sunday dinner never did seem right while David was away at school," Nancy mused as if talking to herself.

"The rest of us were here, Mama," Lucinda reminded her.

"We sure were, Mama," Tad said, looking up from his plate.

"I know, but I don't like it when any one of you is away. The Sunday you and Lucinda and David ate dinner with the Taylors, I was so lonesome I couldn't enjoy what I'd cooked."

"I reckon we'd better enjoy eatin' together while we can. 'Cause, with this war, the boys will soon both be gone," Lewis said, forgetting his wife's request that they not talk about the war.

"Papa, you've upset Mama," Lucinda said as her mother pushed back her plate.

"It's all right, Cindy. I'm not hungry anyway," Nancy said as she got up and started to the kitchen.

Lucinda watched her go, then left the table and followed her. She found her standing by the back window, looking out across the field Papa had plowed last week for a corn patch. Lucinda saw tears in her mother's eyes, and she went to her and put her arm around her shoulder. "Papa didn't mean to upset you, Mama. Why don't you come back and eat your dinner?" she pleaded.

"Lucinda, I'm not upset with your papa. I just know that what he said is true. We're not all going to be together much longer, and by the time the war's over, we may never all be together again."

"Don't say that, Mama. It ain't like we're not good hardworking, God-fearing people. Surely there won't anything happen to Tad or David."

"I know we're God-fearing and hardworking, Lucinda. God knows I've tried to raise you younguns right, but a musket ball don't know the difference in them that's good and them that ain't."

"We can all pray, Mama."

"I know, but sometimes we have to pay for what we've

done. Your Papa voted for Mr. Lincoln when he run for president because he was born in Kentucky and his wife was from Lexington. I told him at the time that Mr. Lincoln would get us in a war over the slaves."

"The preacher said at church this morning that it ain't the President's fault. He said that Stowe woman, writing that book, *Uncle Tom's Cabin,* is the cause of the war. He said something about her book waking up the conscience of the nation," Lucinda continued.

"Then I wish she had never wrote it. I hate to see colored people in slavery, but I don't want my boys killed over them."

"Some of the men at church were really het up over what the preacher said this morning."

David had been listening from his place at the table, and he got up and started to the kitchen. "There's nothing anybody can do to keep the war from coming," he said as he entered. "Making slaves of human beings is not right, but there's a lot of people who don't understand that. It's going to take war to stop slavery."

"Now, David, you listen here," Tad called irately from the dining room. "Them Yankees ain't got no cause to come down here and tell us how to run our business. I say every state has the right to run its own affairs." His chair scraped the floor as he pushed it back from the table and got up.

Lucinda ran to stop him. "Don't say any more, Tad," she pleaded. "You know how stubborn David can be, and Mama's already upset."

"We ain't got no cause to fight the war in this house before it hardly gets started," Lewis Perry said loud enough for all to hear. He rose from his chair and walked to the kitchen, standing tall and straight.

Lucinda thought her papa always looked two inches taller when he was angry.

They all fell silent as Lewis looked around the room.

He observed them all for a minute, then went to the hall and took his hat and blue denim jacket from the hall tree, where he had left them when he came in to dinner. He put them on and left the house by the front door. His footsteps resounded loudly as he walked the length of the big porch and down the side steps. Lucinda thought his heavy tread sounded almost angry.

"I see Papa going to the barn," Tad said, looking out the side window. "There's probably something that needs doing out there, so I'll go out and help him."

"Tad, tell Papa I'm going over to the Taylors. I told Verna I'd be back after dinner," David called as Tad went out the kitchen door.

"I'm glad you're going," Nancy said, turning to David. "Maybe by the time you come home, you and Tad will both have cooled down."

"Mama, I'll help with the dishes," Lucinda volunteered, and she went to the dining room and started clearing the dirty dishes from the table.

"I wish the Taylors had never moved here from the North. They've not been a good influence on David," Nancy said as Lucinda brought the dirty dishes to the kitchen.

"I wish they hadn't either, Mama. I ain't never understood them, and I can't make myself like Verna."

"I've been wishing David would get over her, but I wonder if he ever will," her mother said as she carried hot water from the back of the stove and poured it in the dishpan.

"When we get through with the dishes, I'm going out to the barn and help Papa and Tad with whatever they're doing," Lucinda announced.

"Lucinda, ain't you never going to grow up and be a lady? Seems like you'd rather do men's work than to work in the house."

"I don't know, Mama. Anyhow, with the war, the

boys will soon be gone, and I reckon me and you will both have to help Papa all we can."

"There you go talking about the war again. I wish we could forget it and that it would just go away."

"I wish it would too, Mama." She put her arm around her mother, and kissed her on the cheek. "I won't stay long at the barn, Mama. Soon as I see that Papa and Tad can finish whatever they're doing without my help, I'll come back and keep you company."

"I wish you would, Cindy. All this war talk has upset me no end."

"I'm sorry, Mama. I really will hurry." She looked thoughtfully at her mother for a long minute. Then she ran up to her room to dress in her outside work clothes.

"I won't be gone long, Mama," she promised again as she came running back down the stairs.

Her mother watched her go out and listened to the door bang behind her. Then she listened to her footsteps as she went down the steps. She wished that she had not gone.

An hour later, as Lucinda was returning to the house, she saw David walking rapidly along the lane toward home. She crossed the yard and waited for him by the front gate, holding her arms crossed tight against her breast to shelter herself from the wind.

"How come you're home so early?" she called when David was in hearing distance. "You had a falling out with Verna or something?"

"Verna and I have broken up," David stated coldly as he reached her.

"David, I didn't think that would ever happen," Lucinda exclaimed.

"It's her family's fault. They're all upset over the war, and they started criticizing Mama and Papa and Tad and you. They said you would all side with the South, and Verna even said she thought I'd turn Rebel. That's when

I walked out."

"They ought to know that you're for the North, David."

They walked a few steps toward the house then paused to talk.

"I am for the Union, Lucinda, but I won't tolerate Verna and her family criticizing my family, no matter which side they're for."

"I'm not sorry you broke up with Verna, but I am sorry you're going to fight for the North, David. I'm sure Tad will be fighting for the other side," Lucinda said soberly.

"I'm sorry it has to be that way, Cindy, but we have to save the Union. It will be the end of the nation if we don't."

"You'll at least wait until you're called up, David?" Lucinda insisted.

"I could wait, but I'm not going to. The Union needs men now. It won't take long to crush the rebellion if there are enough volunteers. Even allowing time to train new recruits, the rebellion will be over in three months."

"David, in three months you and Tad could both be killed. Don't volunteer," Lucinda pleaded, near tears.

"There's nothing you can say that will change my mind, Lucinda. If enough men will volunteer, we may not even have to fight. We can blockade the South so they can't get supplies, and we can simply starve the Rebels into surrender."

While they were talking, Lewis and Tad came from the barn on their way to the house. They were near enough to hear David's last remark.

"I doubt that it will be that easy, David," Lewis countered.

"Them professors up East has put a lot of high sounding ideas in his head, Papa, but they're wrong," Tad said bitterly. "I'm going to join with the South. What do you think of that, brother?" he ended, glaring at David.

"I just hope we never meet on a battlefield," David cried in an angry voice.

"Now both of you calm down," Mr. Perry ordered. "We're not goin' to fight the war here on the farm, and both of you can forget about fightin' on either side, unless you're made to."

Tad and David looked at each other coldly, but neither of them spoke.

"Why don't both of you do what I'm planning to do? Wait and see who's winning, then join that side." Lucinda teased, trying to ease the tension.

David looked at her for a long minute, and the trace of a smile crossed his sensitive face. "I wish it was that simple, Lucinda." He opened the door and went in the house. By the time the rest of them entered he was going up the broad stairway.

"Are you going to church tonight, Nancy?" Lewis asked when the sound of David's footsteps reached his room.

"I didn't go this morning, Lewis, and I hate to miss again tonight, but people will be talking about the war. Like as not the preacher will be preaching about it again, and I don't think I can stand to be reminded of what's happening."

"I don't think I'll go either," Lucinda said. "That stuck-up Verna Taylor will be there, and I don't want to listen to her talk. There's no telling what she'll be saying."

"We may not have much time left to be together, so I'm going to stay home with the rest of you," Tad decided.

"Then, I'll cook us a good supper, and we'll all eat together, if everybody agrees not to mention the war."

"I'm with you on that, Mama, and I'll help you cook," Lucinda offered.

"Me and Tad will go back to the barn and feed and milk early so we can have more time together," Lewis said.

"That's a good idea, Papa," Tad agreed.

A short time later, Lewis and Tad left for the barn, and Lucinda went to the kitchen window and watched them go. She was thinking that soon she and her papa would be doing the chores without the help of Tad and David, for they would be gone to the war.

Chapter 2

*T*he family sat long at the table that night, eating chicken and gravy, hot biscuits with fresh-churned butter, and fruit and vegetables Nancy and Lucinda had canned last summer. From the cellar there were Irish potatoes and sweet potatoes. The Irish potatoes they served mashed and the sweet potatoes they had candied. They talked, teased, and laughed while they were eating, avoiding all mention of the war as Nancy had requested.

David was depressed because of his breakup with Verna, and he had the weight of what he knew he must soon do on his mind. Still he made a gallant effort to be as sociable as the others.

"I made some pumpkin pie," Lucinda announced when they had all eaten until they were stuffed.

"I hope you whipped some cream for toppin'," Tad said.

"Mama did that. She has better luck at whipping cream than I do."

"Then I'll have a big piece of pie."

"The rest of you?" Lucinda asked.

"You know they'll all eat pumpkin pie," Lewis responded.

"I'm stuffed, but I'll have a small piece, Cindy," David answered.

After they had finished eating their pie, they still lingered at the table talking, loathe to end this time together. David was the first to arise.

"If the rest of you will excuse me, I'll go up to my room. I have some things to go through, letters and such from Verna . . . some things I want to return to her."

"You sound like this is final, David," Lucinda observed.

"It is, Cindy. I've found out that Verna and her folks don't respect me or my family, so I'm through with her."

"I'm sorry, David, but I've never been able to get to know that family," Nancy remarked.

"Don't worry, David. A handsome guy like you will find another girl before the week is out," Tad teased.

"Sure you will, David, without any trouble at all. I know some girls at church who would give anything if you'd notice them. I could. . . ."

"Never mind, Cindy. When I need your help, I'll let you know," David cut in as he was leaving.

"I'll see you in the morning, David, if you don't come back down before bedtime," Lewis called after him.

"Sure, Papa. Good night, everybody."

They all called good night to him, but he was already going up the stairs.

"That was a good supper, Nancy," Lewis said, turning to her.

"It sure was, Mama," Tad agreed. "There ain't nobody that can cook like my mama."

"I don't know what to make of all this praise. You men usually don't say anything about the food," Nancy returned, smiling.

"This was a special occasion, Mama, and I'm going to do the dishes for you without being asked," Lucinda declared, and she arose and started clearing the table.

"Thank you for offering, Cindy, but I'll help you," Nancy responded.

Tad stood up and stretched, then followed Lucinda to

the kitchen. "Cindy, I don't know what this family would do without you," he said.

"Now what brought that on, big brother?" she asked, standing on her tiptoes and pretending to look down her nose at him.

"You're so full of life, Cindy, and you cope with things, even when the rest of us can't."

"Well, if that's all you followed me in here for, you just go somewhere out of my way." She made a face at him.

"I know when I'm not wanted, so I'm gone," he growled in mock anger.

She slapped him on the shoulder, and he shook his fist at her. Then he returned to the dining room, looking for his father. Lewis was gone, so he went to the parlor thinking he might be there. When he did not find him there, he went out on the porch and looked about the yard. Then, by the dim light of a crescent moon, he saw him leaning against the poplar tree where they had met and talked so many times since he was a small boy.

He had helped his father set that tree when he was only six, and from that day it had been their tree. They had met beside it to talk so many times through the years.

Lewis was looking across the low, rolling hills to the north as if lost in thought.

"Papa, I didn't know you were out here," Tad said as he joined him.

"I came out to think, Tad. This war really has me worried."

"Me too, Papa. It looks like there would be enough people with brains in this country to work things out without us going to war."

"I was just thinking the same thing, Tad. The Almighty never intended for men to settle their differences this way. This war is the Devil's way of trying to destroy our country."

They fell silent, and the sounds of the cold, April wind sweeping the grass and sighing through the big cedar tree in the corner of the yard reached them. One of the horses whinnied in the barn, and Ol' Jack, one of their mules, hammered on his stall with his front hooves. He was always doing that, but Ol' Beck, the other mule never did. An owl called from the thicket in the valley, and a dog barked from a neighbor's yard beyond the ridge.

"The moonlight sure makes the hills and hollows look pretty. There can't be no place as pretty as Kentucky," Tad observed. "I don't know why David ever went East to school."

"I reckon he thought he could get a better education in New York than he could here. The school up there is supposed to be one of the best in the country for training doctors."

"And now David will be going North to fight for the Union."

"All his life, David's been worried about the slaves, and since he went up East to school he's been worse. He says he wants to save the Union, but I think he wants to see the slaves freed more than anything."

"David has changed, Papa. Since he's come back, I can't even have a conversation with him without it ending in an argument," Tad lamented.

"David has always been different from you and Cindy. I never have understood him, but your mama has. Reckon she's the only one that ever has."

"I know, and she's the only one he'll listen to."

"Verna and her family has been a bad influence on him. Thank God, that's over, but I reckon they broke up too late for David to come to his senses."

"I think you're right, Papa, and I think he'll join the Union Army soon as he can."

"And you'll join with the South."

"Not right away, Papa. Kentucky is a neutral state so far, so I'm going to wait and see how things work out. I may not even be needed."

"David thinks the South won't put up much of a fight."

"David is wrong, Papa. I believe the South will win the war."

"I've been hopin' the North and the South would work things out."

"Papa, they never have been able to agree over this slavery thing, and they won't now. The whole country is going to be tore apart by this war, and, when it's over, I think there'll be two countries, and I don't know which one Kentucky will be in."

"I think I'll go up and have a talk with David. I know I can't talk him out of joinin' the Union Army, but I want him to know that we all love him no matter what happens."

"Tell him for me that, even though he's going to fight for the North, he's still my brother."

Tad stayed where he was after his father had gone in, looking across the valley to the strip of woodland on the next ridge. The trees had put out the early leaves of spring, and they looked silver in the moonlight. The wind chilled his cheeks and bit through his light jacket. He drew it tighter around him, thinking that he ought to go in. The front door opened behind him, and he turned and saw Lucinda standing in the doorway, silhouetted against the light of the room behind her.

"Cindy, you almost spooked me," he said.

"That's not true, Tad. I know you ain't afraid of no living thing on this earth." She closed the door and stood with her arms across her breast, hugging herself against the cold.

"You're the one that ain't afraid of nothin'," he said.

"I reckon I ain't, but I've been thinking."

"Thinking what, Cindy?"

"I'm glad I don't have a sweetheart."

"What about Nathan Wills? Ain't he your sweetheart?"

"You know he ain't. That was just kid stuff. I sort of got to like him that summer when he visited his cousin Susie Jones and her folks on their farm. We never did any more than grin at each other. He was only ten, and I was just nine. I ain't seen him since that summer."

"You did write to each other for a time," he persisted.

"Unhuh. We still do, but it ain't never been serious."

"Then I agree that you don't have a sweetheart, Cindy, and I know that you ain't never cared about a boy in your whole life."

"That doesn't mean that I haven't thought about boys. I have as much right to dream as any other girl."

"Then how come you've never had a beau? There's plenty of fellers that would like to have you for a sweetheart."

"The right one hasn't come along, that's all. Of all the boys I know, there's not one I'd waste my time on."

"Then why the talk about you not having a sweetheart?"

"I've just been thinking how hard it's going to be to see you and David go off to war. If I had a sweetheart going, I don't think I could stand it."

"I reckon that might be so."

"I've been thinking about Mama. It's going to be awfully hard on her, with you and David both going off to war. I'm glad Papa is too old to go. It would kill Mama if he had to go."

"I reckon you're right. I hope the war don't last long enough for men Papa's age to be called up for duty."

"Oh, Tad! Do you think that could happen?"

"I don't think it will, Cindy, but it could. Anyway, it's too early to worry about it."

"I reckon you're right, Tad. I'm freezing," she ended,

again hugging herself. "Let's go in and talk with Mama. Papa is upstairs, and Mama is by herself."

"Much as Mama has on her mind, we shouldn't leave her alone any more than we have to. Maybe she won't worry as much if we're around."

He took Lucinda's hand, as he had when they were children, and led her into the house. They found their mother standing by the kitchen window, looking out into the night.

"We came in from outside to be with you, Mama," Lucinda said.

"I'm glad you did. I don't like being alone when it's so dark. I don't mind the kind of dark I see when I look out the window. At least the moon is giving a little light out there. It's the other kind of dark that's bothering me. The night looks bright compared to the darkness I feel."

"I'm sorry, Mama. I shouldn't have left you alone, but I went out looking for Tad."

"Come here, Lucinda," Nancy said, turning half around.

Lucinda went to her mother and put her arm around her shoulder.

"Tad, I want you to come too," Nancy said.

"All right, Mama." He went to the other side of his mother and put his arm around her also. For several minutes they stood, looking out through the window. Nancy was the first to speak.

"Lucinda, you and Lewis will soon be all I have at home," she began. "Tad, I think it will kill me to see you and David go off to war. I love you both, and I want you to know that I'll pray for both of you every day."

"I'll be praying for both of you too, Tad," Lucinda added.

"Mama, I'm not goin' into the army right away. I've already told Papa that I'm goin' to wait and see how things work out."

"You will be going though, Tad . . . sooner or later."

"I reckon you're right, Mama, unless this turns out to be a short war like David thinks it will."

"Oh, Tad, do you think it could be?"

"Mama, much as I hate to say it, I don't think the war will end that soon."

"Then, you will be going, Tad?" Lucinda prodded.

"I reckon I will, though the thought of goin' is killin' me." There were tears in Tad's eyes as he spoke. Nancy and Lucinda saw them, and they both started sobbing.

"I've never seen you cry since you were little, Tad," Lucinda said.

"I cry a lot inside, Cindy." He hugged her and his mother. Then he left them and went back out into the night.

Chapter 3

*T*wo weeks after the outbreak of the war, the day came when David was to leave to enlist in the Federal Army. During those two weeks every member of his family had tried to persuade him to at least delay enlisting until later in the year. But all their pleadings had been in vain, and the dreaded morning came when David was to go to a recruiting station beyond the Ohio River where he would enlist in the Army of the Ohio.

David insisted on getting an early start, for he planned to ride Charcoal far toward Ohio today. So the family arose at an early hour. Nancy and Lucinda started cooking breakfast at once, and Lewis and Tad went to the barn to do the morning chores.

Meanwhile, torn between his love for his family and what he saw as his duty, David remained in his room, fighting back his sadness and packing the few belongings he would take with him in his carpetbag.

Lewis and Tad soon finished at the barn and returned to the house.

"Breakfast is ready," Lucinda said as they entered. "It will be on the table by the time you men wash your hands."

"Everything is peaceful outside this morning," Tad commented, as he started pouring water in the washbasin. "The trees are in full leaf. Early flowers are bloomin', and the robins are chirpin' and hoppin' around in the yard."

"It doesn't seem right for the country to be at war, when spring is bringing new life to everything," Lucinda exclaimed.

"I don't understand why we have to have a war," Nancy said sadly.

"It's over them niggers," Tad said bitterly.

"I heard that, Tad," David lashed out as he entered from the hall where he had just deposited his carpetbag. "I say that's not what the war's about. If the southern radicals have their way, we won't have a country, so we have to fight to save the Union."

"We'll have none of that," Lewis cut in. "Mama and Lucinda have cooked a good breakfast, and I want everything peaceful while we eat."

"Remember how we ate breakfast the day David left for college. We were all so happy and excited that day. Let's pretend he's just going away to school again," Lucinda suggested.

"I will be going to school . . . sort of," David responded. "I ought to learn a lot if I can get in a medical corps."

"I fed Charcoal so she'll be ready for you to saddle and bridle," Tad said as they set down at the table.

"What are you going to do with that mare when you get where you're going?" Lewis asked.

"If I can't get in the medical corps, I'm going to try to get in the cavalry. If I do that I'll need her. If I don't I'll sell her."

"I just can't bear the thought of you being in the army, David," Nancy said in a half sob.

"It's killing me to leave you, Mama. . . . and the rest of you, but I know my duty," David said, looking around the family circle.

"Maybe the war will be over before it hardly gets

started," Lucinda spoke up, breaking the awkward silence that followed.

"We'd better pray so we can eat," Lewis said. Then he bowed his head and prayed briefly in his quiet way.

"You write home every week," Nancy said to David near the end of breakfast, breaking the silence she had maintained while they were eating.

"I will, Mama, and I'll be looking for letters from home every week."

"Papa and Tad are no good at writin' letters, but I'll write real often and keep you up on everything," Lucinda promised.

"I'll write, and I'll pray for you, David," his mother told him.

David turned away to hide his tears.

"I'll go saddle and bridle your mare," Tad offered, and he arose to go.

"Thank you, Tad." David struggled hard to blink back unwanted tears; then he turned away. "I forgot something," he mumbled as he left the table. In a moment his footsteps resounded through the house as he ran upstairs to his room.

"I'm going to wait in the parlor till David comes back down," Lewis said.

"We'll come in a minute and wait with you," Nancy told him.

When David reached his room, he looked down at his bed for a long moment, thinking how many years he had slept there. He recalled how his mother used to kneel with him each night as he said his prayers.

He hadn't prayed much since he started dating Verna Taylor, he realized. Though her folks attended church, they didn't take much stock in praying, and he had come to the place where he didn't either. He would do better in the future, he promised himself as he took a final look around his room.

Verna's picture looked back at him from the dresser, causing a lump to rise in his throat. He wished he hadn't forgotten to put it with the things he'd mailed back to her. He placed it face down in the bottom of his dresser drawer so it would not cause his mother or Lucinda unhappy thoughts when they came to clean his room. At last he picked up his carpetbag and hurried downstairs. Nancy and Lucinda met him in the hallway and walked with him to the parlor where his father was waiting. Nancy was weeping quietly.

"David, I hate to see you fight for the North, but I appreciate a man standin' up for what he believes," Lewis said.

"Papa, this is tearing me apart, but the future of our country is at stake, and I can't live with myself if I fail to do my duty."

"I don't understand your sense of duty, son, but I won't stand in your way."

"I'm afraid I won't never see you again, David," Lucinda sobbed.

"Don't talk like that, Cindy," he said almost savagely. "Of course you'll see me again. This is going to be a short war, so I'll be home sooner than you think."

"I think I'll die if you and Tad ever meet in battle," Nancy sobbed, dabbing at her eyes with her handkerchief.

"You pray that we won't, Mama."

Feeling that he could bear no more, David looked out the front window to see if Tad was coming with his mare. To his relief he saw that he was just riding her up to the front gate.

"I have to go," David said gruffly. "Tad's here with my mare." He shook hands with his father, gave his mother a quick kiss, hugged Lucinda, then started out.

Lucinda clung to his arm and went out with him. White-faced and silent, Nancy took Lewis' arm and they followed David and Lucinda out. When David reached the mare, he paused and turned to his mother. She threw her arms around him, buried her face on his chest, and sobbed uncontrollably.

David set down his carpetbag and put his arms around his mother. "I love you, Mama, and I'll write to you every week," he promised.

"David, when will I ever see you again?" Nancy asked brokenly.

"It won't be long, Mama. I'll be home on leave before I go into action. Besides the war will soon be over."

Lewis finally succeeded in getting Nancy to let go of David. Then David turned to Lucinda and gave her a hug and a quick kiss on the cheek. He shook hands with his father and Tad, then mounted Charcoal. "Good-bye, all of you," he called as he turned the mare and started her galloping along the lane toward Mackville Pike.

Silently they watched him ride out of sight.

"Well, he got the early start he wanted," Lucinda said, breaking the silence.

"Reckon he'll pass through Perryville before the stores are open. Folks won't hardly notice him on the road," Lewis commented.

"Wonder when he'll get to Ohio?" Nancy asked.

"He'll have to spend the night on the way, so I reckon he won't get there before late tomorrow," Lewis calculated.

"So far from home, and that's only the start. I just feel that I'll never see him again," Nancy said sadly.

"Oh, I think this war is going to be the death of us all," Lucinda sobbed, standing apart.

"Thank God, you won't be going away to fight, Cindy," her father said.

"Mama and Papa, let's go in the house," Lucinda said, taking them both by the hands and leading them in as if they were children.

Chapter 4

"*I* sorely miss David," Nancy said as she was leaving for church with Lewis and Lucinda and Tad the next Sunday morning.

"I reckon David will be listening to some chaplain preach today," Lewis suggested, hoping to mollify his wife.

"We should have had a letter from him by now," Lucinda sighed.

"I guess they've been trainin' him and the other recruits pretty hard," Tad suggested.

"I wish there was room for all of us to ride in the buggy," Nancy said as they reached the front gate.

"I'd much rather walk, and I reckon Tad would just as soon walk," Lucinda exclaimed.

"I thought you'd want to walk, Cindy. That's why I didn't saddle and bridle Ol' Joe and Ol' Jack," Tad responded.

"You young people can walk if you want too, Tad, but I'm glad you harnessed the mare to the buggy and brought it out front for me and Lewis," Nancy told him as she was getting in the buggy.

"Unhitch Katy for us, Tad," Lewis said as he also got in the buggy.

Tad unhitched the mare, and, before Lewis could pick up the reins, she started along the lane as if she knew where she was going.

Tad and Lucinda started walking in silence, watching their parents in the buggy. After the buggy turned onto Mackville Pike and went out of sight, they still talked little, for their hearts were too heavy for their usual small talk and banter.

When they came in sight of the church, the mare was already hitched at the rail, and their parents had gone inside. Verna Taylor was standing on the church porch apparently waiting for them to arrive.

"I don't want to see Verna Taylor after what she said to David the last time he went calling on her," Lucinda said to Tad in an undertone.

"Maybe she's changed her tune, since David joined the Union Army," Tad answered softly.

"Well, she'd better."

"Just wait till I join up with the South. I reckon that will change the tune on her fiddle again."

"Hush, Tad. She'll hear you."

"Hello, Lucinda. You too, Tad," Verna greeted. "Have you heard from David?"

"Not yet, Verna. I reckon he ain't had time to write," Lucinda answered.

"I reckon he ain't wrote to you either, Verna, since you and him had a fallin' out," Tad said, looking closely at her.

Verna's face reddened, and she bit her lip to keep back an angry retort. "I'm sorry about that. I see now that I was wrong about David, but I'll bet the rest of you will side with the Rebels," she said caustically.

"Lucinda ain't said which side she's on yet, but, me, I'm a born Southerner, and I reckon I'll die one," Tad said as he and Lucinda reached Verna.

"Tad!" Lucinda scolded, knowing that he was trying to bait Verna.

"I'm sure you will," Verna said coldly. Then she

flounced through the church door and banged it shut behind her.

"You shouldn't have said that, Tad. You've made her
mad, and you know how she and her family can hold a
grudge," Lucinda reproached.

"I ain't courtin' no favor from Verna or her family.
They're Yankees, and I don't want no truck with them. I
say it's a good thing that David broke up with her."

"I'm going to tell Papa on you," she teased. "Come
on, let's go in the church."

They entered the church and parted company. Tad
went to sit with some young men near his age in the back
of the church, and Lucinda went to sit with some young
ladies who were sitting in the pews behind their parents.
Lucinda noticed that her parents had taken their usual
place in the pew beside Jim and Nelly Crabtree and their
daughter. Mary, who always sat beside her mother, smiled
a welcome to Lucinda as she sat down.

A moment later Mrs. Sanders took her place at the
organ, and old Brother Petree came to the rostrum with a
hymnbook in his hand.

"We'll stand and sing the doxology," he announced
in a quiverish, wizened voice.

Mrs. Sanders took time to adjust her hat, put on her
glasses and place the hymnbook on the organ to her satis-
faction. Then her jeweled fingers came down on the keys,
and the organ responded uncertainly. After the opening
refrain Brother Petree led the congregation in singing.

Lucinda started singing with her usual full voice, but
halfway through the first line she noticed that very few
people were singing. Then she noticed that the families
known to be for the South, the Broyles, the Edwards, the
Tates, the Fergersons, the Crabtrees, and her own parents, were on one side of the church. Those known to be
pro-Union, the Wrights, the Fullers, the Andersons, and
the Taylors, were seated on the other side. On both sides

the men were sitting sullenly in their places, not looking at anyone on the other side, but some of the women were glaring at each other across the aisle. Others kept their eyes downcast. Surely this was no way for people to behave at church, Lucinda thought, and she again started singing.

She was one of only a few who participated in the service that morning. Other hymns were announced but few people sang. Announcements were made but few paid attention. The offering was received, but almost everyone ignored the passing of the plate.

Lucinda watched her father put his offering in the plate as usual and was proud of him.

At last Brother Western came to the pulpit and opened the big Bible that lay on the stand.

"I read from the Word of God," he announced in a thunderous but reverent voice. He paused for effect, then he started reading: *The Lord is a very present help in time of trouble.*

He looked up from the Bible and his eyes swept the congregation. "People, we are in a time of trouble," he began. "As all of you well know, our country is involved in a terrible war. Therefore we especially need the present help of The Almighty at this time. Now I'm not taking sides in that which is dividing our country, but people on both sides are going to need the present help that only God can give."

Lucinda glanced around and saw that people on both sides of the church were now glaring angrily at the pastor. Apparently people on both sides were angry because he was not taking sides with either the North or the South. She shrugged and turned her attention again to what the pastor was saying.

"I'm not sure how any of us can long remain neutral in the conflict that has gripped our nation, but neutrality is the official position of the Commonwealth of Kentucky—at least so far. So I feel that I am on solid ground in not taking sides."

People leaned forward to catch what the preacher would say next.

"It is rumored that ministers may be forced to sign an oath of allegiance to the Union or be put in prison."

"They ought to be if they won't sign it . . . the last one of them," Jackson Taylor muttered loud enough for everyone to hear.

Lucinda glanced at the Fullers and the Andersons and saw that they were nodding agreement. Others turned and looked at Mr. Taylor in anger.

"I have always been a good citizen, but my first allegiance is to a heavenly country," the pastor continued as if he had not been interrupted. "As your pastor, I want to serve all the people, regardless of which side they are on. So I have no intention of signing an oath of loyalty for either side. My manner of life for all the years ought to be sufficient recommendation for anybody. My business will continue to be, as it has been in the past, to point people to the God who is a present help in the time of trouble. I—"

"I say, you're not fit to be a preacher if you won't support the Union," Jackson Taylor interrupted, rising to his feet.

Several of the men seated near him shouted, "Amen."

"I say, we don't need no Yankees, like them Taylors, coming down here from the North to tell us how to run our business," a man in the back, whose voice Lucinda did not recognize, shouted angrily.

"I've got something to say," another man shouted.

Lucinda turned and saw a stranger in the back of the church rising to his feet. He was holding a clenched fist above his head.

"I was just passing through and stopped for church, but I say that a preacher who won't stand up for the Union ought to be run out of the country," he shouted angrily.

"Sir, please sit down," the pastor thundered.

"He's got as much right to speak his mind as the rest of us," Mr. Wright, a man who had always been outspoken against slavery, said loudly.

"Thank you, sir," the stranger said, looking around arrogantly. Then he slowly sat down.

"If there is further disorder, I will personally take out a warrant for the arrest of the perpetrators thereof," the pastor growled.

There followed a chorus of "amens" from one side of the church and a loud stamping of feet from the other.

Brother Western looked around uncertainly, but when he spoke his voice was firm. "The congregation is dismissed. We'll have church again when you have learned to behave yourselves in the house of God," he announced, and he closed the big Bible with a thump, stalked from the pulpit, and left by the back door.

Murmured voices, some of approval and some of dissent, filled the void. The stranger arose and left the church, and Jackson Taylor followed him. Outside he engaged the stranger in conversation. Then he called the Wrights, the Fullers, and the Andersons, and they all went across the road and gathered around the man. At once he started talking and gesturing wildly, but he kept his voice low so that others could not hear what he was saying.

The angry voices inside the church slowly subsided, and the rest of the people started leaving. Those who had buggies hastened to them and drove away. Those who had come on horseback went to their horses and left at a gallop. Soon only a few young people remained on the church porch, talking.

Nancy and Lewis spoke briefly with John and Jane Edwards, and Lucinda paused to visit with Mary. When they left the church they saw the men who had gathered across the road.

"Looks like them that's for the North is brewin' up trouble, so we're leavin'. You and Cindy had best hurry on home too," Lewis said to Tad as he hurried Nancy to the buggy.

"Tad and I will see you and Papa at home," Lucinda said to her mother.

"All right, Lucinda, but you and Tad hurry. I don't trust that strange man. There's no telling what he might do."

"I'll take care of Lucinda," Tad promised.

While Tad and Lucinda were talking with Mary and a few other young people, the group of men across the road broke up. Then Verna and her mother, who had been standing apart, joined Mr. Taylor, and they left without a word.

Most of the young people simply ignored them, but Lucinda watched them go. She wished she could reach out to Verna in friendship, but she knew it was not possible. She had never liked the girl, though, before she and David had broken up, she had been friendly with her for David's sake. Now the war had come between them, and there could be no reconciliation until the war was over—if then.

The talk of the remaining young people was subdued, with none of the usual high-spirited talk and laughter. They were troubled, and their hearts were so heavy that all gaiety had gone out of their lives. They soon said their sad good-byes and started home also.

"After all the trouble in church this morning, I wonder if there won't be fighting in our community before the war's over," Nancy said to Lewis as the mare turned on the lane to their house.

"What happened at church is a shame, but I think that's about all the war we'll ever have around here. Kentucky is a neutral state," he responded.

"About as neutral as our pastor, I suppose, and you see how far it got him," Nancy countered.

"I reckon you're right about the pastor. All he did was make enemies."

"Do you think Brother Western may have to go to jail for wanting to stay neutral?" Nancy asked after a moment.

"It wouldn't surprise me if he does. Anything can happen in these times," Lewis responded.

"I'm still afraid there'll be fighting right here in Boyle County."

"There ain't nothin' in this county for men to fight over, Nancy. The war will be fought in big towns where there's navigable streams and railroads."

"Boats come up the Kentucky River, Lewis."

"Yes, Nancy, but, when they do, there ain't nowhere for them to go except back to where they come from. I reckon there could be some fightin' at Frankfort or Louisville," he conceded grudgingly, "but it won't come near us."

They fell silent then, and neither of them spoke until they turned on the lane for home. Then Nancy broke the silence. "Lewis, this war frightens me," she said.

"I don't like it either, Nancy, but there was no way the South could avoid it."

"Lewis, has Tad been talking to you?"

"Tad don't have to talk to me. I know it's wrong for people in the South to have slaves, but the North ain't got no right to tell the South what they can or can't do."

"Lewis, if you had to sign an oath of allegiance to the Union or go to jail, what would you do?"

"Nancy, I don't rightly know."

"I know one thing. I'll be glad when this nightmare is over."

"So will I, Nancy," Lewis responded as he stopped the buggy at the yard gate for Nancy to get out.

When Tad and Lucinda reached home, their father was coming from the barn, after unhitching and feeding Katy.

"I'm going to run up to my room and change so I can help Mama with dinner," Lucinda said as they entered the house.

"And I'll go up and change into my work clothes so I can bring in some water and some wood for the cook stove," Tad returned.

Chapter 5

"I'm worried about Tad," Nancy said to Lewis one morning while he lingered at the breakfast table, drinking a second cup of coffee, after Tad had gone out to the yard. "He's not like himself, and every morning after breakfast he goes out and walks about in the yard, looking like the end of the world has come."

"I reckon he's troubled over the war, but he won't talk about it," Lewis rejoined.

"I think he doesn't want to join the army, but he feels that he's duty bound to do it."

"When he does enlist, it will be for the South."

"I know, and he may be worried that he and David will meet somewhere on a battlefield," Nancy said.

"You may be right," Lewis agreed.

"And part of his trouble may be worrying over the church," Nancy suggested. "Tad won't say much, but you know how he loves the church."

"I reckon the trouble at church upset Tad more than it did the rest of us."

While they talked, Tad continued to walk in the yard, fighting his own battle. The conflict at church had made him aware of how deep the division in the country was. It had also made him realize that the issues that divided the North and the South would only be resolved on the battlefield. And with that realization had come the conviction that this was not going to be a short, easily-won war.

Other young men were hastening to enlist, just as David had, but, unlike many of them, he recoiled at the thought of war. The very thought of having to shoot at other men was abhorrent to him, but slowly and painfully the conviction came that he could not stay out of the conflict.

This morning his walk led him to the backyard, and he looked out across the acres of corn he and his father had planted. It was just beginning to come up and would soon need attention. He thought of the other crops, the wheat, the hemp, the sugar cane, and the garden, to say nothing of the hay they would have to cut and put up. He was glad his father did not raise tobacco. They had enough work to do without it. Caring for what they were growing and for all the livestock entailed a lot of work. That meant that he was needed at home, and the thought of leaving his father and mother and Lucinda to do all the work troubled him. In the meadow, beyond the cornfield, cattle were grazing around the crest of the hill. From that high point, the ground sloped gently to Hope's Creek. He could just see the tops of the tallest trees that rose from the valley where Hope's Creek followed its meandering course. The trees were bowing before the wind, dislodging the black birds that had perched there. They were flying in circles and protesting noisily.

As a boy he had trapped along Hope's Creek and along a smaller stream in the next valley. David had never trapped with him. He had been more interested in reading books, drawing pictures, and practicing the piano. David had taken to music even more than Lucinda, though she had quickly and easily learned to play the piano.

He shrugged, thinking it was strange that he had none of their talent. Maybe he was only meant to be a farmer. That was all right with him. He loved the farm . . . always had. He enjoyed watching a pair of mules plod patiently across the field pulling a turning plow, and he enjoyed watching the black soil turn from the moldboard of the plow. He loved to plant things and see them grow, and, like Papa, he delighted in the livestock they had on the place. It was a pleasure to feed and care for them, and he liked to watch the hogs and the calves grow and to dream of the money they would fetch. He did not want to leave the farm and go off to war, but he was convinced that the freedom of people in the South was at stake.

After he enlisted, it was possible that he would never return home. The thought saddened him, but it did not cause him to waver from what he saw as his duty. His life and the lives of the members of his family would never be the same if the Yankees won the war. He shuttered to think what life would be like under their control.

He had been slow coming to this decision, and, now that it was made, he was worried about the work his family would have to do without his help. Papa could not possibly do all the work, and he could not easily hire the help he would need. Most of the young men were already gone, and the older men who would be left would have more work than they could do.

Perhaps Papa could hire Nigger Henry, the freed slave who owned a little farm adjoining theirs, though he was old, and he had his own little farm to look after. Lucinda would help all she could. She had always worked with him and David and their father. She liked farm work, and she could do more work than David any day. Even Mama would have to help outside after he was gone, though she was not as strong as she used to be. That was an added worry, but there was no help for it.

He walked slowly back to the front yard, still lost in thought. The issue of slavery had never troubled him greatly. His father had never owned a slave, so he had never given much thought to slavery except when David brought it up or when he was reminded that Nigger Henry and his wife, Mandy, had once been slaves. The real issue in this war, as far as he was concerned, was the Yankees trying to force their will on the South.

He paused and looked down the hill to the valley below the barn, and his eyes came to rest on an old, decaying, walnut tree. He recalled shooting a squirrel out of that tree with his papa's musket. It had been a good shot, for he had shot from a distance at a squirrel he could barely see. He had always been a good shot—like Papa.

"I'd make a good soldier, if I had the stomach for it," he said aloud. "Anyway, I have to join the army, so I reckon I may as well go in and tell Mama and Papa and Lucinda that I think the time has come for me to go." He turned on his heel and went resolutely into the house.

"You didn't walk long this morning, Tad," Lucinda observed, looking up from the dishes she was washing.

Lewis looked up from an old newspaper he had started reading, and Nancy turned from the churn she was filling with milk to be churned into butter.

"I've been tryin' to make up my mind what I have to do, and finally I have decided," Tad responded.

Nancy caught a quick breath, and Lewis laid aside his paper and stood up, looking at him.

"You are going off to war!" Lucinda exclaimed.

"I don't want to go, Cindy, but I know that I have to. It's goin' to take every able-bodied man in the South to whip them Yankees, so I've decided that I have to go."

"I knew this was coming, Tad, and I've been trying to reconcile myself to it," Nancy said soberly.

"When are you going, Tad," Lewis asked.

"I think I'll go the first of the week."

"I've been wishin' you'd wait till the crops are laid-by," Lewis said, almost if he were making a request.

"Why don't you at least wait that long?" Nancy insisted.

"If they're goin' to make this a short war, I reckon

they need all the help they can get now," Tad replied.

"I don't see how one man can make that much difference," Lucinda joined in, anxious to keep Tad at home as long as possible.

"All right; I'll wait till the crops are laid-by," Tad agreed at last. "I've been worrying about all the work you all will have to do after I'm gone."

"I appreciate you being willing to wait that long," Lewis said, and he placed his hand affectionately on Tad's shoulder.

In the following weeks hot weather came to Kentucky. The crops grew rank and green, and Lewis and Tad cultivated them. Lucinda, always wearing her big, floppy, straw hat and a cotton work dress, helped in the fields or at harvesting the garden and helping Nancy can and stow what she had canned in the cellar.

Meanwhile rumors were rife in Kentucky of war preparations, of young men enlisting for the Union, and of young men enlisting for the Confederate States. There were rumors of all kinds of atrocities, many of which were later proven to be untrue. Accounts from newspapers were considered more reliable, and usually they were.

In early July word was circulated through Kentucky towns and communities of a Confederate camp, called Camp Boone, that had been formed across the Tennessee line, near Clarksville, and young Kentucky men started going to Tennessee to enlist. Some traveled alone, often on foot or on horseback. Others traveled in groups, often walking and camping out at night. That started Tad thinking again that he should enlist, but he had promised to stay and work until the crops were laid-by.

Surely a few more days would not make that much difference, he thought, trying to reconcile himself to the delay.

By mid-July word was out that twenty-six companies

had formed the 2nd Kentucky Infantry at Camp Boone. That made Tad even more anxious to enlist. A few days after that, the news of the Confederate victory in the Battle of Manassas swept the country. Then more and more Kentuckians left the plow to enlist for one side or the other, but the victory of the Confederates made Tad think that the war would soon be over, and that led him to re-think his decision.

Perhaps he would not be needed in the war after all. If he did enlist, it was possible that the war would be over before he finished his training. On the other hand, if he did not enlist, those who had would look upon him with disdain, and that troubled him. Finally he decided that the time for him to go had come.

He said as much to Lewis as they worked in the field one day, and Lewis agreed that he could go at the beginning of the coming week. The crops would be laid-by then, and the work on the farm would be slack until the beginning of harvest.

Tad was relieved that at last his decision was made and he would go and serve with others who had already enlisted, but it was not to be.

Late that afternoon, as he and Lewis were feeding the stock, a thunderstorm broke above the barn, and rain poured upon the tin roof, roaring like an avalanche. Thunder rumbled across the heavens, and lightning danced across the sky. Then a sudden flash of lightning illuminated the dim interior of the barn, and a loud clap of thunder sounded as if it were crashing through the roof. Ol' Joe, startled by the flash of lightning and the sound of the thunder, loped through his open stall door and knocked Lewis over the tongue of a plow that had been parked in the barn.

"Papa, are you all right?" Tad called anxiously when he saw Lewis sprawled on the ground with his legs on the tongue of the plow.

"My leg is hurting, and I'm sure I broke it," Lewis replied calmly.

Tad ran to his father and soon determined that indeed his leg was broken.

"It's broke all right. You just lay there. Don't try to move while I go get Mama and Lucinda to come and help me get you to the house. Then I'll ride to Perryville and get Dr. Montgomery to come and set your leg," Tad told him.

"Never mind going for Nancy and Cindy, Tad. Help me get up on my good leg, and I'll use you for a crutch and hobble to the house," Lewis insisted.

"Are you sure you can do that, Papa?"

"You ain't never seen me helpless have you? My leg has started hurting something fierce, but, with your help, I'll make it to the house."

It wasn't easy, but Tad finally got Lewis up on his good leg. He put his arm around his waist. Lewis put his arm across Tad's shoulder, and they started slowly and painfully to the house.

"Mama, Papa's hurt, and Tad's helping him to the house!" Lucinda cried when she chanced to look out the window and see them coming.

Before her mother could answer, she was out the door and running to meet them. "What happened?" she cried when she was within hearing distance.

"Ol' Joe knocked Papa over a plow and broke his leg. Cindy, you get on the other side and help me get him to the house."

Just then Nancy reached them. "How bad are you hurt, Lewis?" she asked, searching his face.

"Broke my leg is all, Nancy."

"Oh, Lewis, does it hurt bad?"

"Bad enough, but I can bear it."

"After we get him to the house, I'll go for the doctor," Tad said.

"Lucky I wasn't hurt worse," Lewis said, trying to keep Nancy from worrying.

"You sure you don't want me to help you get in bed before I go after the doctor?" Tad asked after they got Lewis in the house and seated in an overstuffed chair in the parlor.

"No, you go on. I'll be all right," Lewis told him as Nancy and Lucinda carefully placed a stool under the broken leg.

"I'm glad we got the crops laid-by. I reckon that, even with my broke leg, I'll be able to help Nancy and Cindy do what has to be done, once Dr. Montgomery gets it set," Lewis looked up to say to Tad as he was leaving.

Tad paused only a moment. "Don't worry about that, Papa. I'll not enlist in the army until your leg is mended." He left to go for the doctor without waiting for Lewis to reply.

The first of September, Dr. Montgomery removed the splints from Lewis' leg and told him that he would soon regain full use of it. That day Tad started getting ready for his long delayed departure to enlist in the army.

He would travel light, taking only what he could carry in a carpetbag. Some young men, going into the army, carried the family gun with them, but he would leave the musket for Papa to use. He might want to go hunting someday. Surely the army could furnish him a weapon. After Tad was packed and ready, he still delayed some days, dreading to tear himself from his family.

Then, when he read in the *Louisville Journal* that General Buckner had taken Bowling Green and that recruits were rushing to join him, he finally decided that the time had come for him to go.

"I'll leave Monday," he said after reading the article. "It says here that men from all over the Bluegrass are going to Bowling Green to enlist, so I'll go too."

"We'll take you to Perryville, and you can catch the stagecoach to Bowling Green," Nancy said.

"I'll go along to help see you off, Tad, but if I was a man, I'd be going with you," Lucinda told him.

"Then it's a good thing you're not a man, Lucinda. Somebody has to stay and help Mama and Papa with the work."

"I'll do that, Tad. Remember, I learned to work outside when I was a little kid."

"Tad, I'm going to cook you a good dinner today. It may be the last home-cooked meal you get for a long time," Nancy told him.

"I appreciate that, Mama. I'd like fried chicken and gravy, and I'd like one of your blackberry pies, if you have some canned blackberries left in the cellar."

"Ain't the chickens a mite big for fryin'?" Lewis asked.

"Papa, remember that old hen that set out in the weeds and hatched off that late bunch of little chickens? They've growed big enough to fry. I saw a young rooster yesterday that's just the right size," Lucinda declared.

"And I do have some blackberries left," Nancy answered, smiling. "I saw them when I went to the cellar one day last week."

"Papa, do you have any work for me to do before I leave?" Tad asked.

"No, Tad. We finished the chores before breakfast, and I'm going to take the rest of the day off and spend it with you."

"I'm glad, Papa. After dinner, if it's all right with you, I'd like for us to walk over the farm. I want to see everything one more time before I leave."

"Sure, Tad. I'd like to walk over the farm myself. I ain't seen all of it since I broke my leg."

"I'll go too, Tad, if you don't mind," Lucinda cried excitedly.

"Sure, Cindy. I'll be glad to have you, but that will leave Mama alone."

"I'll come along too, if you promise not to walk too fast," Nancy responded.

"Now that we have that settled, I'll help you with dinner, Mama," Lucinda offered.

"Then you go out and show Tad that chicken you saw so he can catch it. And, Tad, you bring in a load of wood while you are outside."

"I will, Mama. I never thought the day would come when I would enjoy carrying wood for the cook stove."

The morning passed with the family visiting and working together. Soon the big kitchen was filled with the aroma of cooking food, making them grow hungry before the food was ready.

When everything was cooked to its delicious best and had been put on the dining table, they all sat down to eat. Their enjoyment was mingled with sadness, but they ate and talked, savoring every fleeting minute they had together.

"Cindy, we'll leave the dishes, so Tad and your papa won't have to wait on us," Nancy said as they finished eating.

"I'm glad, Mama, 'cause I'm anxious to get started," Tad said.

"I'll be ready in a minute. I just have to get my big straw hat to keep the sun off my face. I always have been bad to freckle," Lucinda said as she arose to go to her room.

"Bring my hat too, Cindy," her mother called after her.

In minutes they all left the house and crossed the yard to the side gate.

"Let's go through the barn first," Lewis suggested.

They reached the barn, and Tad lifted the latch and opened the door. "Remember how David and I used to play marbles in the driveway?" he asked, turning to Lucinda.

"Yes, and I remember how you used to make me sweep the dirt and the straw out of the way so you would have a clean place to play. Then you wouldn't let me play till David got tired and went to the house."

"You were a better marble shot than me or David either one, that's why," he reminded her.

"Look at the pigeons up in the eaves, Tad. Remember how you used to climb up and get the young pigeons out of the nest just before they were big enough to fly?" Nancy asked.

"And I'd dress them so you could fry them for me," Tad reminisced.

"All except the one I would beg you into letting me keep for a pet," Lucinda reminded him.

"Those shoats are going to be butchering size, come November, and you won't be here to help, Tad," Lewis said as they paused by the pigpen.

"Don't keep reminding me of all the work we'll have to do," Nancy pleaded.

They passed through the barn and went out into the sunlight again. Then they walked to the top of the hill in the meadow.

"We can almost see the whole farm from here, because this is the highest spot on the highest hill," Lewis said.

"I never noticed that before. I suppose it's because I hardly ever come up here," Nancy said.

"I can see the cattle in the back field, all except the ones that are down by the creek," Tad commented.

"Want to go back there?" Lewis asked.

"If it's not too far for Mama and Cindy to walk."

"You know it's not too far for me, brother," Lucinda reminded him.

"I'd like the walk, if we don't go too fast," Nancy

said.

As they started down the hill, a field lark rose from the grass and flew away, singing its plaintive notes. A bit farther on, a rabbit jumped from a clump of tall grass and raced away, curving around the sloping ground below them. From the top of a dead locust tree, a woodpecker hammered, trying to make a hole in the hard wood. In the clover blossoms at their feet, bees were gathering honey. Grasshoppers were springing from the grass and flying a few feet and landing in another hiding place.

"Everything is so alive and so beautiful," Nancy exclaimed.

"After I'm gone, I'll remember everything we've seen and everything we've said on this walk," Tad commented as they continued down the hill toward the creek.

"I looked back this way from the yard this morning and remembered how I used to trap along the creek in the wintertime," Tad remarked.

"And I remember how upset we all were the day you came back from your trap line smelling like a skunk," Lucinda reminded him.

"So do I. The teacher sent me home from school that day."

They reached the creek and stood by a deep pool watching minnows dart in the sunlight with their sides flashing golden glints of light.

"The farm is so peaceful and so beautiful, I wish I didn't have to leave," Tad said sadly, still watching the minnows.

"So do I, Tad," Lewis agreed.

"I'll pray every day that the war will soon end so you and David can both come home, Tad," Nancy promised.

"You do that, Mama, and I'll be prayin' too," Tad said as they turned and started back to the house.

Chapter 6

After Tad had gone off to war, Lewis and Nancy and Lucinda carried on as best they could, though the work was hard, the hours long, and their hearts heavy.

Each morning they got out of bed before dawn and dressed for the day. Then Lucinda and Lewis went to the barn to feed and milk while Nancy cooked breakfast. When they had finished the chores, Lewis and Lucinda returned to the house, and they all sat down together for breakfast. Then Lewis prayed over the food, always including David and Tad in his prayer.

They talked little while they ate and they ate of necessity, hardly tasting the food, for their minds were on the war and on the work they must do today without the aid of either of the boys. Besides, they were worried about the division in their community, and in their church, and they were worried about the dangers they knew Tad and David were constantly facing.

Each day they hoped for letters from the boys, and they were always relieved when a letter came from either of them. They were especially pleased when they received letters from both of them. For a time they were less worried. On days when no letters came, they were disappointed and not a little worried.

One night in mid-October, Lewis and Nancy and Lucinda went to the parlor after supper and sat down to talk as they often did. As they talked, the light from the lamp on the mantle fell on Lewis's face, accenting every line. With a shock, Lucinda realized that she had never seen her father look so tired or so old.

Papa is really not that old, she thought. She looked at her mother, wondering if she looked as old and tired as her father did. The light was on the side of her mother's face, and it revealed that she was pale and that she looked very sad. She doesn't look like she will ever smile again, Lucinda thought sadly. I must do more to help both of them.

"I'm glad the war has not come near us," Lucinda said, trying to cheer them.

"We can't say that anymore," Lewis commented. "There is fightin' in Kentucky now."

"And it's too close for me," Nancy sighed. "I haven't slept easy since General Buckner took Bowling Green."

"That's one thing that really put a bee in Tad's bonnet to join up," Lewis commented.

"I wish he'd write again. I'd like to know for sure where he is," Nancy said.

"So would I," Lucinda agreed. Then, still trying to console her parents, she added, "I'm glad there's no troops closer than the ones at Bowling Green."

"That may not always be true, Lucinda. I read in the paper the other day that General Grant has brought the Army of the Ohio to Paducah, and he hopes to gain control of all of Kentucky," Lewis answered.

"Papa, you've always said there's nothing in Kentucky to fight over," Lucinda reminded him.

"I've done a heap of readin' lately, Cindy, and I've learned that General Grant wants control of the rivers. Whoever controls Kentucky will control the Kentucky River, the Ohio River, and part of the Mississippi. Besides, the North wants to move their armies through Kentucky on their way south."

"But, Papa, surely there won't be any battles fought near here," Lucinda insisted.

"I hope not."

"I wish the North would leave Kentucky alone," Nancy said distraughtly.

"I still believe what Papa said in the beginning. I don't think there's much in Kentucky for the Yankees to fight over. It ain't like we had as many slaves as they do in the South," Lucinda elucidated.

"I hope you're right, Cindy, though I don't think you are," Lewis said.

"Lewis, I'm going to bed," Nancy announced. "I'm tired, and all this talk of war is making me nervous." She arose to go as she was speaking.

"I'm ready to go too," Lewis responded.

"You all go ahead. I'm going to read a few minutes before I come up to bed," Lucinda told them, and she went to the bookcase to select a book. She returned and settled down to read, but she could not become interested in what she was reading, so she soon laid the book aside and also went upstairs to her bed.

"We ain't heard from either of the boys lately," Nancy said to Lucinda as she came in from the barn a few mornings later.

"Tad is probably still in training, and David said in his last letter that he is in General McCook's III Corps, and he thought they would soon be on their way to Louisville. So both of them must be all right," Lucinda consoled.

"It still worries me that David and Tad may someday meet in battle."

"You ought to be glad that the fighting in West Kentucky is over, and that there's not been any fighting where David is," Lucinda reminded her.

"I know, Cindy, but I still worry. I can't sleep at night

for worrying."

"We'll have to do a lot of praying and trusting, Mama."

"I know, Lucinda, but my faith is weak, especially since we stopped going to church because of the hard feelings between the members."

"I know, Mama. When I went last Sunday, I could tell that the church is really divided. People on both sides were cold to me. I suppose David enlisting for the North made the people who are for the South mad, and Tad enlisting for the South made the others mad."

"I reckon the Petrees is the only ones that can understand. They've got two grandsons enlisted in the Union Army and two more enlisted with the South."

"They've stopped going to church too, Mama. I heard that some of the men went to Mr. Petree and told him they didn't want him leading the singing any more, so the whole family has stopped going."

Just then Lewis came in. "Is breakfast ready?" he asked. "I want to hurry and eat. After breakfast I'm going to drive the calves to the back pasture. The grass is gettin' short in the field where we've been keeping them."

"Breakfast is ready, all but putting it on the table," Nancy answered.

"I'll help you drive the calves, Papa, soon as I help Mama clean the kitchen," Lucinda volunteered.

"I'll do the kitchen so you can go on and help your papa," her mother responded as she put the eggs on the platter with the ham she had fried.

"I'll pour the coffee, Mama," Lucinda offered, but she did not skip to the task as she had in the past. She smiled ruefully, remembering how happy and how full of energy she used to be. Surely she was not becoming an old woman before her time.

"Lewis will you take time to read from the Bible and pray before we eat?" Nancy implored. "Seems like we don't get any spiritual help since we've stopped attending church."

"I'll get the Bible, Mama," Lucinda offered. She arose and went to the parlor and got the Bible from the library table and returned and handed it to Lewis.

"Since we've not been goin' to church I've been readin' the Bible some at night, after your mama has gone to bed," Lewis said as he took the Bible from her hand. "The country is in such a mess that we need strength from somewhere." He started turning the pages of the Bible.

"Here's what I was huntin'. I read this last night, and it seemed to help me. It's in the book of Habakkuk. *But the Lord is in his holy temple: let all the earth keep silence before him.* In the next chapter it says, *O Lord, I have heard thy speech, and was afraid: O Lord, revive thy work in the midst of the years, in the midst of the years make known; in wrath remember mercy.*" He closed the Bible and laid it aside.

"Seems like to me that we need the revival the prophet was praying for," Nancy commented.

"Christian people on both sides ought to pray for God's mercy on our poor, sufferin' nation," Lewis said.

Tears were stinging Lucinda's eyes as she looked at her father. She had never known him to be much interested in praying and reading the Bible before. She looked at her mother and saw that there were tears in her eyes also. She watched her father bow his head. Then she bowed her head also, but she did not pray. Instead she listened to him as he prayed. He almost broke down as he prayed for David and Tad, but he soon recovered and continued his prayer, praying that the war would soon end and that people would get right with God.

They were all subdued when the prayer ended, and they ate their breakfast almost in silence.

Lucinda was the first to arise when they finished eating. "Mama, I'll help you with the dishes until Papa is ready to go after the calves," she said as she started picking up the dishes and silverware from the table.

"I'll go let the stock out while you help your mama, Cindy. Then I'll come by for you," Lewis told her as he arose to go.

In the coming weeks Lucinda and her mother harvested the remainder of the garden and brought in the pumpkins they had raised in the cornfield. They did their chores, and kept up on the news, and wrote daily letters to the boys. During the fall harvest they worked from sunrise until dark, then fed and milked by lantern light. After a late supper each night, Lewis and Nancy fell into bed exhausted. Even Lucinda went to bed earlier than usual.

In due time they picked the corn and put it in the crib. Near the end of October, they made molasses. Jim Crabtree and his boys, John and Ned, who were both too young to go to war, came over to help.

Lucinda and Nancy both went out to help. Lewis and the Crabtrees made a pit and put the sorghum box over it. They cut the cane and stripped the leaves from the stalks. Then they hitched the mules to the tongue of the sorghum mill and started them going round and round, turning the mill. They fed the stalks through the mill and caught the green juice the mill pressed from them in a bucket. They poured the juice in the sorghum box and built a fire under it. Smoke poured from the hole at the other end of the box, and the fire roared and crackled.

The mules continued to walk round and round. The mill kept turning, and juice continued to pour into the bucket. Each time it was filled, one of the boys emptied it into the sorghum box. The smell of cooking molasses soon mingled with the smell of wood smoke, filling the air with a heavy, smoky sweetness.

Before the war, the day they made sorghum had been a hilarious one. Neighbors had come to help, and in the afternoons, after most of the work was done, they had stayed to visit and to enjoy the stir-off. While they visited, they carved small paddles from scraps of lumber, and, when the molasses had almost finished cooking, they used the paddles to scrape away some of the delicious foam that collected along the edges of the box. Then they sat down to lick the foam from the paddles. But this year no one came to the stir-off.

"This is the saddest stir-off I've ever seen," Lucinda said when the molasses was nearly finished and the sun was going down.

"Maybe by next year the war will be over, and just maybe people will get over their hard feelings and come back," Nancy suggested.

"I doubt that they will, Nancy. The hurt runs too deep for that," Lewis told her. Then he turned away and started dipping the molasses from the box and ladling it into jars to be stored in the cellar.

"Oh, I see someone coming," Lucinda cried, shading her eyes against the setting sun. "It's Mary Crabtree, and she's so grown-up, I hardly knew her."

"She was a pretty little girl, and now she's growing into a beautiful woman," her mother responded.

Lucinda glanced and saw that Mary's father and brothers were not near enough to hear. "Mary would be a good sweetheart for Tad," Lucinda suggested.

"Cindy, you know that Tad has never taken a fancy to any girl."

"I know, but by the time he comes home from the war he might, and Mary just might be the one he'll take a liking to."

"Oh, Mary, I'm glad you've come," Lucinda called to the girl, for she was now too near for them to continue to speculate about her future.

"I couldn't miss the stir-off. Besides I was dying to see you and your mother," Mary returned as she joined them.

"See, I brought my paddle." Mary went to the molasses box and started scraping the sticky foam from the edge.

"Just a minute, and I'll get a paddle and join you," Lucinda laughed.

As the sun was going down, the work was finally finished, and, in the gathering twilight, the Crabtrees unhitched the mules from the tongue of the mill.

"Take them to the barn and unharness them. Then put them in the stall. I'll feed them later," Lewis instructed.

"You go ahead and feed them, Papa. Mama and I will carry the molasses and put it in the cellar," Lucinda offered.

"Leave the five gallon can for the Crabtrees," Lewis called.

"John, you stay and help the women," Mr. Crabtree said to his oldest son.

"All right, Pa," John said. He shrugged, looked at Lucinda and smiled. "I didn't want to help with the mules nohow," he said, and he picked up the largest container of molasses and walked beside Lucinda as she carried two of the smaller containers to the cellar.

"I'll help," Mary volunteered as she picked the one remaining jar and started carrying it toward the cellar.

Chapter 7

*E*arly in December newspapers carried lists of the most suitable gifts to buy for men in the military, regardless of which side they were on.

"Look Mama!" Lucinda cried when she saw the article in the *Louisville Journal.* "It says here that there's a shortage of blankets and overcoats and warm socks for soldiers this winter." She handed the paper to Nancy, pointing to the article.

Nancy took the paper and walked to the window and held it to the light.

"Lucinda, it says that soldiers may actually suffer from the cold this winter and that there is a shortage of these items in the stores. And it says that prices are high because of the war."

"I noticed that. It also said soldiers need revolvers."

"I'd hate the thought of buying guns for my boys," Nancy returned.

"Mama, they may need them for self-defense," Lucinda suggested.

"You have a point there. Being well-armed might keep them from getting killed."

"Mama, we'll have to go shopping before people buy up everything."

"It's a good thing Lewis sold two of our calves last week. That will give us some extra money for shopping."

"Papa's at the barn. I'll run out there and show him the article. Maybe he'll take us shopping today—or tomorrow at the latest," Lucinda said as she took the paper from her mother's hand and started to the barn on a run.

"What's the big hurry, Cindy?" Lewis asked when she entered the barn, panting for breath.

"Mama and I want to go Christmas shopping, Papa. We need to buy some things for Tad and David while there's time to mail them if they can't come home for Christmas."

"I hadn't thought of that, Cindy, but it's still plenty early."

"The mail is awfully slow since the war, Papa. Besides, with the cold weather, there's things David and Tad need right now. It says here in the paper that there's not enough blankets or overcoats or warm socks for the soldiers. For all we know Tad and David may be suffering from the cold."

"Let me see that paper," Lewis said, reaching for it.

She handed him the paper and pointed to the article.

"The light ain't too good in here. Let's go open the door so I can see to read it."

Lucinda skipped to the door and pushed it open. "Hurry and read it, Papa," she urged. "It's cold with the door open."

Lewis caught up with her and took his time reading the article. Then he handed the paper back to her. "Looks like you've made your point," he said.

"Can we go today, Papa? Mama wants to go."

"I never can say no to you when you get your mind made up, Cindy. Anyhow, I reckon the boys will need blankets and coats. I'm glad I sold them calves," he added as an afterthought.

"Thank you, Papa. I'll go tell Mama so she can start getting dressed to go. Where will we go shopping? They don't have much in Perryville."

"I reckon we'll go to Danville. Lexington would be better, but that's too far to go in one day."

"We'll hurry and get ready, Papa. It's been forever since we've been off the place! I think I'll go wild with excitement."

"You're wild enough as it is, girl," he called after her, for she was already running toward the house.

In less than an hour Lewis had hitched the mare to the buggy and brought it out to the yard gate. Lucinda met him with a stone she had heated in the oven and wrapped in a blanket. "Cold as it is today, we'll need this hot rock to keep our feet warm," she said as she put it in the floor of the buggy. Then Nancy came out and they all climbed into the buggy.

"I notice you and Cindy have both put on your heavy coats," Lewis observed.

"Yes, and we'll need them on a cold day like this."

"I put on my heavy coat before I went to harness up Katy," Lewis said as he pulled the buggy rug over their laps.

"We'll have to hurry or we'll be in the night getting home. Then it will really be cold," Nancy replied.

"I'll hurry the mare. Get up, Katy. We've got a ways to go," Lewis called as he whacked the mare on her back with the reins.

When they reached Danville, Lewis drove the mare to the back of the general merchandise store, got out and hitched her to the hitching rail.

More excited than she had been since the beginning of the war, Lucinda sprang from the buggy and turned to help her mother step down.

"Never mind me. I can still get around," Nancy laughed good-naturedly as she too alighted.

"You women seem mighty anxious to spend my money," Lewis teased as they started down the alley toward the front of the store.

"Now, Papa admit it; you're just as anxious to shop for Tad and David as we are," Lucinda bantered.

Lewis only smiled as he continued along the alley with them.

Inside the store they found that the merchant, Mr. Smith, had little to sell.

"It's hard to get merchandise since the war, and people have already bought up most of what I had," he told them.

"Maybe we should go to Lexington," Nancy suggested.

"That's a long drive in a buggy," Lewis objected. "Traveling men that call on me say there's less in Lexington than there is here."

"There's more stores in Lexington," Lucinda spoke up brightly.

"That's true, but there's also more people to buy what they have. You might as well save yourself the trip."

"Since we're here let's see what we can find," Nancy decided.

They went to the coatrack and looked through the few coats Mr. Smith had in stock. To their surprise they found a coat that would fit David and another that would fit Tad. They were disappointed that there were not more to choose from, but they decided that the ones they had found would be all right. Lewis winced when Mr. Smith told him the price, but he bought them anyway.

They soon found two warm blankets. "I'm almost afraid to ask the price of these," Nancy remarked.

"I don't have many, and I don't know when I'll get more, but the price on these is not bad. I bought them before the war, and I haven't raised the price," Mr. Smith told them.

"We'll take them," Lewis said without waiting to hear the price.

After that they shopped for socks and for some other small items. Then they shopped separately, each buying gifts for the others.

"That's all except the revolvers. We'll have to go to the hardware store for them," Lewis said when they had finished shopping.

"I hear he's almost sold out," Mr. Smith said.

Lucinda and Lewis exchanged disappointed glances.

"Maybe it's for the best," Nancy exclaimed. "I don't like the idea of buying guns anyway."

"Now you wouldn't want your sons to be unprotected if they get in a tight place, would you?" the merchant asked. "Guns is not my main line, but I've been selling a few since the start of the war. It just happens that I have a few revolvers left." He opened a case and brought out a tray of pistols of one sort and another.

"I like the looks of this one. It don't look so heavy and unwieldy," Lewis said, pointing to one of the revolvers.

"That's a .36-caliber Whitney Navy Revolver, but lots of men in the army prefer it to the heavier army pistol. Like you said, they're not too heavy to handle."

Lewis picked up one of the navy revolvers and balanced it in his hand. Then he held it at arm's length and looked down the barrel. "I think these will be all right," he said.

"Since you had to pay so much for the coats, I'll make you a special price for these," Mr. Smith said. "You can have two of them for twenty dollars."

"I think I'll see what they have left at the hardware store before we buy," Lewis said, thinking that the price was high.

"I'm sure he don't have any guns like these, but you can go and see what he has if you want to. Tell you what, though, to save you the trouble, I'll cut my price by one-fourth. You won't find a price like that anywhere else."

"We should hurry, Lewis. It will be dark before we get home," Nancy reminded him.

"Cut the price to five dollars each, and I'll take them," Lewis told the merchant.

"You drive a hard bargain, but I'm going to let you have them," Mr. Smith agreed. "I'll add up your bill," he said as some other customers came in.

When the figures were added, Lewis checked them carefully. Then he took his folding pocketbook from his pocket and paid the merchant.

Mr. Smith tied up their purchases and they returned to the buggy and started home.

The next day Lucinda wrote a long letter to Tad and another to David, telling both of them about all that was happening at home and urging them to come home for Christmas if possible. She asked them to write at once and tell them if they could not come home so they could mail their presents. Anxious days followed while the family waited for answers to her letters.

David's letter arrived first. He was now in Louisville, not a great distance from home, but because of the shortage of medical personnel he could not get a furlough. He was mailing gifts for each of them and one to be forwarded to Tad, because he did not know his address.

Lucinda covered her disappointment as best she could. Lewis said little, but Nancy was distraught.

"Maybe Tad can come, Mama," Lucinda said, trying to comfort her.

"I'm not going to get my hopes up, Cindy," Nancy replied disconsolately.

That night a heavy snow fell, and the next morning, shod in rubber boots, Lucinda waded through it to the mailbox. She returned to the house excited, and held the letter over her head for her parents to see.

"Tad thinks he can come home for Christmas," she announced. "I opened his letter and read it the minute I got it. They are planning to furlough a lot of the men for

Christmas, and his captain is going to put in a word for him. I just know he'll get to come."

"Read the letter to us," Nancy requested.

"All right, Mama." She leaned against the wall and read the letter through without pausing.

Nancy's face was aglow, and Lewis was smiling broadly when she finished.

"We're going to have the best Christmas we've ever had, in spite of the war, and in spite of David not being able to come," Lucinda exulted.

"We'll make it the best one we can," Nancy agreed.

"I'm going to the woods this very day and cut a Christmas tree and bring it home and put it up," Lucinda declared. And, without further adieu, she went up to her room, put on her heavy work clothes, and left to go after the tree.

Lucinda picked up an ax at the woodpile and laid it across her shoulder, as one of her bothers would have done. Then she started across the fields towards Hope's Creek in the deep snow. The cold wind stung her face and tears ran down her cheeks and froze, but she did not turn back. When she reached the top of the hill, she started down the other side, half-sliding, half-walking, and half-falling toward the narrow valley where Hope's Creek flowed. When she reached the valley, she went into a thicket of trees to get shelter from the wind.

For a few moments she paused, stamping her feet to warm them. Then she walked along the creek until she found a cedar tree that was just the size and shape she wanted, and with two deft strokes of the ax, she cut it down.

She looked around for some mistletoe, but all she could find was high in hardwood trees. She got some stones from the edge of the creek and threw them at the mistletoe, but they fell far short of the mark. After a few tries, she gave up and started looking for something else she could use for decoration.

Soon she saw some buckbushes with red berries on them. "These will be just right," she told herself, and she quickly cut down all the buckbushes she could carry. Then she picked up the trunk of the tree she had cut and started back to the house, dragging it and carrying the ax and the buckbushes.

She had almost more than she could carry, but she struggled on, for she did not want to make a second trip.

Nancy was watching from the back window when Lucinda came in sight at the top of the hill. "Lewis, you better go help that girl. She's bringing half of the forest home with her," she called.

Lewis came from his chair by the fire to join her at the window. "I see what you mean," he said. "I'll put on my coat and boots and go help her."

"Looks like you've got more than you can carry," Lewis said when he met Lucinda.

"Papa, I'm glad you've come. I guess I did get carried away, but I was enjoying myself cutting these bushes with the pretty berries on them. Now I'm out of breath," she panted.

"Here, I'll help you." He took the ax and the trunk of the tree she was dragging.

"Thank, you, Papa. I was about ready to leave the tree and come back for it later."

"I'm glad Nancy saw you coming with all this load, Cindy. You go on in the house, and I'll stop at the wood-pile and trim the lower branches off the tree and square the trunk and put a stand on it," Lewis said as they reached the yard gate.

"I'll be glad to get in out of the cold, Papa," she replied, and she hurried to the back door and started stamping the snow from her feet.

Her mother heard her and opened the door and handed her the broom.

"Thank you, Mama," she said, dropping the buckbushes on the ground. She took the broom and swept the snow from her feet.

"I'm glad you brought plenty of those bushes with the red berries," her mother said when Lucinda picked up the buckbushes and started inside.

"I thought they would help make the house look like Christmas."

"They are pretty," her mother agreed.

Lewis soon brought the tree in and stood it in the corner of the parlor. "Nice looking tree," he commented as Nancy and Lucinda came to see it.

"I can't wait to decorate it," Lucinda declared.

"We better get dinner first, Cindy. It will be past time to eat before we get it on the table."

"I guess I can wait. Anyway, after all that tramping in the outdoors, I'm hungry. Come on, Mama, and I'll help you get dinner."

After dinner Lucinda went up to the attic and dug out the homemade Christmas decorations they had stowed there after Christmas last year. She came down singing, and her voice echoed through the hallway.

"Looks like you've already got the Christmas spirit," Lewis remarked as she set the box of decorations on the sofa and started going through them.

"I'll really have it when Tad gets home," she responded.

"I'll watch while you women put the pretties on the tree," Lewis said, and he sat down in the big horsehair chair.

"You would!" Lucinda teased as she and her mother set to work.

When the decorations were all on the tree, they stood back to admire it. "It's a beautiful tree," Nancy said, smiling as she had not smiled since the boys had gone away.

"What a jolly time we'll have when Tad gets home,"

Lucinda exclaimed.

"I'll enjoy having him home, but I wish David could come too," Nancy said, and the smile left her face.

"Mailing his presents ought to help some," Lewis suggested.

"I guess you're right," Nancy agreed. "We'll wrap them this afternoon, and Cindy can take them out to the mailbox in the morning."

"I'll go in time to meet the mailman so we will be sure the packages are on their way," Lucinda said.

Tad wrote that he would arrive in Perryville on the afternoon stagecoach Christmas Eve, and Lucinda and her mother grew so anxious they could scarcely wait for him to come. Lewis said little, but each day he checked another day off on the calendar.

Two days before Christmas, Nancy and Lucinda started preparing food for Christmas dinner. Even Lewis was pressed into service, picking out hickory nut kernels for the nut cake that was one of Tad's favorites.

On the day Tad was to come home, they had a hurried breakfast, then continued with last minute preparations. Lucinda scurried here and there, humming merrily to herself, and doing the work of two women. Noon came almost before they realized it, and they sat down for a quick bite to eat.

"Mama, there's not room for all of us in the buggy, so I'll stay and work on dinner while you and Papa go get Tad," Lucinda volunteered while they were eating.

"Lucinda, I know how much you want to go meet Tad, so I'll stay and let you go."

"No, Mama. You're the one who ought to go. I don't mind staying home."

"Nancy, you ought to go, Tad will be expectin' you," Lewis told her.

Without further objection, Nancy took off her apron

and went upstairs to dress. She came back ready to go as the clock was striking one.

"You and Papa will get there just in time if you hurry," Lucinda looked up from her task to say. "Papa has already gone out to the buggy."

"Good-bye, Cindy," Nancy said as she was going out the door.

Lucinda watched from the window as her parents left. Then she went back to her tasks.

It was mid-afternoon when she heard the buggy returning, and ran to the window, and saw it coming down the lane. Nancy was seated in the middle with Lewis and Tad on either side.

Lucinda snatched up her sweater from a chair, threw it on, and ran out, reaching the front porch just as the buggy stopped at the gate.

"Hello, Tad. Welcome home," she screamed, waving at him with both arms.

"My one and only sister," Tad called. "My, I'm glad to see you."

"Oh, Tad, Tad, I thought you'd never get here," she cried.

"Lucinda, you'll catch your death of cold, running out here wearing only that sweater," Nancy reproved as Lucinda ran out to the gate.

Tad bounded from the buggy, and ran to meet Lucinda. "Glad to see you, Cindy. There ain't another man in the army got a sister like you." He gave a bear hug. "Just a minute; I forgot to get my carpetbag." He hurried back to the buggy to get it.

"Let's go in out of the cold," Nancy said. She got out of the buggy, and Lewis started Katy to the barn.

Tad took his mother's arm, and Lucinda hurried to meet them and took her other arm. Together they went into the house, and the aroma of cooking food met them.

"I haven't smelled food like that since I joined the

army. You didn't cook all that for me?" Tad asked on a rising inflection.

"Most of it is for tomorrow, Tad, though we will have a good supper tonight," Nancy responded.

"We invited the Crabtrees over to eat with us tomorrow," Lucinda butted in.

"Jim and Nelly and Mary are coming, but John and Ned are visiting their grandparents," Nancy hastened to add.

"Well, all I have to say is, the way you all cook, they're in for a good meal," Tad observed.

"Ain't nobody can cook like our mama," Lucinda said.

"You're not so bad at cooking yourself, Cindy," Tad exclaimed. "I wish David could be here, though I'm not sure we'd get along since we're fightin' on different sides."

"Of course you would, Tad. After all you are brothers," Nancy insisted.

"I'm goin' up to my room and leave my carpetbag. Be back in a minute," Tad said, and he started bounding up the stairs.

The next morning, after a good breakfast and an extended time of talking around the table, they went to the parlor to open their presents. Lucinda got the presents from under the tree and passed them around. Then they all opened their presents, with expressions of pleasure and words of appreciation. There were even some tears of joy and a few hugs.

The clock in the hall started striking just as they finished, and Lucinda began picking up the clutter.

"It's ten o'clock already," Nancy exclaimed.

"Where has the time gone, Mama? I haven't finished making the pies yet," Lucinda exclaimed.

"And I have to see to the fire. I want that turkey to finish cooking. . . . and there's the dressing and the cranberries to finish," Nancy said, springing up and hurrying to the kitchen.

"I hear the Crabtrees coming," Lucinda cried as the clock was striking eleven-thirty.

Tad went to wait on the porch until their buggy stopped at the gate.

"Good morning, neighbors," he greeted.

"You ladies come in, and I'll go with Jim to the barn to put the horse in out of the weather," Lewis called as he joined Tad on the porch.

"Need my help, Papa?" Tad asked.

"No, Tad. You had best walk the ladies to the house so they don't slip in the snow."

"Guess you're right, Papa." He walked with his father to the gate just as Mary and her mother reached it.

"You ladies walk carefully. There are icy patches in the snow," Tad warned.

"If you don't mind, I'll hold onto your arm, Tad," Mary said timidly.

"Then, I'll hold to his other arm, and if one of us falls, we'll all go down together," her mother laughed.

Tad was surprised when Mary took his arm, yet he thought he should not be. The Crabtrees had been friends for years. Still, he was pleased, and he felt a thrill as Mary walked beside him. He glanced at her furtively, and, with a start, realized how attractive she had become since he had last seen her.

Lucinda met them at the door and promptly took charge of Mary and her mother, ushering them in, relieving them of their coats and hats, and bidding them to sit down and take off their winter boots.

Tad now found himself useless, so he retired to a chair by the fireplace in the parlor. Nancy came from the kitchen briefly to greet Nelly and Mary.

"Mary and I will come out and help you with dinner," Nelly offered.

"Lucinda and I have everything almost finished. You

sit by the fire and warm yourselves. I know you must be frozen from your drive in the cold," Nancy said.

"I'll punch up the fire," Tad said, getting up. He picked up the poker and rearranged the logs until they started burning busily. When he sat down again, he was pleased to see that Mary had chosen to sit in a chair near where he had been sitting. She was looking at him pensively, and he thought her cheeks had a trace of heightened color, though he was not sure that the cold wind had caused it.

Lewis and Jim soon came from the barn and sat down near the fire without pausing in the conversation they were having about the war. Nelly sat quietly listening. Tad wanted to say something to Mary, but could think of nothing to say. That was strange, he thought, for he had never had difficulty talking with Mary before.

Nancy soon called them to dinner, and they all filed into the dining room where Nancy and Lucinda were standing, one at each end of the big table.

"Be seated," Lewis invited.

"Nancy, you and Lucinda sit down and eat with us. We're not company, so there's no need of your serving us," Nelly insisted.

"We'll pass the food around first. Then we'll eat with you," Nancy replied.

Soon everyone but Mary had their plates loaded with turkey and dressing, steak and gravy, canned peas and corn, sweet potatoes, and Irish potatoes, and cranberries and apple sauce. Most of them sampled all three kinds of bread, corn bread, biscuits, and crackling bread.

"Mary, you're not eating anything," Nancy observed when she saw that her plate had little on it.

"I'm just not started yet," Mary responded, blushing and making a pretense of putting more food on her plate.

Tad saw that she was blushing and thought that she was beautiful. *I'd ask her to be my sweetheart if I didn't have to go back to camp,* he thought.

After the dinner was finished off with pie, and nut cake, and canned grape juice, they all retired to the parlor. The parents sat by the fire and talked and grew comfortable and sleepy. But Lucinda kept Mary entertained by bringing out the stereoscope and showing her the collection of pictures they had bought at the General Merchandise Store in Danville for the entertainment of the family and their guests.

Lucinda had already seen the pictures a hundred times, but she viewed them along with Mary to be polite, and Tad looked at them just so he could be near Mary.

Late in the afternoon, the Crabtrees decided they should be going, and Jim and Lewis went to get the buggy. Nelly and Mary dressed for the outside, and, when Jim drove up to the front gate, they started out, insisting that Nancy and her family visit them soon.

"You will come with them, Tad?" Mary asked softly in an aside while the others were talking.

"I wish I could, Mary, but I have to go back to camp."

"I almost forgot. When are you going back?"

"I have to go tomorrow."

"So soon?" she asked sadly.

"That's the way it has to be. I was just wondering, Mary, when I go back, will you write to me?"

"I'll be glad to, Tad, but you have to write me first."

"I will, Mary. I'll write to you the first thing after I get back to camp," he told her warmly.

"Come on, Mary," Jim called as he ushered Nelly, still talking to Nancy, toward the buggy.

Tad walked to the buggy with Mary, then timidly held her hand as she got in.

"Good-bye, all," Tad said. Then more softly, for Mary's ears only, he said good-bye again.

Jim turned the horse along the lane, and the Perrys watched the buggy until it was out of sight.

Chapter 8

*T*he coming of the new year offered no promise of an early end to the war. So the Perrys started the year as they had ended the last one, thinking of all the work they had to do and worrying over the future of the country. And each day they worried about the safety of Tad and David.

By late February the weather was mild enough for Lewis to start turning the ground in the fields he planned to plant, and it remained mild and dry long enough for him to finish in record time. March brought rain and wind and snow. That slowed his work, but the first of April mild weather returned, and he started cultivating the ground to make it ready for planting.

When the weather became warm enough to start planting, Lewis started working in the fields early each morning. Nancy and Lucinda joined him soon after they finished the necessary work at the house, and they all worked until the setting of the sun, taking only time to eat a hurried meal at noon.

After the crops were planted, there was a brief respite while they waited for the seed to germinate and the plants to appear above the ground. When the plants were large enough to start cultivating, they were kept busy in the fields from early morning until the setting of the sun.

They still watched each day for the coming of the

mailman, and when he came into sight, Lucinda would start running to meet him. He would hand her any mail he had for her family, and if there was a letter from Tad or David she would hold it high overhead for her parents to see. If there were letters from both of them, she would hold up both arms and wave them. Then she would hurry back to the field and arrive red-faced and short of breath.

On the days when no letters came, she would walk back to where her parents were waiting under the big oak tree at the end of the field and sit down with them to rest.

The mailman brought the *Louisville Journal* each Monday. On that day they would read the *Journal* page by page, searching for every scrap of news about the war. After they had finished reading it, they would discuss any battles that could possibly involve either of the boys. Then they would talk of David and Tad, wondering where they were and what they were doing. From their infrequent letters they could not easily keep track of their movements, but they were thankful that, as far as they knew, neither of them had been in any really big battles.

At last they would place the paper under a rock so the wind would not blow it away. Then they would drink from the jug of water they had brought from the spring and stashed in the shade of the tree that morning and go back to work.

One day late in the summer, Lucinda met the mailman and got a letter from Tad. Usually she hurried back to the field and let her mother open the letters from both boys, but today she had a premonition that prompted her to open Tad's letter at once. She vacillated for a moment, then tore open the letter and scanned the first page. There were the usual greetings and reports on where he was and what he was doing, but halfway down the page she stopped short and her hand went to her heart.

"No it can't be," she cried. Then, sobbing, she ran back to the field to rejoin Lewis and Nancy.

"Mama, Papa, I—have—a—a—letter from—Tad," she cried between breaths when she was near enough to be heard. "I felt like I ought to open it, and when I did I saw why. Tad says that Nathan Wills has been killed in a battle in Virginia."

"Oh no, not that fine boy! I can't believe that he's been killed," Nancy cried.

"Tad said in his letter that he couldn't believe it."

"It's a shame for a fine young men like Nathan to be killed," Lewis said.

"I'm sorry, Cindy. He was the only sweetheart you ever had," Nancy remarked.

"He was the only boy I ever saw that I cared to take a second look at, Mama, but we were only children when I was struck on him."

"I'm glad he was only a childhood sweetheart," Nancy said.

"I think I might have fallen in love with him if I had been older, Mama."

"Haven't you been corresponding with him ever since that summer when he came from up from Georgia to visit his uncle's family?" Nancy asked.

"From time to time, but we haven't written for ages. Now I never will hear from him again," she said sadly.

"I'm sorry, Lucinda."

"Mama, I know a Christian girl is not supposed to hate, but I hate this war, and I hate the Yankees."

"I know how you feel," Lewis told her mildly.

"I wish I didn't feel that way," she responded, wiping the tears from her eyes.

The last week in August they started harvesting the poor crops they had grown, for the summer had been unusually dry and the crops had done poorly. The following Monday, when Lucinda met the mailman, she got the usual Sunday paper and a letter from Tad and another from David. Immediately she started back to the field, waving both arms above her head. "I have two letters," she called when she was near enough for her parents to hear.

"Hurry, Cindy, I can't wait to read them," Nancy called, getting to her feet. Then she hurried to meet her. "Open—David's—letter—first, and we'll read it as we walk back," Nancy panted when they met.

Lucinda tore open David's letter, and scanned down the page. "He's still in Louisville, but he says there's talk that they will move out soon. Oh, Mama, I wonder if that means he will soon be in battle."

"Is he still serving with General Crittenden's Corps?" Nancy asked.

"I suppose he is. The letter didn't say."

They walked on a few steps as Lucinda tore open Tad's letter. Then they paused as she read it. "Tad says that he is still in General Powell's Brigade, and they are still in Kentucky."

"It's terrible that they are both in Kentucky—so close to home, and neither one of them has come to see us."

"Nancy, do you and Cindy intend to bring the letters and tell me what's in them?" Lewis demanded.

"I'm sorry, Lewis. I just couldn't wait to find out what David and Tad are doing."

They hurried to join Lewis in the shade of the tree, and Nancy sat down beside him, but Lucinda remained standing with her back against the tree. While Lewis and Nancy listened, she read both letters aloud. Then they spent some time discussing what the boys had written.

"Well, let's see what's in the paper," Lewis said at last.

Lucinda handed him the front section, then she started looking through the remaining pages.

"I see that there was a battle at Richmond last Saturday!" Lewis exclaimed. "It says that Major General E.

Kirby-Smith defeated the Union forces led by General 'Bull' Nelson."

"Lewis, Richmond is not far away!" Nancy exclaimed with alarm.

"I reckon it's forty miles from Perryville, maybe less."

"That's too close for me," Nancy remarked.

"Do you think the fighting will come any closer, Papa?" Lucinda asked.

"Like I've always said, Cindy, there ain't nothing in Boyle County for them to fight over. Most likely, if there's more fightin' in Kentucky, it will be at Louisville or Frankfort. Frankfort is on the Kentucky River and Louisville is on the Ohio."

"Frankfort is not far away, Papa."

"And it's the capital. If the North can take Frankfort, they can make sure that the state won't side with the South."

"Frankfort is too close for me," Nancy said, shuttering.

"I hope that neither David nor Tad ever have to fight in Kentucky," Lucinda said.

"I pray they won't, but there's no tellin' what the future holds," Lewis responded.

"Oh here's something," Lucinda exclaimed, still looking at the paper. "It says here that Rev. Western has been called in for questioning. He is accused of not being loyal to the Union."

"I hope nothing happens to him," Nancy said.

"They could put him in the federal prison at Nashville," Lewis commented.

"Oh the poor man! We've not been going to church lately, but I still love him and his family," Nancy cried.

"I doubt that he'll sign any pledge," Lewis said.

"Why not, Papa? He's not going to take up arms for the South."

"The Lord knows he's tried not to take sides, but I

reckon that ain't good enough for the Federal Government."

"Why can't he just sign the pledge that he's not against the government in Washington?" Lucinda asked.

"I reckon that wouldn't be good enough. They want him to sign that he's for the Union, but he wants to serve the people on both sides."

"I pray he doesn't have to go to prison. I don't know what will happen to his wife and little girl if he does," Nancy worried.

"Ain't much we can do except keep on workin'," Lewis said, and he got up and started back to the field.

The next Monday, as they again sat in the shade reading the *Louisville Journal*, Lucinda suddenly looked up from the section she was reading. "It says here that they let Brother Western go," she said. "They just gave him a warning not to give aid or comfort to the enemy."

"I'm glad. I respect him as a pastor, and he's a stabilizing influence in the community," Lewis commented.

"His wife needs him more than we do," Nancy added.

"Seems like there's no end of trouble. Only the Lord knows how or when this will all end," Lewis commented as he arose to go back to work.

Sadly, and without comment, Nancy and Lucinda arose and followed him back to the field.

Chapter 9

Weary months passed after Tad returned to his company, and Lewis and Nancy and Lucinda struggled on, burdened with ceaseless toil and with worry about Tad and David. Each day seemed unbearably long, and the weeks and months dragged beyond belief. Finally the long summer drew to an end, and the time of harvest was upon them.

One day the first week in October, Jim Crabtree came to the barn on horseback while Lewis was feeding. "I've got bad news, Lewis," he greeted, making no move to dismount. "Yesterday afternoon in Perryville, I heard that soldiers are all around us, and they are moving this way."

"Why would they want to come here?" Lewis countered.

"Don't know, but that's the talk. A traveling salesman at the hardware store said he had seen Union soldiers on the Springfield Pike. They were moving toward Perryville. And a farmer who lives over toward Danville said he'd seen Rebel troops bivouacked over his way."

"I never have thought they'd come to Boyle County."

"Reckon I didn't either, but they've come. I come by to tell you in case you have anything you need to do before they get here."

"I don't reckon there's much a man can do."

"Just thought I'd let you know. I'd better go tell the

other neighbors," he said, and he turned his horse and galloped away.

Lewis hurried to the house to tell Nancy and Lucinda what Jim had told him.

"What are we going to do if fighting breaks out near the house?" Nancy almost sobbed.

"If that does happen, we'll have to stay out of sight till it's over," Lewis responded.

"Maybe we could hide in the cellar," Lucinda suggested.

"Not a bad idea, but I can't imagine you hidin' from anything," Lewis said, looking at her with raised eyebrows.

"I read in the paper that soldiers have been raiding farms and taking what they want—horses, cows, hogs—anything that's loose," Nancy said. "Sometimes they don't even offer to pay for what they take."

"We'll just have to take that chance if they come this way. There's no place we can hide what we've got."

"I'm not worried, Mama," Lucinda said after what was a long silence for her.

"You never worry about anything, Cindy," her mother scolded.

"We'll cope some way. We always have."

"But this is different, Cindy. This is war!" Nancy exclaimed.

Lucinda did not want to admit it, but she was worried, and that night, for the first time in her life, she slept poorly, and the next morning, she arose with a feeling of dread.

Papa had been wrong about fighting not coming to Kentucky, she realized. Brother Western, and other preachers like him, had not been able to stay neutral. Now it appeared that the state could not either. In the past it had been a comfort to Mama when Papa had assured her that war would never come near them. Mama had so much to worry about, she had taken comfort in what Papa had told her. Now that small comfort was gone.

They should have known that Kentucky was going to be involved when President Lincoln had General Nelson to set up a recruiting camp at Camp Nelson. Besides they had had other warnings. In September they had read that General Braxton Bragg had crossed Cumberland Gap and was marching toward Glasgow, and that Major General Don Carlos Buell was marching with six divisions toward Bowling Green. But they had still hoped the war would not come to Boyle County.

Lucinda sighed heavily, then started dressing for the day. When she finished, she went downstairs and joined her mother in the kitchen.

"Your papa has gone to feed and milk, and we have to hurry breakfast," her mother greeted as she entered.

"What's the big hurry, Mama?"

"Papa and I are going to Perryville this morning to get a few things we need before the soldiers come any closer. He wants to get an early start."

"Don't you want me to go, Mama?" she asked.

"Of course I'd like for you to go, Cindy, but Papa is going to load the buggy with groceries and wheat seed. He needs the wheat to sow in the cornfield when he gets through picking corn."

"I guess there wouldn't be room for me with all that in the buggy," Lucinda agreed. "What do you want me to do while you and Papa are gone?"

"You can pick what's left of the fall garden, Cindy, though it's been so dry this summer that there's not much to pick."

"And it's still dry. Papa says we're almost out of water for the stock. All that's left is a few water holes in Hope's Creek."

"Your papa worries too much."

"Should I go and help him at the barn, Mama?"

"You had better help me with breakfast, Cindy. Your papa should be almost finished by now."

"When did Papa decide to go to Perryville?"

"He must have decided in the night. He said we'd better go today, because this may be the last chance we'll have until the soldiers leave."

"That's true, and I know there's things we need from town."

"Don't worry while we're gone, Lucinda. We'll hurry right back."

"I'll be busy, Mama, and that will keep me from worrying."

Lewis Perry looked grim when he came in from the barn a few minutes later. "I hope the war don't come no closer than it has already," he said.

"You always said there's nothing in Perryville worth fighting over, Papa," Lucinda reminded him.

"Nothing but the water in Chaplin River and what little is left in Hope's Creek. It takes a lot of water for all the men and horses in one army, let alone two."

"Papa, aren't you and Mama afraid you'll get caught in a battle before you get back?" Lucinda asked anxiously.

"I worry about that," Nancy spoke up before Lewis could answer.

"Even if the soldiers come this way, they won't be here for another day or two. An army can't move fast with all their supplies and artillery," Lewis explained.

After breakfast, Lucinda cleared the table and washed the dishes while her mother dressed and her father went to the barn and hitched Katy to the buggy. He drove up to the front gate just as her mother came downstairs ready to go.

"Lucinda, I have some cream and eggs to sell in Perryville. Will you help me carry them out?" her mother asked.

"Of course, Mama." She walked ahead of her mother to the pantry.

"I'll get the cream, Cindy," Nancy said as Lucinda picked up the basket of eggs.

They left the house together, and went to the buggy, and loaded the cream and eggs. Then Nancy got in, and Lewis started the mare toward Mackville Pike.

Lucinda watched them go and listened to the clip, clop of the mare's hooves and the crunching of the buggy wheels in the gravel. Gradually the sounds diminished, and soon the buggy turned on the Mackville Pike and drove out of sight.

For a long while Lucinda looked the way her parents had gone; then she went back into the house. The house had never seemed so large and empty as it did this morning. Nor had it ever been so noisy. The wind had started blowing, and with every gust the house rattled and groaned and made popping sounds. It was almost as if it had come alive and was protesting.

She tried to estimate how long her parents would be gone. It shouldn't take them long to cover the three and a half miles to Perryville, and after they got there they would both hurry. Mama would sell her cream and eggs while Papa went to buy the wheat. It would take some time for the cream to be weighed and tested for butterfat, but it wouldn't take long for Mama to buy the few groceries she would need.

Lucinda knew the grocery list by heart. . . . a box of matches, a box of soda, a can of baking powder, some salt, some lard, a bag of flour, a can of salmon, a can of oysters for soup, maybe nutmeg and vanilla extract, and a can of coal oil. She counted them off on her fingers. Mama's list was almost always the same, but she always wrote one out anyway.

While Papa was at the feed store, he would likely buy some salt for the stock, and he might pick up a twenty-five pound bag of flour from the mill. He would carefully load what he bought in the buggy. Then he would meet Mama at the store and carry the groceries out for her. He would crowd them in the limited space left in the buggy, and they would start home.

How long would it take them to do everything? and how long would it take them to get home? It was not likely that they would eat in town. *They would be too hurried for that, so they should be home by early afternoon,* she reasoned. Lucinda wanted to finish her work before they returned, so she got the broom and started sweeping the pantry floor. After that she made room for the vegetables she was going to harvest.

She put the rest of the house in order, then put on a worn cotton dress and some old shoes, and a wide-brimmed straw hat. She attempted to tuck her red-gold hair beneath the crown, but unruly, frizzy strands fell around her face. Finally she gave up, pushed the strands of hair away and let them hang. Then she picked up a bucket and went out and crossed the backyard to the garden.

There wasn't much to harvest—a few late tomatoes, some bright red pods of pepper, and some stunted winter squash. She dug in the potato hills and decided there were not enough potatoes to be worth digging. They had harvested enough potatoes from the early planting anyway. There were a few late beans, but the beetles had ruined most of them.

She gathered what she could from the garden and put it all in the bucket, except the squash, and carried it to the pantry. Then she got a bushel basket from the barn to put the squash in. She carried the basket of squash to the cellar beneath the house and set it on a shelf, then returned to the house and put away the few vegetables she had gathered.

When it was almost noon, she started preparing lunch,

killing time with each task, and hoping her parents would be home by the time it was ready. Despite her efforts to delay lunch, it was finally ready, and still her parents did not come. So she put all she had cooked on the back of the stove to keep it warm, and sat down to wait. More than an hour passed, and still they did not return. So Lucinda sat down and ate, though she was too worried to be hungry.

Suppose the soldiers had moved faster than expected. Suppose they had already reached Perryville. Would they detain her parents? Or would they give them safe passage?

Finally she pushed back her plate, and got up, and cleared the table, and carried them to the kitchen. She got warm water from the back of the stove and washed them. She also washed the ones that had been left over from breakfast. When she finished, she went to the hall and looked at the big clock. It was past two.

"It shouldn't take them this long," she said aloud, and her voice echoed through the house.

There was nothing more to do, so she went outside and walked about in the yard. The afternoon sun was warm upon her. The trees were brown and red and gold, for an early frost had tinted their leaves. Goldenrods were blooming in the fallow field beyond the garden, and purple ironweed blooms were visible above their gold.

Lucinda went to the hammock that was stretched between two big maple trees in the side yard and started it swinging, toying with it. Then she decided to get a book and lie in the hammock and read. She went to the bookcase in the parlor and selected a copy of *Lena Rivers* a friend had loaned her at church. Her friend had told her that it "was a real good book."

She returned to the hammock and laid down. The hammock was comfortable, and the dry wind fanned her cheeks. She looked up through the leaves of the maple tree and saw patches of blue sky. A buzzard was hanging in the sky, but, as he drifted with the wind, a maze of golden leaves obscured him from her view.

She turned to the first page of the book and started reading. After she had read a few pages, she closed the book with her finger marking her place and rested it on her chest. She was too concerned about her parents and too concerned about the opposing armies that were approaching Perryville to keep her mind on what she was reading.

For a time she lay listening for the sounds of the mare and buggy coming along the lane, but the only sounds she heard were the wind fanning the leaves above her and the chirping of a lone bird in the tree.

"It's still early," she assured herself, thinking that soon she would hear the hoof falls of the mare and the clatter of the buggy wheels on the graveled drive.

She tried again to get interested in the book, but she still could not keep her mind on what she was reading. Finally she gave up, rolled out of the hammock, and went back to the house. She put the book back on the shelf and went up to her room. Determined to keep herself busy until her parents returned, she set to work cleaning her room with a vengeance. She changed her bed, swept the floor, and dusted the furniture. Then she rearranged her clothes in her wardrobe. All the while she kept listening for the return of her parents, though now she had begun to believe that surely something had detained them.

Lucinda looked at her windows and remembered that she had not washed them since spring. "You need washing," she said aloud to the windows. Then she went downstairs to get water, soap, and some cloths. Soon she returned and started washing the windows.

"I'll get a ladder and wash the outside tomorrow," she told herself as she climbed into a chair to reach the upper sash of her big front window. She smiled as she recalled the fuss her father had raised the last time she had climbed a ladder to wash her windows on the outside. Even her mother had joined him, telling her that she was old enough to begin acting like a lady.

Lucinda worked on the windows until they were shining clean on the inside. Then she raised the lower sashes, one by one, and reached outside and washed them. Finally she could find nothing more to do to her room, so she went downstairs and walked through the house, looking for something to do there. She found nothing that really needed doing, and she was too worried to simply make work.

She went to the living room and looked out the window. The sun was almost down, and it was painting the clouds in hues of red and orange and gold. The shadows of the big trees were creeping across the yard. With a start she realized that it was time for her to go to the barn and feed and milk. That would keep her occupied for a time.

When Lucinda finished at the barn, she returned to the house, carrying a basket of eggs and a pail of milk. She set the eggs on the table in the pantry. Then she strained the milk, filled a crock, and set it on a table to sour for churning. She put the rest of the milk in two-gallon syrup buckets and carried them out to the springhouse and put them in the water so the milk would be kept cold.

The sun was dropping below the horizon as she returned to the house, and when she entered she saw that the shadows were gathering in the big rooms.

"There's no use waiting until it gets dark to light the lamp," she said aloud as she picked up the lamp from the mantle and started to the kitchen. There she lighted it and placed it in its accustomed place on a shelf.

She was not hungry, but she decided to cook supper anyway. She was convinced now that her parents would not come home tonight, but she decided to cook supper anyway—just in case they did.

She built a fire in the cast-iron range, and, while it was getting hot, she mixed the ingredients for biscuits. While she was rolling the biscuits out, she heard the sounds of the fire in the range, but there was no sound of the mare and buggy on the lane.

She cut out the biscuits, placed them in the baking pan, and put them in the oven. Then she went to the pantry and got some potatoes. She returned, peeled them, sliced them, and put them in a skillet to fry. She sliced some ham and placed it in another skillet and put it on the stove. Then she filled the coffeepot with water, put coffee in it, and put it on the front of the stove to boil.

The oven was now getting hot, so she put the biscuits in to bake. Then she put the ham and potatoes on the front of the stove. The smells of frying ham and boiling coffee soon filled the room. When supper was almost ready, she piddled at unnecessary tasks, hoping that her parents would come home.

When supper could be delayed no longer without spoiling it, she opened the oven door and pulled the biscuits out so they would stay warm without burning. She put the skillets and the coffee on the back of the stove so they would stay warm. Then she went to the front door and stood in the darkness, looking forlornly along the lane.

"Nothing has happened to them," she told herself firmly. Then she went out on the porch and sat down in the swing and started gently swinging.

A dog barked on a neighboring farm. Crickets and katydids filled the night with their sounds. A bat fluttered and dipped in the night air. An owl hooted in the thicket behind the barn. The clock in the hall struck the hour, and she counted its chimes. It was eight o'clock.

Her parents would have been home long ago if they

were coming, she realized. Numb with worry, she got up and went indoors, locked the front door, then went to the other outside doors and locked them.

Without eating a bite of the supper she had cooked, she picked up the lamp and climbed the stairs to her room. She placed the lamp on the mantle, then she knelt by her bed and prayed for her parents and her brothers.

A great while later, she put on her nightgown and put out the lamp and got into bed. But she did not soon fall asleep. Instead, she lay staring up into the darkness of her room and listening to the clock in the downstairs hall strike the hours and the half hours of the night. In the early hours of the morning she fell asleep and dreamed of shadowy armies, fighting across a field covered with a huge American flag.

Chapter 10

*L*ucinda awoke at daylight the next morning with a sour taste in her mouth and with fear in her heart. Her first thought was of her parents. *Could they have come home during the night without her hearing them?* she wondered. For a moment she lay listening for any sound that would tell her they were home. The only sound she heard was something on the roof—perhaps a squirrel or a bird. She yawned, got out of bed and dressed, then went down to the kitchen.

She had no desire for food, so she decided to do the chores before she ate breakfast. She picked up the milk bucket and stepped outside, and, to her dismay, she heard horses neighing and men shouting in the distance, but they were too far away for her to understand what the men were saying.

Soldiers must be encamped on that long ridge to the west, she guessed in alarm. A moment later, more faintly, she heard men and horses in the other direction. In sudden shock she realized that soldiers from both the North and the South were nearby. They must have been nearer than her father had thought when he and her mother left for town yesterday. That was why they had not returned. Fervently she hoped they were all right.

Suddenly there were musket shots in the distance. They were followed by the still more distant boom of a cannon. She should be in terror, she realized, but, aside from her worry about her parents, she was coldly calm. Anything could happen, she knew, yet she felt detached, as if the presence of the armies did not concern her.

As she hurried on to the barn, she thought of her brothers and hoped that neither of them was out there with the troops. Inside the barn, she could no longer hear the men and horses, and she heard no further sounds of guns or cannons, but she made sure that the door was closed and latched.

"I wish they would simply go away," she said testily as she hurried to her tasks.

After Lucinda finished feeding the stock and milking the cows, she started back to the house. Outside the barn, she again heard the men and horses. They sounded nearer than before. That meant they were on the move.

She paused at the back door of the house to listen, and her eyes roamed about the yard. The maple trees were beautiful with their leaves tinted golden-yellow and red. She lifted her eyes to the cornfield behind the house. The cornstalks were stunted from the drought. Their dry leaves were pale yellow, and they fanned in the morning breeze.

Sparrows landed in the fence row, chirping noisily, and pigeons wheeled above the fields and landed on the barn roof. A hen cackled in the henhouse. Pigs grunted as they fed in their pen, and sheep grazed peacefully in the field behind the barn. It seemed impossible that on such a day and in such a place men could fight and die.

She made a hopeless gesture and went in. She put the milk in syrup pails and carried them to the springhouse and set them in the water beside the ones she had left there the night before. There was no way she could use all that milk. With all her heart she hoped that her parents had not been detained by nothing more than soldiers blocking the road. If that was what had happened, surely they had stayed with friends in Perryville last night. It was not likely that they could come home today, and she could only hope that they were safe.

When Lucinda returned from the springhouse, she was still not hungry, but she decided to eat anyway. The fire in the range had gone out, so she went to the woodpile and brought in kindling and put it in the wood box. She made a second trip and brought in a load of wood. She took her time cleaning the ashes from the firebox and building a fire. While it was getting hot, she emptied the coffeepot, refilled it with water, dumped in some coffee, and set it on the stove. She got out the dishes and silverware she would need and set them on the breakfast table.

When the stove was hot, she put the food on to warm. When it was ready, she brought her plate and put a small quantity of food on it. She poured herself a cup of coffee and sat down at the breakfast table to eat.

When she finished eating, she washed the dishes and put them away, then paused, wondering what to do next. Her impulse was to saddle Ol' Joe and ride to Perryville and try to find her parents, but she realized that would be a foolish thing to do. Since they could not come home, it was not likely that she could reach Perryville.

Perhaps she should start cleaning downstairs. Mama would be pleased. Besides, cleaning the house would help her to forget the loneliness of the big empty rooms and the danger that threatened from without.

For a moment she vacillated, not really wanting to get involved in housecleaning. Then, on an impulse, she went up to her room and dressed with care, as if she were expecting company. It was possible that some neighbor might come to the house. Or some member of the military might come. In sudden panic she hoped that soldiers would not come to pillage the place.

After Lucinda finished dressing, she brushed her hair, and dusted powder on her face, and went back downstairs. She paused at the foot of the stairs, shrugged, then went out on the porch and leaned against one of the big white columns, listening to the sounds that were coming from beyond the hill to the west. Men were calling to each other, but their words were faint and unintelligible. Horses were neighing, and Ol' Joe was answering them from his stall.

Soon she heard horses and wagons on the move, and, beyond the ridge she saw dust rising. Soldiers were coming in her direction! To the northeast, she heard more horses and wagons. She turned and saw a distant cloud of dust rising there, beyond the trees in the valley. The other army was also on the move!

She walked out into the yard for a better look, and to her alarm she saw more dust rising in the direction of Perryville. "There must be soldiers everywhere," she cried, aghast, and for the first time in her life she felt a tremor of fear.

The sounds to the east became louder, and horses and wagons appeared, moving across the top of a distant hill. They came down the hill and into the woods, and she lost sight of them. But she could still hear them coming toward her. Dismayed, she waited, watching and listening, hardly believing that the armies were about to fight so near that she could see them. And Papa had said so often that it would never happen here.

She looked toward the Mackville Pike, wishing she would see her parents coming home, but she turned away, biting her lip in disappointment.

It was time to let the stock out of the barn, but she feared that they would be frightened by the noise of battle. They could be injured if the fighting was nearby. She had best leave them in the barn, but they would need extra feed and water.

Glad for something to do, she went back to the barn, and, taking care not to spoil her Sunday dress, she spent half an hour putting out extra hay and corn for the animals. Then she made several trips to the springhouse carrying water to them. She filled the drinking buckets Papa had put in each stall and poured water in the trough for the hogs.

"I wouldn't have put on my good dress if I had known I'd have all this to do," she said to the hogs. The largest of them grunted, as if in reply.

She went to the stall where they kept the mules. Ol' Beck, the tamest of the mules came to her, and she reached over the side of the stall and petted her. "You're frightened too, Beck, I suppose," she said as she stroked her neck.

Suddenly it occurred to her that perhaps she could see what the armies were doing from the vantage point of the attic in the house. Instantly she ran to the house, and, without stopping to catch her breath, she ran up the back stairs to the attic.

The smell of unpainted wood and dust and decay assailed her nostrils as she hurried past the clutter, that had accumulated in past years, on her way to the southwest window. When she reached the window, she looked out, and, to her dismay, the big chimney at the end of the house blocked her view. So she hurried to the window at the other end of the attic, but there the big maple tree in the side yard also blocked her view.

Disappointed, she turned away and went down to her bedroom and stopped beside her bed, feeling lonely, helpless, and out of control. After a while she knelt by her bed and prayed and wept softly. Then she arose and went down to the front door and opened it and looked out. All was now quiet, and she dared hope that the soldiers had all gone away. She looked along the lane again, still hoping to see the bay mare and the buggy bringing her parents home, but again she turned away disappointed.

She closed the door and went to the kitchen, thinking it was almost time to eat again. She would warm up the leftover food again, and she would try to eat more than she had at breakfast.

There were still some embers in the range, so she put wood on them and watched until a tiny blaze started curling upward. Then she put the caps back on the stove and walked the floor while waiting for it to get hot.

Soon the flames were crackling merrily, and she felt the heat from the range, so she put the food on to warm.

"I'll put some water on to heat before I eat," she said aloud, for the sound of her voice seemed to make the house less lonely.

When the food was warm, she put it on the table and sat down to eat. She still had little appetite, but she stayed at the table anyway, mincing with the food.

"I had best wash the dishes, so they won't be dirty when Mama and Papa come home. I'll go out of my mind if I don't stay busy," she told herself.

The clock in the hall struck one o'clock. When it struck one-thirty, Lucinda was still killing time in the kitchen. At last she could find nothing more to do, so she decided to go outside and see if the soldiers had gone away. She pushed open the outside door, and again she heard the sounds of the armies, but now they were muted, as if they had moved away. That gave her reason to hope there would be no battle, but in her heart she knew that the danger had not passed.

She went out in the yard and wandered about, feeling the warm autumn sun upon her. Then, on an impluse, she decided to cross the valley below the house and climb the next hill. Perhaps from there she could see whether the soldiers were leaving or not. Even if they were not, they would be too busy to notice her. Besides, she would keep out of sight among the trees.

She ran into the house and put on a pair of comfortable shoes and her wide-brimmed hat to keep the sun off. As always, loose strands of hair fanned around her face, looking like burnished gold in the sunlight.

She crossed the yard to the front gate, let herself out, closed the gate behind her, ran down the hill to the narrow valley and crossed it, and started up the hill. She paused once for breath, and while she was resting she heard a man shout a sharp command.

There followed shouting and the sound of running feet. Half frightened she ran the remaining distance to the hilltop and took cover in a stand of hardwood trees. Then she saw soldiers in blue taking up a position directly in front of her. The men were no more than fifty yards away, and she scanned each face carefully, wondering if David could be among them. She was relieved when she did not see him.

At that moment she heard wild screams from a wooded valley to the north. She turned and saw galloping horses, ridden by gray-uniformed cavalrymen, emerge from the woods on a gallop. They crossed a shallow valley and started up the rise toward the line of Union soldiers. Almost suffocating with excitement, she watched them come.

The galloping horsemen, screaming wildly, were holding drawn swords above their heads. The sunlight was glinting on the polished steel, and the horse's hooves were pounding the parched earth, and the dust was rising in a cloud behind them and hanging in the air. The dust moved with the horses as they galloped.

A cavalryman on a huge black horse was riding slightly ahead of the others, and a Rebel flag was waving above his head.

"The Rebel Flag!" she murmured, forcing herself to keep her voice low. Thinking that the riding men did not pose a threat to her, she stayed where she was, watching.

The horses swept up a rise through scattered trees, and the men in blue started firing at them. Their muskets sounded like popcorn popping, only they were louder. A horse stumbled and fell, apparently hit by a musket ball.

His rider was thrown from the saddle and landed on his back. He did not get up.

"They are really shooting at them!" she cried, and her eyes grew wide with shock. She covered her mouth to keep from screaming, but she did not move from her place.

The charging men drew pistols and fired point blank as they swept through the line of Union soldiers. Some of the Confederate soldiers reholstered their pistols and drew their swords and started slashing the Union soldiers, wounding and killing men before her eyes. Some of the men screamed in pain. Others fell without a sound.

The clatter of firing muskets filled the air. Another horse fell, wounded. His rider leaped free and continued to fight on foot until he found a horse without a rider and mounted him.

The riding men galloped away as rapidly as they had come, leaving a dozen Union soldiers on the ground, dead or seriously wounded. A Rebel cavalryman was lying on the ground, not moving. Apparently he had taken a rifle ball and was dead. Lucinda was frozen with horror, scarcely believing that men had been wounded and others killed before her eyes.

A shout from the west caught her attention, and she turned and saw many more soldiers in blue uniform, as if they had arisen out of the earth.

"I hope David is not up there," she whispered frantically.

Shots came from the other direction, and she turned and saw Confederate forces marching out of the woods in the valley.

Tad! she thought, and her hand flew to her throat. *Could he be among those marching men?* With all her heart she hoped that he was not.

She watched the men cross the valley, take up positions behind a fence, aim their muskets and rifles, and start firing. The guns made a loud, cracking sound and bullets whizzed through the air, sounding like angry bees. Blue smoke, mingled with the airborne dust. The smell was acrid and choking. Men shouted and screamed, and some cried in pain.

Lucinda could feel her own heart beating, and the first fear she had ever known assailed her. Suppose a stray bullet should strike her. Suppose her parents should come home and find her dead. She should run home, but if she did she would never know what happened. So she simply moved deeper into the trees and continued to watch the battle.

The Rebel soldiers started tearing away the fence and pouring through the openings and charging up the hill.

A sharp command from the Union side caught her attention, and she turned and saw more Union forces marching down the hill to join those already in place.

She jumped when a cannon boomed from the top of the ridge, but she did not cry out. *Surely the cannon would kill every Rebel soldier in that advancing line,* she thought.

The muskets and rifles were now cracking steadily from both sides. Musket balls and rifle bullets were whizzing through the air. Some of them struck the ground, not twenty feet from where she stood, and some of them cut through the trees above her head. They sounded like a scythe in a briar patch. Others were cutting men down, and they were falling like ironweeds before a blade wielded by a strong man.

Cannons were now booming steadily, and cannonballs were roaring through the air. Some of them were striking the trees above her, and breaking off branches. Dumfounded, she watched the branches fall to the ground. Other cannonballs hit the ground, and Lucinda felt the vibrations from them. Blue smoke from the guns and cannons drifted in the air and burned her nostrils.

Gaping holes appeared in the line of soldiers before

her, and she realized that some of the cannonballs had struck the men. Her heart almost failed, but still she did not run away.

Lucinda jumped with each deep-throated boom of the cannon. She covered her ears with her hands, but she could not shut out the terrible sounds. A stray cannonball could hit where she was standing, she realized. If that happened, even the trees would not keep her from being killed. She hugged herself in fear, but she gritted her teeth and stayed where she was.

The men in gray charged up the hill, firing, reloading, and firing again.

Union forces returned their fire. The cracking of muskets and the booming of cannons continued until blue smoke almost obscured the fighting men, but she could still see men falling near her. Some crawled slowly and painfully away. Some, though they could not stand, continued to reload and fire into the enemy line. Some of the fallen men did not move.

The Confederates continued to advance in the face of the withering fire. Then a sharp command rose above the noise of battle, and the Union troops fell back. Halfway up the hill they panicked, then turned and fled. Lucinda had no way of knowing that these were unseasoned troops, facing real battle conditions for the first time. She only hoped that was the end of the battle.

Fresh troops soon joined the retiring line, and they made another stand. The Rebels continued to charge toward them, firing, reloading, and firing again.

Soon the Union forces retreated again, this time pausing to fire as they went. More men fell on both sides. Some of the wounded limped to the rear. Medics appeared from nowhere, and started carrying men away on stretchers. Some wounded men were loaded on wagons and taken away, but the dead were left where they had fallen.

Pale and shaken, Lucinda screamed for them to stop,

but her cry was lost in the noise of battle. She now wanted
to run away, but her feet refused to move.

The Union forces continued their retreat over the hill.
Some of them took refuge in a cornfield, others behind
trees, and still others behind stone fences. From their hiding places they continued to fire their weapons.

Commanding officers rode up the hill on beautiful
horses to a vantage point for observation. Then teams of
horses pulled cannons out of the woods and into the open.
At the top of the hill each team circled and stopped with
the cannon they were pulling pointed toward the Union
forces. The drivers quickly unhitched the teams and took
them out of the way.

A command rang out and men aimed and fired the
cannons at the men who had taken cover. The cannons
boomed and belched smoke and balls of iron. The soldiers reloaded them as fast as they could, then fired again.
The infantry continued to fire into the cornfield and at
the men who had taken shelter behind the trees and the
stone fence.

The withering fire drove the men from their cover,
and they fled and struggled over a fence and retreated
beyond the hill.

It was almost over, Lucinda decided, and, regaining
the use of her legs, she started running toward home as
fast as she could. As she ran she heard a fresh outbreak of
cannon fire, and, with every boom, she jumped and ran
faster. Frightened and broken by what she had seen, she
did not stop running until she reached the valley below
the house. There she rested briefly, then ran along the
valley to a point behind the barn. Then she started up the
hill, keeping the barn between her and the house so her
parents would not see her if they had come home in her
absence. When she reached the barn, she paused again to
catch her breath and to listen for the sound of her father
inside. She did not hear him, so she opened the door and

looked in.

The mare was not in her stall, and the buggy was not where they kept it. Her parents had not returned. That meant that she would have to spend at least one more night alone.

That gave her grave cause to worry. *Suppose some soldier, taking refuge from the battle, should come to the house. What dangers would she face? And what could she do?* There was little she could do but hide inside the house and keep the doors locked until she was sure the soldiers were gone, she realized.

She pushed the barn door closed and leaned against it, trying to bring her emotions under control before she went in to see how the animals were faring.

Chapter 11

*A*s Lucinda entered the barn, the gelding put his head over the side of the stall and nickered softly.

"Poor Ol' Joe," she said to the horse, and she went to him and stroked his neck. The big horse was trembling, and she realized that the noise of battle had frightened him.

"It's all right, boy," she said, though she knew that nothing was all right, and she doubted that anything in the world would ever be right again.

She went to the stall where they kept the mules and saw that they were standing close together in the corner, trembling. She went to the cows' stall and looked at them. They looked back at her with large, frightened eyes. Even the hogs were not grunting contentment, as they usually did. Instead, they were piled on top of each other in the far corner of their pen.

Lucinda started talking aloud to the animals, as much to calm her own fears as to calm them. "You all still have plenty of feed . . . and there's water. I don't think any of you have eaten a bite or drunk a drop of water all day, but I think all the banging and booming will soon be over and you can calm down."

A sudden loud booming of cannons made her jump with fear, and she decided that she ought to go to the house and lock herself in until the fighting ended. So she left the barn and started hurrying to the house.

In the distance she heard the rifles and muskets cracking and the cannons booming. The fighting had moved
farther to the west, but she heard voices in the field where
she had watched the battle. She listened closely, but she
heard no sounds of battle. Instead she heard the cries of
wounded men, and she heard horses and moving wagons, or ambulances. They could be picking up the
wounded to take them to a field hospital, or they could be
pulling the cannons away. There was little talking, but
occasionally a man spoke with authority.

Soon the horses and wagons started moving away,
some to the west and some to the east. She wondered if
both sides were picking up their wounded. That would
be a sight to see, she decided—two armies, so recently
engaged in killing, now bent on saving lives.

At the back door she paused to listen, still trying to
determine what was happening. At times the muted sounds
were almost drowned by the sounds of the continuing
battle to the west. At other times she heard the mingled
sounds of gentle talk, cries of pain, and more moving
vehicles.

Suddenly, without taking time to think, Lucinda
started running back to the scene of battle. She did not
stop until she reached the place where she had stood earlier while watching the battle.

To the west wagons and ambulances were moving
over the ridge, but there was no sign of the Rebels. If
they had been collecting their wounded, they had already
gone. She turned to the battlefield and saw that it was
littered with the bodies of the dead, from both the Union
Army and the Confederate Army. The ground was also
littered with rifles and swords and canteens and slouch
hats that had fallen from the heads of dead or wounded
men. Some cannons had also been left behind.

The sight of so many dead bodies filled her with an

unutterable disgust. *Why had this happened? How could men be trained to so callously shoot and kill one another?*

She wondered when they would come to bury the dead. Surely they would bury them after they had taken care of the wounded. Many of the dead men's eyes were open to the sky, and the sight of them filled her with anguish. In sudden anxiety, she wondered if one or both of her brothers could be lying out there—dead.

She did not want to be near the dead men, but she had to know if her brothers were out there. So she climbed the fence and started across the field, determined to look into the face of every dead man she could before their comrades came back to bury them.

Cautiously she approached the nearest dead soldier and saw that he was young and handsome. He would have looked as if he were asleep had it not been for a great, bloody gash across his throat. Suddenly ill, she turned away and ran behind a tree and bent over, retching violently. When her sickness passed, she straightened and brushed the tears from her eyes.

"I don't know how I can bear the sight of another dead man or the stench of the battlefield, but I have to make sure that my brothers are not out here," she told herself sternly as she wiped her face with her handkerchief.

Faintly she heard the horses and wagons in the distance as she again started her walk among the dead.

"I'm glad they're gone," she said, talking to keep up her courage.

Several times she thought she was going to be sick again, but she forced herself to continue her search. A brief glance at the face of each lifeless man was enough to tell her that he was not one of her brothers. There were so many of them, she wondered if she could bear to look at them all. Surely the sight of them would cause her to have nightmares for the rest of her life.

After half an hour of wandering among the dead soldiers, she could bear no more, and she turned away and started running in the direction that she thought was home. The hill seemed steeper than she remembered, but she ran on, intent on getting away from the dead soldiers. Finally she paused for breath, and she saw that she had run far up the hill, almost to where the Union soldiers had made their last stand before she had gone home.

With a startled cry, she turned and ran back down the hill. She soon came to a ditch that had been washed in the field by the rains of other years. She attempted to leap across it but missed her footing and fell into it. Shaken, she struggled to her feet and attempted to get out of the ditch, but the ditch was deep so she started along it, trying to find a place where she could climb out.

A few feet ahead, tall weeds had grown up and fallen across the ditch, effectively blocking her way. She turned and started back. Then she heard someone moaning in a low voice.

"I didn't hear anything. There's no one out here but dead men," she cried.

Then she heard another moan, louder than the first one.

"There is someone alive out here!" she exclaimed. "But where?"

"Over here. Water!" a low, anguished voice responded.

"Where?" she cried again, looking around.

There was a long pause. Then the voice responded, "In the ditch."

She looked up and down the ditch. Then she looked beyond the fallen weeds. There she saw a place where the weeds had been crushed, as if someone had fallen on them.

"I think I see where you fell, but I don't see you," she called. "Where are you?"

"Don't know . . . weeds above me . . . can't see . . . need water." The voice fell silent.

She called again, but the voice did not answer. She stood on tiptoes and looked over the weeds. Then she saw the soldier lying on his back in the ditch. Weeds were crushed into the ditch beneath him, and more weeds almost covered the ditch above him.

She called to him again, trying to keep him talking, but he did not answer. *Had he died?* she wondered. *Perhaps he was only unconscious.* Forgetting her good dress, she crawled out of the ditch on her hands and knees and ran to the place where the soldier had fallen. Through an opening in weeds, she saw that he was wearing a blue uniform.

"He's a Yankee!" she mouthed in silent shock. The Yankees had taken David from his family, and they had killed Nathan, and, no doubt, this one would have killed Tad if he had had the chance.

She turned angrily away. *Let him die,* she thought. *No one saved Nathan.* She took a defiant step away from the wounded soldier, but she paused when she heard him moan again.

"Water . . . water," he called hoarsely.

The thought of doing anything for a Yankee soldier appalled her, but her woman's heart made her pity him. For a moment she stood vacillating, wondering what she was to do. *They've stopped looking for the wounded, and there's no telling when they'll come back to bury the dead,* she thought. *When they do come back, they may not find this soldier, and he will die out here alone. I'll never forgive myself if I don't try to save his life.*

She was angry because she was in this position, but she started tugging the weeds aside anyway. When they were out of the way, she saw the soldier's pale, anguished, blood-streaked face, and her heart went out to him. His hat had fallen from his head, and his blond hair was matted with blood.

If he didn't look like a dead man, he would be handsome, she thought.

"Stop it," she commanded herself in an angry whisper. She had no business thinking such thoughts in the midst of the dead that lay around her. Besides, it should not concern her what a Union soldier looked like.

The soldier's eyes were closed, but if he ever opened them they would be blue, she thought. Nathan Wills had blue eyes, and there was something about this soldier that reminded her of him.

The soldier had said he wanted water, so she would find water for him if possible. Not far away she saw a canteen attached to the body of a dead soldier. There should be water in it, but she dreaded to take it from the body of the dead man. She would have to forget her queasy stomach and her innate dread of dead bodies, for the wounded soldier might not live long enough for her to go to the house and get water.

She went to the dead soldier and dropped on her knees beside him. She struggled with the unfamiliar fastenings, and when the canteen came free she shook it. Water sloshed inside. Thankful that it was not empty, she ran back to the wounded Yankee.

"I have brought you some water," she said as she dropped on her knees beside him.

His eyes twitched, then opened to narrow slits, just wide enough for her to see that they were blue as she had expected.

"Just a minute," she said, as she removed the cap from the canteen. "I'll hold your head up if it don't hurt you."

She put her hand under his head and gently raised it, watching his face for any sign of pain.

He opened his mouth and she pressed the canteen to his lips. He drank thirstily. Then he closed his eyes again.

"Are you all right?" she asked.

His only response was the slight movement of his right eyelid.

"Maybe I can call a medic," she offered without stopping to think that she could not easily reach the Union forces.

He did not answer, so she climbed out of the ditch and started running up the hill the way the Union Army had retreated.

In her haste she stumbled and fell, skinning her knees and tearing her dress, but she got up and ran on. Her knees were stinging, and she felt blood running down her legs, but she did not stop. She was panting for breath, but she pressed on until she reached the fence at the top of the hill and saw a cloud of dust in the distance. The armies still were fighting, so there was no way she could go to them for help. If anything were to be done for the soldier, she would have to do it.

She started running back down the hill. Pain stabbed at her side, but she struggled on until she reached the soldier.

How could she move him? And where could she take him? she wondered.

"Soldier, are you still alive?" she demanded.

He did not answer, but again she saw his right eyelid lift slightly.

"You're alive all right. I hope you can hear me. I'm going to go get someone to move you to a place where you can be cared for."

She turned away and started running toward home. As she ran she wondered how she would move the soldier and where she could take him. Papa would never consent to a Yankee soldier being in his house. Besides, since Papa and Mama were both gone, it would not be proper for a single girl to take a man to her house, even a wounded one. Besides, if she should take him there, the neighbors, whose sympathies were with the South, would never forgive her.

If he should die while she was gone, that would solve her problem, but, if he were alive when she returned, she would have to do what she could for him, even though Papa would be furious, and Tad would hate her, and Mama would say nothing in her defense for fear of angering Papa. Only David would take her side, and he was too far away to help.

As she continued toward home, she thought of Nigger Henry and his wife, Mandy. It was not far across the fields to their house and perhaps she could get them to help.

Nigger Henry and Mandy had found their way to their community from the South and bought the little farm where they now lived, after their master had freed them. They never had said, but surely their sympathies must be with the North. They should be willing to help, and they would not talk.

When Lucinda reached home, she was glad to find that her parents had still not returned. Fervently she hoped that they would not come until she had found a place for the soldier.

She went to the barn, and, even though the gelding was still restless, she saddled and bridled him. Then she mounted the sidesaddle, and rode across the farm at a gallop to the gap in the fence that opened near Nigger Henry's cabin.

Mandy was standing in the doorway, shading her eyes with both hands when Lucinda rode up.

"Law, Miss Lucinda, what yo' in such a all-fired hurry 'bout?" she asked. "Yo' runnin' from de war? We been layin' low all day an' listenin' to all dat shootin'."

"I have to see Henry. Is he here?"

"He's in de barn. He's—"

"Thank you." She turned the gelding toward the barn and spurred him to a canter.

"Henry, Henry, I need your help," she called when

she reached the barn.

"Yes, ma'am. I's a-comin'," Henry called in return. The barn door opened, and Henry, stooped and old and gray, emerged, looking at her and squinting at the fading light of the afternoon sun.

"Miss Lucinda, what's done gone and happened 'sides de war?" he asked.

"Henry, there's a wounded soldier on the hill over there." She pointed toward the field of battle. "They missed him when they were looking for the wounded. Now they're gone, and he'll die if we don't help him."

"What yo' want me to do, Miss Lucinda?"

"I need you to help move him so his wound can be treated."

"Is they any dead bodies about? Miss Lucinda. I don't like bein' 'bout no dead people."

"There are some dead bodies, Henry, but they won't hurt you."

"I don't know 'bout dat, Miss Lucinda. I sho' don't like bein' round no dead people. Is dat wounded soldier from de South?"

"He's a Yankee, Henry. Please hurry, he may be dying."

"Miss Lucinda, if I help yo' save a Yankee, de white people 'round here will hang me." He shook his head firmly. "No ma'am, Miss Lucinda. I won't do it."

Mandy had just arrived and was listening.

"I hear what yo' say, Henry. Yo' might be right 'bout de white people hanging yo', but yo' can't let a man die dat's been fightin' fur our country widout doin' what yo' can fo' him. I reckon Miss Lucinda is takin' a chance, same as yo' would be, and she ain't backin' down," she said emphatically.

"Law me, what can I do, Mandy?" Henry demanded.

"I reckon that soldier needs movin' like Miss Lucinda say, and he needs some doctorin'. Now yo' hitch up de mules to de sled and go fetch that Yankee so's I ken doctor him. Yo' hear?"

"Where yo' think we is goin' to put a full grow'd Yankee soldier?" Henry asked, shaking his head dejectedly.

"Yo' do what I say, Henry, an' I'll fix de place to keep him out o' sight till he gets well. Now you get."

Henry went back in the barn and to the stall where he kept the mules. Sullenly, he brought them out and started putting the harness on them.

"Mandy, I'm going back to the soldier. At least I can take him some fresh water from our house, and I can tell him that help is on the way. Tell Henry to come straight past our house, then to go across the valley and up the next hill. He'll see my horse hitched to the fence, and I'll be watching for him."

"Yes, ma'am, Miss Lucinda. I'll tell him, an' I'll make him hurry."

Chapter 12

*L*ucinda galloped the gelding home and dismounted
at the springhouse. While she was tying him to the limb
of a tree, she noticed that the sounds of battle were now
in the distance. Relieved, she hurried to the house and
got an empty syrup pail to carry water in and a cup for
the soldier to drink from. Back at the springhouse, she
filled the bucket with water and pressed on the lid. Then
she remounted the gelding and rode back to the fence at
the top of the hill.

She took pains not to spill the water as she dismounted
and hitched the horse. Then she climbed the fence and
hurried to the soldier.

He was lying just as she had left him, with his eyes
closed, and his face ashen. The sight of him caused pain
to stab at her heart, for she thought he had died while she
was gone. Then she saw that his chest was moving ever
so slightly, and she breathed a sigh of relief, though she
feared that he had lost consciousness.

"Soldier, are you awake?" she asked.

The fingers on his right hand twitched slightly.

"Soldier! Are you awake?" she called again.

His eyes came half open, and she thought they were
the bluest eyes she had ever seen. She moved to him, and
his eyes followed her. "What is your name, miss?" he
asked weakly.

"I'm Lucinda. What is your name?"

"Martin. . . . must be an angel," he murmured softly to himself, and he closed his eyes again.

"I brought you some fresh water," she said loudly, trying to arouse him.

"Thanks," he responded, and he opened his blue eyes again.

She set the bucket on the ground, pried the lid off, and filled the cup with water. Then she knelt beside him, as she had before, and lifted his head and pressed the cup to his lips.

He drank the cup dry, then smiled wanly.

"Help is on the way," she told him. "A negro man is coming with a team and a sled. We are going to move you, and a negro woman is going to treat your wound. She has treated wounded men before."

"I would have died if you hadn't come," he murmured as he drifted back into unconsciousness.

She placed her hand on his forehead and found that he was burning with fever. "I wish Henry would hurry," she said aloud. Then she arose and walked back to the fence to see if he was in sight. To her relief, she saw him coming down the hill in front of her house with the mules and sled. She watched until he crossed the valley and started up the hill. Then she went back to wait by the soldier.

While she was waiting, the enormity of what she was doing dawned upon her. Everyone she knew, except David and the Taylors, would hate her if they learned of this. Yet she knew that, no matter what happened, she could not leave the soldier to die alone. If he were David, or Tad, she would want someone to help him. If he had a family, they would want her to do what she could for him, so she really had no choice.

She soon heard Henry coming and arose to go and meet him. "I'll be back in a minute," she told the soldier as she was leaving.

Henry was taking a panel out of the fence when she reached him. "I hears cannons boomin' and muskets poppin' ober de hill. Yo' don't think de fightin' might come back dis way, do yo'?" he asked uneasily.

"I'm sure it won't, Henry, but we do have to hurry. Let me help you with the fence."

"Yo' needen mind with dis ol' fence, Miss Lucinda. I'll get it out o' de way in a minute," Henry answered.

"I'll help and it will save time."

"Yo' had best go back and stay wid de Yankee. I'll manage dis ol' fence," he told her patiently.

"You're right. He might need me," she agreed, and she ran back to the soldier.

She was still looking down at Martin when Henry stopped the mules so the sled was alongside the ditch where he was lying. Henry kept his eyes on Martin so he would not see the dead soldiers scattered over the field.

"It won't be easy to get him on de sled widout hurtin' him," he said.

"I'll help you lift him, Henry."

"Yo'll get your pretty dress all bloody, Miss Lucinda."

"Don't worry about that. I've already ruined it. Let's hurry and get him loaded and leave before somebody sees us."

"I brung dis ol' quilt, and I'll put it in de ditch 'side o' him. Den, we ken roll him over on it."

"Then what will we do?"

"We'll get holt o' the corners and drag him out o' de ditch if we is strong enough."

"Let's try, Henry. Please hurry!"

"I's hurryin', Miss Lucinda," Henry said patiently as he spread the quilt beside the soldier and started pushing it under him.

"Now, Miss Lucinda, maybe us boof ken roll him over on de quilt," he said at last.

She knelt beside Henry, and together they rolled the soldier on the quilt. He groaned, but he did not regain consciousness.

"Now we'll boof get holt o' de quilt and pull," Henry said.

It took all the strength Lucinda had, and Henry grunted as if he were straining himself, but together they rolled the soldier out of the ditch.

"How are we going to get him on the sled, Henry?"

"I'll get holt o' de corners o' de quilt at de head and lift. Yo' ken get holt at de feet."

Together they lifted and pulled until the soldier was on the sled. He grimaced with pain more than once, but he did not cry out.

Then Henry started the mules back toward home, and Lucinda ran ahead to the gelding. Henry did not stop to repair the fence but continued across the fields, walking beside his mules and guiding them in the direction of the Perrys' barn.

Walking and leading Ol' Joe, Lucinda hurried until she caught up with the sled. Then she walked behind it, still leading the gelding, and kept her eyes on Martin. From time to time she looked around to see if anyone was watching them. She was relieved that no one was about.

The soldier made the trip better than she expected, though he had winced with pain each time the sled lurched over a stone or a rough place. Finally they passed the barn and she breathed a sigh of relief, because it shielded them from being seen from the house, should her parents return.

Henry turned the mules toward his place, and she was greatly relieved when they came in sight of his cabin and saw Mandy standing in the doorway.

When they reached the gap, Mandy came out to meet them. She took one look at Martin and motioned them on to the barn. "He sho' look like he needs lookin' after," she said as she fell in step with the sled.

Henry stopped the sled at the barn door, and Mandy hurried to open it.

"I fixed him a place in de strippin' room. They ain't no room fo' no soldier in our house," she explained after Henry drove the mules inside.

"The stripping room? Will he be all right in there?" Lucinda asked with concern.

"Yo'll see. Dey's a stove in dar so's we ken make him a fire, an' I took down our bed and brought it out here fo' him, an' . . ."

"Now where does yo' think we's goin' to sleep, Mandy?" Henry grumbled as he went to close the door.

"Yo' shut your mouth, Henry. We ken sleep on de flo' like we used too. And I put a cover over the window, so's nobody can look in, an' I brung a lamp so's he won't be in de dark," Mandy continued as if Henry had not interrupted.

Lucinda tied Ol' Joe to a post. Then, fearing what she would see, she followed Mandy into the stripping room. Henry followed also, looking dazed.

"See how I fixed it up," Mandy said, beaming. "I eben carried all the tobacco stalks out, and I swept de flo'."

The lamp Mandy had set on a table was burning, and its light was falling warmly on the worn rag carpet she had put on the floor. Lucinda was relieved to see that there were clean sheets and covers on the bed that Mandy had set up in the corner of the room.

"Henry, bring de sled up close to de strippin' room door," Mandy ordered.

Without a word, Henry did as he was told. Then with Mandy's help they carried the soldier in and laid him on the bed.

"I didn't have time to build no fire," Mandy explained.

"Henry, yo' build one, so's he don't get cold when night comes on. 'Sides, I'm goin' to need plenty o' hot water so's I can tend to him."

"Shouldn't we call a doctor?" Lucinda asked.

"An' have dem Rebel sympathizers kum an' lynch us all?" Mandy demanded sharply. "I's treated plenty o' wounded men in my time, an' I ken treat this un."

"Is there anything I can do to help?" Lucinda asked.

"Beggin' yo' pardon, Miss Lucinda, but I wants yo' and Henry boof out o' my way, soon as he brings in de water. Yo' can wait in the barn, an' I'll tell yo' how de soldier is, soon as I sees how bad he's hurt."

Lucinda stayed in the stripping room, looking down at Martin, while Henry was bringing in the water. She realized that there was nothing more she could do, and she started wondering what she had gotten herself into and why she had involved Henry and Mandy.

"Now yo' and Miss Lucinda go, 'cause I's got work to do," Mandy said when Henry had brought the second bucket of water.

Lucinda took a last look at Martin. Then she went out and waited in the driveway, biting her nails and watching Henry unhitch the mules and put them in their stall. After he finished he came and sat down on a nearby lard can he used for carrying feed to his stock.

"Thank you for helping, Henry," Lucinda said. "I could not have moved him without your help."

"Yo' is welcome, Miss Lucinda. I just hope dey ain't no Rebels eber finds out what we done."

"We'll keep it a secret, Henry. I don't won't anybody to know either, not even my parents."

They fell silent then, and she listened to Mandy's heavy tread on the plank floor of the stripping room.

A great while later Mandy came out, drying her hands on her apron and wiping the perspiration from her face with her sleeve. "The bullet done gone clean through him,

Miss Lucinda," she announced.

"Oh, Oh," Lucinda cried, feeling as if a bullet had pierced her own heart. "Is he going to die?"

"He ain't dead yet. Dat means he ain't shot in de heart or de lungs. He's bled a lot though."

"Then you think he will live?"

"I don't know, Miss Lucinda. I's seen men hurt worse than him get well, and I's seen some not hurt much a-tall that died. De bleedin' is stopped on the outside, but I don't know 'bout de inside. I'll pray fo' him, an' I'll tend to him de best I ken, and I'll feed him when he's able to eat. Dat's all I ken do."

"I'll bring food, and I'll do anything else I can to help," Lucinda promised. "I'm so thankful to both of you. I couldn't have done anything without your help."

"Yo' is welcome, Miss Lucinda," Mandy replied.

"I just hope dat nobody finds out," Henry said, shaking his head.

"I'll come back soon," Lucinda promised. Then she led Ol' Joe from the barn, mounted him and rode home, thinking and worrying.

That night, after Lucinda had gone to bed in her lonely bedroom, she could not fall asleep, for the scenes of the battle kept repeating themselves over and over in her mind. Her knees were sore from her fall, and every bone and muscle in her body ached. Lying there, looking into the darkness, she worried about her parents. *Surely they were all right,* she reasoned. She was glad they had not come home while she and Henry were moving the soldier.

She hoped the soldier was going to live, though he seemed so close to death. She remembered his blood-stained clothes and the way he had drifted in and out of consciousness. If he did live, she wondered how she could take food to him without anyone knowing.

Finally, after she had heard the clock strike twelve, she fell into a troubled sleep. A short time later some new commotion awoke her, and she lay listening to the sounds of horses and wagons and men on the move. At last the sounds grew faint in the distance, but sleep did not soon return to her. When she did fall asleep again, in the last hours of darkness, she slept poorly.

As the early light of dawn was creeping through her window, Lucinda awoke, and her first thought was of the wounded soldier, and she wondered if he had lived through the night.

She sat on the side of her bed and stretched her sore muscles, winced with pain, grimaced, and fell back upon the bed. For several minutes she listened for any sound in the house that would tell her that her parents had come home while she slept. There were no sounds inside, but outside she heard the wind in the trees, and she heard the rooster crow from his roost in the tree outside her window.

At last she got out of bed and dressed and went to the barn and fed the stock and milked the cows. When she came from the barn, she noticed that the sky was overcast, and that it looked like rain. Perhaps the long drought was going to break at last.

When Lucinda reached the house, she decided to skip breakfast and go immediately and see if Martin was still alive. If he was, she would ask Mandy what he could eat. Then she would return and get food for him.

She hurried up to her room and dressed, for in no way did she want Martin to see her dressed in the clothes she had worn to work in the barn. Just as she finished dressing, she heard a horse and buggy coming down the lane.

"Oh, it's Mama and Papa," she cried aloud, glad they had come home, yet disappointed that she could not go to check on Martin.

She ran downstairs and out the front door, arriving just as the buggy drew up at the yard gate.

"Lucinda, we've been worried to death about you," her mother called.

"And I've been worried about you and Papa."

"There were soldiers on the road the day we went to town. They let us pass as we were going, but they refused to let us come back or to send a message home."

"Cindy, I'm glad you're all right," Lewis said as he made Katy turn the buggy wheels so Nancy could get out.

"We heard there was a battle near here," her mother continued.

"There was, Mama, and it was terrible. I could hear the muskets cracking and the cannons booming. It sounded like the end of the world."

"Where did they fight?" Lewis asked.

"It sounded like they were fighting everywhere, but there was a really big battle over that way," she pointed toward the battlefield.

"You must have been scared to death," her mother exclaimed as they started to the house.

"I wasn't really scared, but the noise was awful."

"I'm going to unhitch Katy," Lewis called as he started to the barn.

"Papa, don't you want to get the groceries out first?" Lucinda called.

"There ain't nothing to get out, Cindy," he called back.

"Cindy, we didn't buy a thing. Every store in town was closed and locked. They were all afraid the soldiers would carry off everything they had," Nancy told her.

"Where did you and Papa stay?" Lucinda asked as they reached the house.

"We stayed with the Popes. You remember them. They used to come to our church once in a while."

"Yes, I remember them. They had the freckled-faced boy named Charley. He used to embarrass me to death, winking at me." She opened the door so her mother could enter, then followed her inside.

"Charley has grown up now and gone off to the war. He's fighting for the South. He was in Tennessee the last time they heard from him," her mother said as she removed her coat and hat and hung them on the hall tree.

Lucinda wondered what her mother would say if she knew about Martin. Mama had never been much concerned about slavery, but after David had joined the Union Army her sympathies had been with the North. There was no question what Papa's reaction would be. He would go straight through the roof.

Now that her parents were home, *how was she to get food to Martin?* she wondered. *Some way she would have to go and see about him today, but how?* Mandy might need bandage or medication, and she would certainly need something for Martin to eat.

"Have you had breakfast, Mama?" she asked.

"We ate with the Popes before we left. We wondered if we could get home, but your papa wanted us to try."

"Were there still soldiers on the road?"

"Only a few stragglers, and they were on the move, but we could tell that the army had passed that way. There were things they had dropped, holes they had cut in fences, and cornfields they had stripped. Even the stalks had been trampled in the ground. Lewis was worried to death that they had overrun our farm and carried off everything in sight, but I was mostly worried about you."

"They didn't come near our house, Mama, but I was worried about you and Papa."

"I never would have forgiven myself if anything had happened to you, Cindy. I still feel terrible, going off and leaving a single girl alone like that in wartime."

"I hear Papa at the back door, Mama," Lucinda said. "I must have latched it when I came in from the barn." She ran to let her father in, and her mother followed.

"I'm glad you and Mama got home, Papa," Lucinda said as she let him in.

"I'm glad to be home, Cindy. I'm sorry we weren't here with you while they were fightin'. You could have been killed."

"I knew they weren't shooting at me, Papa."

"Lewis, you know that girl ain't never been afraid of a single thing in her life," Nancy exclaimed.

"I know, Nancy, but war is different," he answered as he started to the living room.

"What are you going to do, now that we are home, Lewis?" Nancy asked.

"I want to go see where they fought, Nancy, and I'll have to hurry. Looks like it's going to rain."

"Why do you want to do that, Lewis?" Nancy asked.

"I wonder if they evacuated all the wounded and if they've buried the dead," Lewis said.

"I think they did, Papa. There was a lot of commotion over that way after midnight," Lucinda answered.

"Just the same, I'll go see," Lewis declared.

"You had better take a raincoat," Lucinda suggested.

"If you'll wait till I change my clothes, I'll go with you," Nancy said. "Lucinda, do you want to go with us?"

"No, Mama. I heard enough of the fighting yesterday to last me a lifetime. You and Papa go on without me." She was thinking that, if she hurried, she could go and see about Martin while they were gone.

"Bring raincoats for both of us," Lewis called to Nancy.

"I will and I'll bring an umbrella too," Nancy replied as she started upstairs to their room.

"Papa, I was afraid all the noise would scare the stock yesterday, so I kept them in the barn all day. I think I'll go let them out."

"You sure you don't want to go with me and your mother?"

"No, Papa, I'll see you and Mama when you get back," she replied as she was leaving for the barn.

Chapter 13

When Lucinda reached the barn, she saw that the mare was still eating the hay her father had put down for her. Leaving her to finish eating, she let the cows and the mules out to pasture. The mules ran from the barn and along the fence row to the dry stream in the back of the pasture. There they paused and pawed at the gravel in the bed of the stream, then they ran to the corner of the field and looked back at her.

The cows walked slowly out of the barn and started grazing the brown grass a few feet away.

Lucinda watched them momentarily, then looked up at the clouds. They had darkened since she had left the house, and there was a feeling of moisture in the air.

"I'll have to hurry before the rain starts," she told herself as she turned toward Ol' Joe's stall. She went in and put a bridle on the horse and led him out. She put the sidesaddle on him and left him standing while she went to the front of the barn and looked out. Her parents were just leaving the house, and she watched them cross the valley and start up the hill toward the battlefield. Relieved that they were gone, she led Ol' Joe out the back door of the barn, mounted the sidesaddle, and started him cantering across the field toward Henry's cabin.

When she reached the gap near Henry's cabin, she dismounted and hitched the gelding, let herself through the gap, and hurried to the barn on foot. She opened the door a crack and looked in. No one was in sight so she went in, closed the door behind her, and stopped, considering what to do next.

The mingled smells of farm animals and hay and tobacco came to her nostrils, and in the muted light in the barn she saw a cat raise his head from a bale of hay where he was sleeping and yawn.

She wondered if she should rap on the stripping room door. If Martin were yet alive, he would not be able to answer the door, she realized. He might even be too weak to call to her, but she dared not simply go barging in on him. After a moment she heard Mandy's heavy footsteps inside the room and called softly, "Mandy, are you there?"

"Law, yes, Miss Lucinda. I's here." She crossed the room and opened the door. "Come on in, Miss Lucinda," she invited.

"Is the soldier all right, Mandy?"

"He done come through de night all right, Miss Lucinda. An' he ain't got no fever. He's powerful weak though." She lowered her voice to a whisper. "An' I wonder if he ain't out o' his head. He keeps talkin' somethin' 'bout a angel comin' fur him." She motioned Lucinda in as she talked.

"I'll have to hurry, Mandy. My parents have come home. They went to see the battlefield, but they'll soon be back."

The soldier heard her voice and turned his head slowly toward her. "The angel is back," he said softly, and a wan, twisted smile crossed his face.

"I'm no angel. I'm Lucinda," she smiled back at him.

"You were an angel yesterday. I would have died if it hadn't been for you. Now I have another angel . . . a black angel." He rolled his blue eyes toward Mandy.

"I'm glad she's taking care of you."

"I know what you're doing for me is dangerous, Miss

Lucinda, but I'm glad you've come to see me."

"I'm glad you're going to be all right. I worried about you most of the night."

"Think of that! . . . a Rebel angel worrying about a Yankee soldier." He smiled faintly.

"I have two brothers in the war. One of them is in the Union Army and the other one is in the Confederate Army. I reckon that kind of leaves me in the middle." She did not have the heart to tell him that she hated Yankees.

"Miss Lucinda, will you write a letter to my mother for me?" Martin asked. "I want her to know that I'm all right." He looked up at her with blue eyes that again reminded her of Nathan Wills. His eyes made it hard for her to remember that he was a hated Yankee.

"It's all right if you don't want to," he said, looking troubled when she was slow to answer.

"Of course I'll write to your mother for you," she answered quickly. "Give me her address." She looked in her purse and brought out a pencil and a scrap of paper.

"Address the letter to Mrs. Morgan Colver. Her address is Cross Station, Ohio. She doesn't have a route number."

"Do you want me to tell her you've been wounded?"

"She'll wonder why I didn't write myself, so you'd better tell her." He paused for breath and grimaced with pain. "Tell her I'll be on my feet in a few days."

"I'll write her tonight, and I'll take the letter out to the mailbox in the morning."

"Yo' ken tell his ma that he's got good keer, 'cause I sho' aim to take keer o' him," Mandy interrupted.

"I know you will, Mandy, and I'll tell his mother that he has the best of care. I won't mention though that we have to keep him hidden because of our hostile neighbors."

"Ain't no way I wouldn't take keer o' him, 'cause he's done got shot fightin' for our country."

"Don't give my mother your address. A letter from her might get you in trouble. Tell her I'll write when I'm better," Martin said, again grimacing from pain.

"I'm glad you thought of that."

"Ma'am, I know what a chance you're taking. You too," he ended, looking up at Mandy.

"We'll be careful, and when you're able to go we'll help you leave without being seen."

"I didn't expect such kindness in the South," he sighed.

"We're more civilized than you Yankees think," she responded sharply.

"No offense intended, Miss Lucinda. If I ever get home, I'll tell my folks how well I was treated in the South."

"I have to go now. My parents were out when I left, but they'll be back shortly, and I don't want them to find out about you."

"Please, Miss Lucinda, don't get yourself in trouble because of me."

"I'll try not, but I will come to check on you again when it's safe."

"I'll be watching for you." He smiled and lifted his pale hand in parting.

She turned away, wishing that she did not have to leave, yet feeling guilty that she was attracted to the soldier.

Mandy followed Lucinda out of the stripping room and motioned toward the outside. Silently they walked through the barn and out into the gray autumn morning. Mandy closed the door behind them.

"Henry, he's down at de garden by de creek pickin' what's left o' de vegetables we grow'd 'fore it rains," she began. "Law, Miss Lucinda, we didn't grow hardly nothin' this year."

"I know. We didn't either. It's not been a good year

for crops and gardens. What do you think about the soldier? Is he going to live?"

"I'm most sho' he is, if I can get somethin' to feed him. I hate to say it, Miss Lucinda, but we ain't got much to feed a sick soldier," Mandy told her.

"I'll manage to get some food to you, Mandy. What do you need?"

"If I had some taters an' milk, I could make him some tater soup. Later on, he'll be needin' somethin' stronger, but soup will do now."

"We have potatoes and milk. How can I get them to you?"

"Yo' know dat big hollow stump at de edge o' de field, behind your barn, Miss Lucinda?"

"Sure, I know where it is."

"Yo' put what yo' ken in it, and I'll send Henry to pick it up."

"All right, Mandy. Do you need other things besides food—like bandages for dressing his wounds?"

"Law, yes, Miss Lucinda. I done tore up our best sheet to bandage him in."

"I'll bring something for bandages, Mandy. Now I do have to hurry. If possible, I'll put some things in the stump before Mama and Papa get back to the house."

"Yo' be careful, Miss Lucinda. Henry, he's some kind o' worried 'bout us keepin' dat Yankee in our barn. An' I don't feel too easy myself. Them Rebels jest might kill us all if they find out."

"We'll have to make sure they don't, Mandy, so I'll only come when it's safe. Now I really must go."

"Good-bye, Miss Lucinda," Mandy said.

When Lucinda reached the gelding, she paused and looked back. Mandy was standing by the barn door watching her with troubled eyes.

Lucinda waved at her, then got on Ol' Joe and galloped toward home. At the top of the hill she stopped the horse and looked back. Mandy was still standing by the barn door watching her. Lucinda waved at her again, and Mandy waved back.

"Mighty spry young woman," Mandy muttered to herself. Then she went back to the bedside of the wounded soldier.

Lucinda circled wide, using the barn as a shield, so her parents could not see her if they had returned. When she reached the barn, she dismounted, stripped the saddle from the gelding, and pulled off his bridle.

The big horse shook his head, then ran across the pasture, snorting. He stopped by a dry, dusty spot in the pasture and pawed in the dust. Then he laid down and rolled in it.

Lucinda watched him briefly, then hurried to the house.

Her parents had not returned, so she went to the front door and looked out to see if they were coming. After making sure that they were not, she closed the door and hurried to the pantry to get some things ready for the soldier. She got some potatoes from a bag and some flour from the bin. She gathered up some small quantities of salt and some lard and a jar of molasses. She put them all in a bag and ran up to her room and got one of her sheets for Mandy to use for bandages.

She hurried back downstairs and again looked out the front door. Her parents were still not in sight, so she picked up the things she had collected and left by the back door. After stopping by the spring to get a bucket of milk, she went out the side yard gate and hurried past the barn and across the field to the stump Mandy had mentioned.

The hollow place inside the big stump was large enough to hold all she had brought, so she carefully placed it inside. She found a large flat rock, struggled with it, raised it on its edge, rolled it to the stump, and put it over the opening. Then, panting for breath, she ran to the barn and went inside just as the rain started pouring. She heard it on the tin roof and was thankful to be inside, though it worried her that her parents were still outside.

"Mama and Papa will drown if they haven't returned," she said aloud. She ran to the front of the barn and looked out and saw her parents were up the rise to the house. They had on their raincoats, and Lewis was holding the umbrella over their heads. Lucinda breathed a sigh of relief, knowing that they would think nothing of it when they saw her coming from the barn.

Then holding her coat over her head, to shield her from the rain, she ran to the house. She entered, put aside her coat and went to the front door and opened it just as her parents arrived.

"We nearly drowned," Nancy exclaimed as Lucinda held the front door open for her and Lewis.

"Did you see the battlefield before it started raining?"

"From where I stopped, there wasn't much to see but some broken wagons and cannons. That was as much as I wanted to see, so I didn't cross the fence with your papa, but he walked all over the place."

"Have all the dead been buried, Papa?" Lucinda asked.

"I'm sorry to say that they haven't, Lucinda. Not the Rebels, at least. It's a pretty gruesome sight."

"And just to think, they're out there in the rain," her mother remarked.

"Soon as it stops raining, I'm going to go see Squire Bottoms. I'm sure he'll want to get some men together and bury them."

"What did you do while Papa was looking over the battlefield, Mama?" Lucinda asked.

"Mostly I just waited. I found these," she ended, holding out some musket balls in her hand. ". . . Minnie balls, I think they call them."

Lucinda winced, thinking how much pain Martin must

have suffered when a heavy lead ball like that had ripped through his body.

"If you'll get out of the way, we'll come in, Cindy," Lewis teased.

"I'm sorry, Papa. I didn't mean to block the door." She moved aside, and Lewis and Nancy entered.

"I'll hang your coats on the back porch to dry," Lucinda offered as they removed them.

"It must have been terrible to be home alone with that battle going on," Nancy said as she handed her coat to Lucinda.

"There was a lot of noise, Mama. . . . muskets and rifles cracking . . . cannons booming . . . men yelling and screaming. And you should have heard the horses. I didn't know horses could make such sounds," Lucinda replied, hoping that would satisfy her mother.

"I'll take care of the coats," Lewis said, folding his coat across his arm and taking Nancy's coat from Lucinda.

"I want to get back to our usual routine and try to forget that this ever happened. I hope war never comes this way again," Nancy continued.

"I think the fightin' has moved away for good," Lewis speculated, as he rejoined them.

Lucinda's heart bounded as she realized that it would be difficult for Martin to get back to his company if the Union Army had left the area.

Lewis and Nancy moved toward the living room, then paused to talk.

"I'm going up and change my clothes so I can get some work done. Maybe work will help me to forget what's happened," she said.

"I reckon I'd better get dressed for work too, though there ain't much I can do while its raining. I wish I'd been able to get the wheat seed I went to town after so I could sow the field before the weather turns cold."

"Now that the soldiers have gone, can't you go back and get the seed when it stops raining?" Lucinda asked.

"I'll wait a day or two. Maybe by then the rain will be over, and maybe all the soldiers, even the stragglers, will be gone."

Lucinda's heart leaped with excitement. If her mother went back to Perryville with her father in a day or two, perhaps she could talk them into letting her stay at home again. If they agreed, that would give her an opportunity to visit Martin again.

"Are you sure they will all leave, Lewis?" Nancy asked.

"I think they will. I believe the Union Army will follow the Confederates until they catch up with them, and next time they'll fight somewhere else."

Chapter 14

When Lucinda awoke the next morning, the gray light of dawn was coming through her window, and heavy rain was pouring on the roof. Her first thought was of Martin. She wished she could go and see him today, but, now that her parents were home, she would have to watch her every move. So it was not likely that she could go.

She listened for any sound that would tell her that her parents were awake, but she heard no movement in the house. Apparently they had overslept. They had probably been too worried to sleep much while they were in Perryville.

Lucinda stretched, then lay wondering how she would manage to get food to the stump for Martin today. *Would it be possible for her to dress and go downstairs without awakening her parents,* she wondered. *And would it be possible to get food for Martin and leave the house without awakening them.*

She quickly discarded the idea. Even if she could collect food without being heard, she would drown in this rain before she reached the stump. Besides, Henry would not know the food was there, and it would spoil. *Perhaps, after her parents had gone to sleep tonight, she could slip out of the house and take food to Henry's cabin,* she thought, and just as quickly discarded the idea, for her father was a light sleeper.

At last, weary with trying to devise a plan, she arose and dressed for the day. To her surprise, as she started downstairs, she saw her father enter the house by way of the front door. He was dressed in his work clothes, and he was dripping wet from the rain.

"Hi, Cindy," he greeted. "I awoke early, so I left your mama sleeping and went back to the battlefield. I found this." He held up a cannonball for her to see.

"Think of them shooting at each other with those things!" Lucinda cried, thinking of Martin. He could have been torn to shreds if a cannonball had hit him. She dared not mention Martin to her father, so she spoke of her brothers instead. "Papa, they may be shooting at Tad and David with cannons for all we know."

"I know, Cindy, and that troubles me."

"Papa, you'd better put on some dry clothes. You'll catch cold."

"I guess I'd better. I'll go change. Then I'll start a fire in the range so you can cook breakfast. Maybe Mama will wake up by the time you get it ready."

"I'll start making the biscuits while you change your clothes, Papa."

"I'll be back in a minute, Cindy," he responded as he started upstairs.

"I'm going to go see Squire Bottoms after breakfast," Lewis said when he came back. "I know he'll want to bury the dead soldiers when it stops raining."

"Do you think the rain will stop today, Papa?"

"I hope it will."

"It's gruesome to think of those soldiers out there in the rain."

"Their comrades must have been in a terrible hurry to get away."

"I think they left in the middle of the night, Papa. That's when I woke up and heard all the commotion," she said as she started cutting out the biscuits.

Lewis finished making the fire and straightened from his task. "After we bury the dead, I want to go to the south pasture and see about the calves. If they're still there, they may be out of grass, though I reckon they have water now that it's started raining," Lewis said.

"The sounds of the battle may have scared them clear out of the county," Lucinda responded.

"Could be. The fence around that field ain't much."

If Mama would only go with him, I could go and take some food to Martin, but she never goes back there, Lucinda thought as she put the biscuits in the oven.

Just then she heard her mother's footsteps on the stairs. "Mama is up, and I don't have breakfast ready," she gasped.

"I'll slice some ham for you to fry," Lewis offered and started to the pantry.

Lucinda looked at him in wonder, for he had never been one to help with the cooking.

"I'll put the skillet on the back of the stove for you to put the ham in, Papa," she called after him.

"Hello, Cindy. I'm sorry to be late getting up. Where's Lewis?" Nancy greeted as she came into the kitchen.

"Believe it or not, Mama, he's slicing ham for breakfast."

"That's nice, and I see that you have breakfast on the way."

"It won't be long, Mama," she said as she filled the coffeepot with water and added coffee to it. "You must be tired from all you have been through this week. Sit down and rest until I get breakfast on the table," she told her mother as she put the coffeepot on the stove and bent to peep into the oven at the biscuits.

"You're the one who should be a nervous wreck, Cindy. I declare, I never cease to be amazed at you. I'll at least set the table while you and Lewis finish breakfast. I'm surprised that you've got him involved."

"I didn't. He volunteered," she said as her father came in with the sliced ham.

Lewis looked at them and smiled and started putting the ham in the skillet. He pushed the skillet to the front of the stove, got the poker, and stirred up the fire. After that he went to the back door and looked out.

"I believe the rain may stop today," he announced when he came back. "The wind is blowing, and it's getting cooler."

After breakfast, Lewis left in a cold drizzle to go and see Squire Bottoms, and Lucinda started clearing the breakfast table.

"I'll help you with the dishes," Nancy offered. "You had everything to do while Lewis and I were gone. I'm still mad at myself for leaving you alone when I knew that soldiers were nearby."

"You had no way of knowing there would be fighting so near home, Mama."

"There's no way I would have left you if I had known."

"Anyway, I'm none the worse for wear, Mama." She was thinking that her mother really would be upset if she knew that she had watched the battle, and had rescued a Union soldier from the battlefield. She wished she could tell her mother about Martin, for in all her life she had never kept a secret from her.

"Something is troubling me, Lucinda," her mother said, claiming her attention.

"What is that, Mama?"

"I'm afraid to tell your papa, but I hope the Union wins this war. It frightens me to think what will happen if the Confederates win."

"Mama! I never dreamed you'd feel that way," Lucinda exclaimed, "though I knew you had a soft spot in your heart for the Union because of David." When the family had discussed the conflict between the North and the South before the war, her mother had usually remained silent, though she did often take David's side when he and Tad got into an argument over slavery. Mama and David had always been close.

"Another thing troubles me. I have always felt sorry for the slaves, and, after David came back from New York and talked with me about them, I decided that slavery was wrong."

"Papa has never owned a slave, but he's always believed that other people should have the right to own them if they wanted to," Lucinda murmured under her breath.

"Since the war has started, he's stronger for the South than ever, and that troubles me. I have disagreed with your father about very few things since we've been married, and I don't like to go against him now."

Lucinda did not speak for a long moment, for she was beginning to wonder if her mother would understand if she told her about Martin. Perhaps she would even help her get food to him.

"I have kept quiet about the war, because I haven't wanted to cause any more division in our family than David has caused," Nancy continued.

"The war is dividing families everywhere, Mama."

"I know." Her mother looked at her with the saddest expression Lucinda had ever seen on her face. It made her want to reach out to her mother, and she tried to understand how she must feel with David and Tad both gone and fighting on opposite sides. She felt suddenly close to her mother, and she decided that it would be safe to take her into her confidence.

"Mama, I don't want to add to your burdens, but I have to talk with you about something," she began.

"What is it, Lucinda? Don't tell me that there's trouble I don't know about."

"Mama, something happened while you and Papa

were gone to Perryville. That is . . ." She paused, for once at a loss for words.

"What is it, Lucinda? Is it something to do with the battle?"

"Well, sort of."

"What do you mean, sort of?" Nancy demanded, looking at her with a half-worried, half-vexed expression.

"Mama, I know I should have stayed in the house while they were fighting, but I went up on the hill and watched the battle."

"Lucinda! You didn't? Weren't you afraid you'd be killed?"

"Not really, Mama. I stayed behind some trees, away from the line of fire."

"Lewis will go out of his mind if he hears about this."

"I hope you won't tell him, Mama."

"Well . . . I'll tell you now that I won't tell him. I don't want to see him to die of apoplexy."

"That's not all I did, Mama."

"Whatever else could you have you done, Lucinda?" Nancy cried, looking at her as if dreading to hear what she would say next.

"Mama, let's go in the living room and sit down," she said at last.

"I think I'd better be sitting when I hear what you've been up to."

They went to the living room and sat down on the overstuffed sofa. Lucinda took her mother's hand before she spoke.

"Mama, let me tell you the whole story before you say anything. Then try to understand," she pleaded.

"What terrible thing have you done, Lucinda?"

"Nothing really terrible, Mama. I'm not sure you wouldn't have done the same thing under the circumstances, but Papa will skin me alive if he finds out about it. And I doubt that Tad will ever speak to me again if he hears what I have done."

Nancy started to speak, but Lucinda plunged on. "After the battle ended, both sides carried their wounded away, but they left the dead laying. Their bodies were strewn all over the place."

Nancy again started to speak, but Lucinda held up her finger for silence.

"Mama, I started wondering if Tad or David could be out there—dead, so I climbed the fence and started looking to see if they were there."

"That was dangerous, Lucinda. Soldiers could have come back. There's no telling what they would have done to you, but I don't see that what you did is anything to be ashamed of," her mother interrupted.

"That isn't all, Mama. I found a wounded Union soldier out there that had been overlooked. I knew they weren't coming back, and I knew he would die if I didn't get help for him. So I got Nigger Henry to help me move him to his barn. Since then Mandy has been treating him, and he is getting better."

"It's good of Mandy to do that."

"Mandy doesn't have food for him, Mama, and yesterday I put food in the big hollow stump back of our barn for Henry to get for him."

"Rebel sympathizers will run Henry and Mandy out of the country, or kill them if they find out, and goodness knows what they'll do to you," her mother exclaimed.

"We must never let anyone find out, Mama. The soldier knows that his presence is a danger to Henry and Mandy and to me. So he'll leave the minute he's able to travel."

"Why are you telling me this?"

"Because I need your help, Mama."

"You got yourself into this without my help," Nancy replied, smiling.

"What would you have done, Mama? . . . leave him

there to die?"

Nancy looked at her soberly for a long moment before she answered. "If I had your courage, Lucinda, I suppose I would have done what you did."

"Will you help me get food to the soldier when Papa is away from the house?" Lucinda asked.

"Lewis will kill me if he finds out, but I'll help you," Nancy responded soberly.

They arose and embraced in a way they had not done since Lucinda was a little girl.

"I love you, Mama," Lucinda said.

"And I love you, Cindy."

"I love Papa too. It's just that I'm afraid of what he will do if he finds out what I have done."

"I know, Cindy, and I'll help guard your secret."

"Mama, I need to take food to the soldier today."

"Then we had better get busy while Lewis is gone," Nancy suggested.

"I'll have to take the food to Henry's house. If I put it in the stump, there's no way to get word to him that it is there."

"I don't think anyone will see you going. Even if the rain stops, people won't be out today."

Lucinda wondered why her heart was pounding with excitement at the thought of seeing Martin when she delivered the food. She knew her face was flushing, and she turned away, hoping her mother would not notice.

Chapter 15

When the food for Martin was ready, Lucinda and her mother packed it in a basket. Then Lucinda hurried up to her room and put on her raincoat and hat.

"I'm ready to go, Mama," she said when she came back down. "I think I'll walk instead of riding Ol' Joe because I don't want to get the saddle wet," she said as she picked up the well-laden basket. "Besides it would be hard to ride and carry this basket."

"Walking won't take much longer, Cindy, but you'll get your feet wet."

"I'll wear my rubber shoes so I won't, and I'll hurry. I have to get back before Papa does."

"I doubt that he'll be back soon. He'll spend time at Squire Bottoms' place, and they may go ask some of the other neighbors to help."

"Just the same, I'll hurry," Lucinda said as she was leaving.

In twenty minutes Lucinda was nearing the cabin where Henry and Mandy lived. Henry saw her coming and waited in the door to welcome her.

"Law, Miss Lucinda, yo' is a sight I likes to see, but not all drippin' wet like dat. How kum yo' is bringin' all dat, 'stead o' puttin' it in de stump?" he asked, eyeing the basket of food.

"There was no way to get word to you if I put it in the

stump."

"How come yo' brung so much?"

"I don't know when I can come again. Mama and Papa have come home. I had to tell Mama about the soldier, but I didn't tell Papa. I brought this while he was away from the house."

"Yo' mama won't tell?" Henry asked, rolling his eyes at her.

"She won't tell, and she'll do what she can to help. I'll have to hurry, Henry," she said as they started to the barn.

"Law, Miss Lucinda, yo' sho' ken move," Henry said, panting for breath, as they reached the barn, and he opened the door for her.

"Mandy, are you there?" Lucinda called when she reached the stripping room door.

"She's dar all right. Dat's 'bout the only place she ever is since we brung dat soldier fo' her to take keer ov," Henry grumbled.

"Sho' I's here," Mandy answered, as she pulled the door open.

"Good morning, Mandy," Lucinda greeted.

"Good mornin', Miss Lucinda. Come on in."

Lucinda entered and saw Martin propped on his elbow, looking up at her with his blue, blue eyes.

"I thought you would never come back," he greeted.

"I came to bring something for you to eat."

Henry entered the stripping room and closed the door and latched it.

"I'm glad you've come," Martin said. "I've been passing the time trying to remember everything about you, but seeing you is much better."

"I mailed the letter to your mother," she said, trying to get the conversation on a more comfortable footing.

"Thank you, Miss Lucinda. I have so much to thank you for."

"I'm glad I found you, and now I want you to get well."

"Not many girls would have done what you did."

"I couldn't leave you there to die, could I?"

Martin dropped on his pillow and groaned.

"You still hurt, don't you?"

"Not as bad as I did. Mandy will soon have me well."

"At fust I didn't know if he'd live or die, but now he's gettin' better ever' day," Mandy said, smiling broadly.

"I hope he soon be able to go," Henry said, lifting the corner of the quilt Mandy had put over the window to look out. "Ain't no tellin' when some Rebel will come by and kill us all."

"Maybe I better leave after dark tonight," Martin suggested.

"Henry, yo' shut your mouf. This soldier ain't goin' nowhar till he's able to travel," Mandy said firmly.

"Someway we'll help you get back to the Union Army when you are able to go," Lucinda told him, though she had no idea how that could be accomplished.

"Thank you, Miss Lucinda. You too, Mandy and Henry," Martin said, looking from one to the other. His eyes came to rest on Lucinda.

She dropped her eyes, knowing that his gaze was making her blush.

"I wish we could have met under different circumstances—before the war started," Martin said.

"It would have been nice," she murmured, then bit her lip, thinking that she should not have said that.

"If I live to see the end of the war, I'd like to come back and visit you, Miss Lucinda. May I come?"

She did not answer at once, but a smile of pleasure crossed her face.

"You didn't answer. Is that because I'm a Union soldier?"

"I—I don't—it isn't that," she stammered. "I would be glad for you to come, but I have a brother fighting for the South. If he lives through the war, I'm sure he would not welcome a man who had fought for the Union. And my father hates Yankees. I'm sorry. I didn't mean to say that."

"Surely people will put the past behind them after the war is over."

"My brother might in time, but I don't know about my father. He's pretty bitter over the war."

"What about your mother, Miss Lucinda?"

"She don't want to go against Papa, but she helped me prepare the food I brought today. I suppose that puts her on the side with the North. And my brother, David, is fighting for the North. Our family is really divided."

"What about you, Lucinda?" It was the first time Martin had called her by name, she realized, blushing again.

"Which side are you on?" he insisted when she did not answer.

"That's what my brothers used to ask me when the war first started. I told them I was going to wait and see which side was winning, then I'd be for that side."

"But that doesn't answer my question."

"I rescued you, didn't I?"

"You probably did that out of sympathy."

"Suppose I did. I still took a chance, and I still may lose all my friends for saving your life."

"I give up. Since I can't pry an answer out of you, I have to assume that you are for the South. That means that you saved me on humanitarian, rather than patriotic, grounds."

"You sound like an English professor," she retorted.

"And you sound like the most evasive and the most beautiful woman I've ever met."

"Yo' ain't goin' to get nothin' out o' Miss Lucinda.

She's been like that all her life," Mandy told him.

"Thank you, Mandy," Lucinda said, realizing that Martin's last remark had made her blush profusely. "I really must go. Papa will be home soon, and I don't want him to find me gone."

"Yo' take keer that nobody don't see yo' leavin', Miss Lucinda," Henry cautioned.

"I'll be careful, Henry."

"When will I see you again?" Martin asked.

"That all depends on when I can get another chance to bring food without Papa knowing."

"I hope that will be soon."

"I hope you continue to improve, though I don't know how I'll cope with you if your vocal powers improve as well. See, I can use big words too."

"I've already guessed that you would be hard to handle in an argument," he laughed.

"Good-bye, Martin," she said, hardly aware that she had called him by name. "Good-bye, Mandy and Henry. I appreciate all you're doing."

"Good-bye, Lucinda. I'll be counting the hours until you come back," Martin said.

She felt her ears growing hot and knew that they had turned red. She wished that she didn't blush so easily, and she was relieved when Mandy and Henry broke in to tell her good-bye. With a nod and a wave, she escaped out the door and started home.

As Lucinda walked home, rain continued to fall. She was glad that the long drought had finally broken, but she wished it wouldn't rain so hard while she was outside.

The ground had become soggy, the trees were dripping wet, and there was not a break in the leaden sky for as far as she could see. That made her start wondering where all the birds had gone. The day before her parents had gone to Perryville, she had seen black birds flying in a whirling mass against the blue October sky. She had watched them until they appeared to be no more than tiny specks in the sky. Now they were nowhere to be seen. The rain was dripping from her hat and running down her back, but she tried not to think about it.

Surely the birds hadn't gone south already, she reasoned, but they would go soon. She wished she could fly away as freely as they could and leave the war behind, even if she had to cross the sea to some distant, sunny island.

She tried to imagine what it would be like if she could fly away like the birds, but she could not long ignore the new warm spot that Martin had caused in her heart.

Was she falling in love with him? she wondered. She had never been in love, not really. Her feeling for Nathan, long ago, had only been the first stirring of childhood interest in a boy.

"That was only puppy love," she told herself indignantly as she blew a drop of rain from the end of her nose. Surely what she was feeling for Martin was not puppy love. She was too grown up for that now. Yet, along with that strange flutter in her heart, there was a feeling she could not fathom. It was not quiet fear or anxiety. It was more like the uncertainty of walking an unknown path in the darkness.

If she should fall in love with Martin, where would that love lead her? she puzzled. She had no idea, but, wherever it led, she felt that she would follow it as faithfully as a mariner follows a star.

She walked on as in a dream, forgetting the pouring rain and the discomfort of the wet garments beneath her raincoat. All too soon she came to the yard fence that surrounded her home, and she knew that her time of walking in a daydream had passed.

She walked past the henhouse, but she did not hear the hens cackling. Nor did she hear Ol' Joe and Katy nickering in their stalls at the barn, for her mind was still back in the cabin with Martin.

As she entered the yard, she saw her father coming home across the field beyond the lane. He looked tired and worried as she had never seen him before. Worry over the war was resting heavily on him, and all the dead men they would have to bury when the rain stopped must be troubling him.

Her mother saw her coming and opened the door for her.

"Thank you, Mama," she said. "I feel like I'm drowned."

"I saw you coming across the pasture, and you looked like you were."

"Papa is coming. I saw him crossing the field beyond the lane."

"He'll be drowned too, so I'll go upstairs and lay out dry clothes for him."

"I'll go up and change. Then I'll help you start dinner," Lucinda said.

During the night the rain stopped. The sudden quiet roused Lucinda from a sound sleep, and she sat up in bed blinking into the darkness. Realizing that the stopping of the rain had awakened her, she fell back upon her pillow, and, in a half dreamy state, she thought of what her papa and the other men must do tomorrow.

The next morning at the breakfast table Lewis said, "I'm goin' to meet Squire Bottoms and some other men this mornin', and we'll bury the dead soldiers."

"I'm glad you all are going to put those poor men out of sight, but I wouldn't want your job," Nancy declared.

"Somebody has to do it, and we'll do it reverently. We'll even say a prayer over them."

"It's a pity you can't have a preacher to come and preach a sermon."

"We talked about that, but any preacher who'd do it would be in trouble. Northern sympathizers would vow that he had done something against the government in Washington. The men who are goin' to help are all for the South, they are not afraid."

"Papa, I'll meet the mailman and see if there's a letter from either one of the boys. Want us to wait until you come back before we open it if there is?" Lucinda asked.

"If there's a letter, you and Mama go ahead and read it. I'll catch up on the news when I get back," he answered as he was leaving.

Lucinda and her mother followed him to the door, and, with a feeling of deep melancholy, watched him walk across the fields toward Squire Bottoms' place.

Chapter 16

*T*he next morning, as the dawn was driving the shadows from her room, Lucinda awoke to the sounds of trotting horses and shouting men. At first she thought that surely she had been dreaming. Then she heard the sounds again, only more distinctly. The sounds were too near to be coming from the Mackville Pike, she realized. It sounded as if the men were in the yard—all around the house.

Frightened, she jumped from her bed, and ran to the window that looked out toward the barn. While she was struggling to get the shade up, she heard her father and mother bounding from their bed with startled exclamations. Lucinda finally got the shade up, and, to her dismay, she saw soldiers entering the barn.

"Papa, Mama, soldiers have gone into the barn," she screamed at the top of her voice.

"I'll bet they're after the horses," Lewis bellowed. "Just wait until I get my clothes on, I'll—"

"Calm down, Lewis. You're not going to go out there and get yourself killed trying to stop them. What can one man do against an army?" Nancy cried.

"Papa, they've just come out of the barn, and they've got Katy and Ol' Joe. They bridled them inside, and now they're putting the saddles on them."

"Where's my gun?" Lewis demanded, and he pulled

on his trousers and ran across the floor barefooted.

"Forget it, Lewis. You can't take on the army," Nancy screamed.

"Two soldiers just got on Katy and Ol' Joe, and they're riding them out the lane," Lucinda wailed. "Oh, I hate to see them take the horses."

"I hope that's all they take," Nancy cried as she entered Lucinda's room. Lucinda saw that she was pale and shaken.

"That's not all they got, Mama," Lucinda said with cold anger. "I saw three of them come out of the smokehouse with all the meat they could carry. They went toward the lane where some more soldiers were waiting!"

"The meat we worked so hard to put up . . . gone!" Lewis spit the words out in hopeless anger.

"Our hams and shoulders and our bacon!" Nancy cried despairingly. "What are we going to eat until you butcher hogs again?"

"Were they Union soldiers or Confederates?" Lewis asked as he and Nancy joined Lucinda at the window.

"What difference does it make, Lewis?" Nancy asked. "This war has turned them all into thieves."

"Mama, you don't mean that. I don't believe Tad or David would steal."

"I still want to know whose army they belonged to. Were they wearin' blue or gray?" Lewis insisted.

"They were wearing blue, Papa."

"Union soldiers!" he hissed. "I might have known. They're all a bunch of thievin' rogues, and David may not be any better than the rest of them."

"Lewis, you've no cause to say that," Nancy said angrily. "I don't really blame the men for taking our meat if they were hungry."

"I suppose they're goin' to eat our horses," Lewis retorted sarcastically.

Lucinda wanted to take her father's side, but at that moment she remembered that Martin was a Union soldier, and she felt that she hated him as she hated all Yankees. Yet she did not believe that Martin was any more capable of stealing than Tad or David.

She looked out the window again and saw that the soldiers were now going out of sight on Mackville Pike.

"I ain't never felt so helpless in my life," Lewis growled, pacing the floor. "There ain't nothin' a man can do to stop an army."

"It's better to do nothing than to get yourself killed or sent to prison," Nancy consoled.

"I don't know how to go about it, but I'll file a complaint with the government," Lewis declared. "Surely the government will pay for this, if ever this war is over."

"Let's go down and cook breakfast, Lucinda," Nancy said. "Maybe we'll all feel better after we eat."

"I'll go build a fire in the cook stove," Lewis said, making a futile effort to control the fury in his voice.

Breakfast that morning was almost a silent meal, for each of them was in a state of desperation, and each was worried in his own way.

Lucinda realized that she and her mother had even more cause to worry than Lewis, for he did not have to worry about a Union soldier hidden in a neighbor's barn. Now she and her mother had even more reason not to tell Lewis about him. And Lucinda felt that she had an even stronger cause to worry than her mother, for she had a strong suspicion that she was coming to care more for Martin than she should. He would soon be going, and that would relieve both her and her mother of the responsibility of providing food for him. Yet she dreaded the day when he would leave.

"I don't hear any more soldiers. I reckon they're gone, so I'll go do the chores, and, while I'm out, I'll see what else they took," Lewis said as they finished eating breakfast.

"I'll help you, Papa, if Mama will let the dishes go till I get back," Lucinda offered.

"You go on and help your papa, Cindy. I'll do the dishes while you're gone," Nancy promised.

"All right, Mama," Lucinda responded as she picked up the milk bucket and followed her father out the back door.

"Looks like they've been in the cornfield," Lewis said angrily, pointing to a gap in the fence. "They must have picked a load of corn before we heard them."

"Wonder if that's all they took?" Lucinda asked.

"I doubt it. They're worse than a band of roving Indians."

"What else could they have taken, Papa?"

"Maybe the calves in the south field . . . if they saw them. I'll go over there and investigate after I finish here."

"I'll go with you, Papa, if you'll wait until I help Mama finish cleaning the house."

"That's a long walk and the grass is wet with dew and we don't have a horse for you to ride," he reminded her.

"I'll go with you anyway, Papa. I'll wear my rubber boots so my feet won't get wet."

An hour later Lewis and Lucinda started across the farm to the south pasture. As they walked past the cornfield, Lewis kept his eyes averted, choosing not to assess the damage done to his crop.

The grass was wet, as Lewis had said, and the refulgence of the morning sun was making every dewdrop sparkle like diamonds. A rabbit sprang from a clump of tall grass and raced up the hill and dropped into a hole beneath a stone fence.

Lewis and Lucinda climbed the ridge to the fence that enclosed the south pasture, and from there they looked down the hill to Hope's Creek. A large sycamore tree, with roots protruding into the stream, towered above it. The sycamore's leaves, prematurely brown from the drought, were falling, windblown, and collecting in clumps along the stream. Some of them were falling into the water that had collected in the bed of Hope's Creek from yesterday's rain, then moving on the surface of the water like tiny, brown sailboats. Lewis did not notice them, for his eyes were searching among the trees, farther down the stream.

"I see a few calves, but I wonder where the rest of them are," he said at last.

"Maybe they're just out of sight, Papa."

"Look!" he cried, disregarding her remark.

She looked the way he was pointing and saw that the grass had been trampled alongside the stream as if horses had passed that way.

"They came this way and took the rest of the calves," Lewis said bitterly. "Look at the hole they made in the fence. That's where they drove them out."

"Maybe the rest of the calves just got out of the pasture, Papa," Lucinda suggested.

"It's not likely. If those rogues found them, they drove them away to slaughter for the army."

They continued along the creek to the calves that were hiding among the trees.

"Only five left!" he muttered, "and they are the scrawny ones."

"Could there be more of them farther down the creek?" Lucinda questioned.

"I don't think so. Them thieving Yankees took the rest of them."

Pain stabbed at her heart as she realized how angry her father would be if he knew the part she had played in saving the life of a Union soldier.

"Maybe they didn't get all the missing calves, Papa. Let's look for them," she suggested, hoping that activity would assuage his anger.

"I think it's useless, but we'll look."

They walked down the stream in silence, looking among the trees for the missing calves.

"They're gone. Let's go and repair the fence," Lewis said at last.

While they were working on the fence, Lucinda wished that she could mend the hurt in her father's heart as easily as they were mending the fence.

The sun grew warmer and the dew dried on the grass while they worked. When they finished, Lewis removed his hat, took out his handkerchief, and dried the perspiration from his face. Then he replaced his hat and looked helplessly around.

"Let's look in the other field," Lucinda suggested.

"It's useless, but we'll look."

They explored farther down Hope's Creek, then walked over the surrounding field. Finally they heard a calf bawl, and they found him hiding in a thicket.

"I don't know how he got in this field, but I reckon he hid and got away from the soldiers," Lewis said.

"Anyway, I'm glad we found him."

"Let's put him in the pasture and drive him back to the other calves. I hope the rascals don't come back and get the rest of them."

"Maybe they won't."

"I hope I never see them again."

They put the stray calf back in the pasture, then started home. They walked in silence, following the fencerow of a fallow field where goldenrods, black-eyed Susans, and miniature sunflowers were blooming. A red squirrel barked from the top of a hickory tree, and a late songbird trilled disconsolately from a thicket. But Lucinda hardly noticed. She was thinking of the problem she and her mother would have providing food for Martin without her father finding out. The raid the soldiers had made on the farm would make caring for him even more difficult than it had been.

Lewis broke the silence when they reached the yard gate and he paused to open it. "I was thinking about going to Perryville tomorrow, but I think I'll wait a couple of days. All the soldiers should be gone by then," he said.

"Surely they will, Papa."

"Lucinda, I hope we never have to see another soldier unless it's Tad," he told her.

She felt her heart skip a beat as she wondered what he would say if he knew she had been carrying food to a Union soldier.

Lewis held the gate open while she passed through. Then she ran across the yard and into the house, calling to her mother that they were home.

"You've been gone so long, I was worried," her mother called from the kitchen where she was starting preparations for dinner. "Did you find the calves?"

"They're all gone but six, Mama. The Union soldiers drove them off."

"Lewis must be furious."

"I've never seen him so angry, Mama."

Lewis entered at that moment and paused to close the door.

"I'm worse than angry, Nancy. If I see another Union soldier cross our place, I'll shoot him on sight, even of they hang me," he vowed.

Lucinda's heart bounded with alarm. She would have to tell Mandy to be sure that Martin did not cross their farm when he left.

Chapter 17

"*L*ewis, say grace," Nancy said when they were seated at the dinner table that day.

"Nancy, I ain't got much to be thankful for since them Yankees have robbed us."

"Lewis, I'm surprised at you," Nancy said, casting a sharp glance at him.

"What do you expect, after them rogues stole what we've worked so hard for."

"We ought to be thankful that none of us is sick and that neither of our boys have been wounded or killed in the war," she reproved.

"The last time I was at church, Brother Western said that we need to do a lot of praying," Lucinda reminded him.

"Then you pray, Cindy. I don't feel like prayin'."

"I'm not good at praying out loud, Papa."

"Then, maybe Nancy will pray."

Without further word Nancy bowed her head and prayed: "Father we're thankful for what we have left. Help us to be humble, and help us to pray for our enemies. Amen."

Lewis glared at her, then filled his plate with beans and potatoes and chicken and gravy and started eating in silence. Nancy and Lucinda exchanged glances, then, they also started eating.

"I'm goin' out and see if them rogues left us enough corn to feed the stock we've got left," Lewis announced when he finished eating. Then he arose and left the table, and picked up his slouch hat, and stalked out of the house.

"Do you think you took enough food to the soldier to last until tomorrow?" Nancy asked after Lewis was gone.

"After what the soldiers did this morning, I don't care if that Yankee starves."

"Lucinda! I don't think you called him a Yankee when you told me about him. I understood you to say that he was a Union soldier," Nancy chided, looking at her archly.

"Maybe I did, Mama, but, after this morning, they are all Yankees to me, though I won't use the swear word some of the men do when they talk about them."

"Your brother is fighting with them, Cindy."

"I wish he wasn't."

"Besides, you have involved Henry and Mandy, so it's up to you to help feed the soldier until he's able to travel," Nancy informed her.

"I wish I had left him to die."

"Cindy! You don't mean that!" Her mother looked at her soberly.

"You're right, Mama, but the sooner he's gone, the better."

"You'll really have to pick your times to take food to him now. I think Lewis will die if he finds out about him."

"Papa said he was going to Perryville tomorrow. Maybe Mandy has enough food to last until then," Lucinda suggested.

"I'll not go with Lewis, so I'll help you get more food together for . . . Did you say his name is Martin?"

"Yes, Mama, but I don't care what his name is. The next time I see him, I'm going to tell him he ought to leave."

"Lucinda! You astonish me! Suppose he's not able to

travel?"

"He's more able to travel now than he was when I found him."

A few minutes later Lewis came in and announced that he was going to visit the other farmers in the neighborhood and see if soldiers had raided their farms. "It may be late when I come back," he told them. Then he went out banging the door behind him.

Nancy looked out the window and watched until he went out of sight across the fields toward a neighbor's house.

"Well, we can cook for your soldier sooner than we expected, and, if we hurry, you can take it to him before Lewis comes back," Nancy said.

"He's not my soldier, Mama. You talk like I'm in love with him."

"Are you?"

"No, Mama, I'm not."

Were you before the soldiers raided us?" her mother asked, looking at her closely.

"Mother!" she cried, raising her eyebrows in feigned astonishment. She hoped her mother did not notice that she was blushing.

Nancy looked at her for a long moment, then shrugged and turned away. "We'd better start cooking for him," she said as she started for the kitchen."

"We don't have to cook for him. All I promised to do is furnish the food. Mandy will do the cooking."

"Don't you think Mandy has enough to do, with nursing him? Besides, I'll bet he's tired of plain cooking. I'm sure that's all Mandy has had time to do. I'm going to bake him a cake."

"Mama! Papa will die if he finds out, only he might kill you first."

"Suppose that wounded soldier was David or Tad. Wouldn't you want someone to be concerned enough to bake them a cake."

"But that Yankee isn't one of my brothers," Lucinda answered sharply.

"The Bible says that we reap what we sow. So I'm going to sow some kindness. Besides, when this war's over, I don't want to have a guilty conscience about this."

"If you say so, Mama. Anyway, I suppose I ought to finish what I started, but I do want that soldier to hurry and leave."

Two hours later, Lucinda left by the back door, carrying a large, well-laden basket of food, including the cake her mother had baked.

Henry was standing in his yard, looking out across the fields as she approached. He saw her coming and met her at the gap and opened it for her.

"Law, Miss Lucinda, yo' sho' is loaded down. Let me have dat," he said, taking the basket from her arm.

"Thank you, Henry. My arm is aching from carrying it."

"Yo' all must think dat soldier is goin' to eat a awful lot."

"I'm not sure when I can come again, Henry. It's not easy for me to get away since my papa is home, you know."

"I hopes dat soldier soon leaves, but, Mandy, she won't let me hurry him."

"You take the food in and give it to Mandy, and I'll be going, Henry," she said.

"Law, Miss Lucinda, ain't yo' goin' in to see dat soldier? He's been a-wishin' fo' yo' to come all day. And Mandy will be some kind o' put out if yo' don't come in and see her."

"Tell Mandy I'm sorry, but I have to hurry."

At that moment Mandy came out of the barn. "Laws-a-mercy, Miss Lucinda, I sho' is glad to see yo'," she called. "I needs yo' to talk to dis soldier, 'cause he's took a mind to leave, and he ain't in no shape to travel yet. Only reason he's still here is 'cause he's waitin' to see yo' 'fore he goes." Mandy walked toward Lucinda as she talked.

"Let him go, Mandy. He's really not our responsibility if he's able to travel."

"Dat ain't the way yo' talked when yo' axed Henry to bring him here, Miss Lucinda," Mandy said emphatically. "'Sides, we ain't finished what we sot out to do yet."

"This basket sho' is some kind o' heavy. I's goin' to take it in and sot it down," Henry said, starting to the house.

"Miss Lucinda, yo' come on in de barn and talk to dis soldier. I can't do nothin' wid him since he got it in his head dat he might get yo' in trouble if he stays."

There was pleading in Mandy's eyes, and Lucinda's heart went out to her. She had involved Mandy and Henry against Henry's better judgment, and it wasn't right for her to walk out on them now."

She paused, thinking what to say to Mandy, and watched Henry leave the house and go to the barn. Then she turned back to Mandy.

"I'm sorry, Mandy, but I don't want to see him," she said.

"How come yo' don't want to see him? Last time yo' was here, I thot yo' was takin' a likin' to him." Mandy's eyes were searching her.

"I could like him a lot if he wasn't a Yankee, Mandy."

"Yo' know'd he was a Yankee when yo' brung him here."

"Mandy, he was wounded, and I thought he was going to die. Besides, something has happened since then that has changed the way I feel about Yankees."

"What does yo' mean by dat, Miss Lucinda?"

"Yankee soldiers raided our place and stole everything in sight. They even stole our horses and drove off most of our calves."

"I's sorry to hear dat, Miss Lucinda, but dis soldier, he didn't have nothin' to do wid dat."

"He would have if he had been able, Mandy."

"I don't know 'bout dat, Miss Lucinda. All people ain't made alike, not eben Yankees. Is yo' goin' to talk to him er not?"

"I don't want to see him, Mandy, but for your sake I'll talk with him."

She walked beside Mandy into the barn just as Henry came out of the stripping room and closed the door behind him.

"De soldier wants to know how come yo' don't come in and see him, Miss Lucinda," he said.

"What did you tell him, Henry?"

"I tol' him yo' was talkin' wid Mandy, and maybe yo'd come in a minute."

"Then I don't have a choice," she said in an angry whisper.

Mandy pushed open the stripping room door and Lucinda entered. Mandy followed close behind her.

Martin was propped up on pillows, half sitting up in bed, when she entered. His blue eyes met hers, and he smiled his welcome. "I thought you weren't coming in to see me," he greeted.

"I really must hurry. My mother and father are home, you know."

"I feel bad, putting you in the position you are in. Besides, I know that as long as I am here Henry and Mandy are in danger. I've been telling her that I should leave, but she won't hear of it. I think she'd tie me in bed if I tried to leave."

"Perhaps you should stay another day or two," she said in a tone that did not convey sincerity. Then she noticed how pale and weak he appeared, and her heart condemned her. "You really should not travel until you are stronger," she added with conviction.

"I'll go soon, regardless. I owe it to you and to them." He indicated Henry and Mandy with a turn of his hand.

"I hope you will soon be well enough to travel. I—I really don't mean that. I—I just want to see you get well," she stammered, for once not able to put her feelings into words.

"After I go, I'm afraid I'll never see you again," he said, looking tenderly up at her.

"Perhaps it will be best if you don't. I'm really a southerner at heart, and there are such deep scars, I'm sure I'll never get over them."

"You have changed since I last saw you," he observed sadly, and he fell back upon his pillows with a groan.

"Union soldiers raided our farm yesterday," she said without thinking.

"I'm sorry." He raised on his elbow, and there was sincere regret in the look that he gave her.

"I never expected Union soldiers to be thieves," she said caustically.

He winced as if she had struck him.

"Armies on both sides are doing that sort of thing, because they can't transport all the food they need when they are on the move," he said after a long pause. "The government will pay later, but I'm sure it looks like stealing to the native population."

"They didn't offer any payment. They simply took what they wanted and left," she said bitterly.

"Don't hold that against me, Lucinda," he pleaded. "I would never take part in such a raid."

"I don't believe you would, but you are in the Union Army, and that makes you one of them."

"One of your brothers is a Union soldier," he retorted.

"I can't help what he does, but I am responsible for what I do."

"So am I, and I tell you again that I would not take part in such a raid."

"I wish you were not in the Union Army."

His hand went to his face, and he looked hurt.

"I may not see you after today," he said after a long pause. "Can't we part as friends?"

"You will not be leaving until you are better?" she gasped, fearing that he would.

"I have no way of knowing when you will return," he replied, ignoring her question. "If I don't see you again, will you at least consider me a friend?"

"It's not easy for enemies to be friends, but I'm glad I saved your life."

"I will always be grateful to you, Lucinda, and, regardless of what you say, if I live through this war, some day I'll come back to Kentucky to see you. You can't do any more than order me to leave."

"The end of the war is too far away for us to think of the future now," she said pensively.

"Just remember that I told you I will come back."

"Good-bye, Martin," she said, arising to go. "I'll see that you have food as long as you are here, but I will not come to see you again. It is too painful."

"There's something I want to tell you before you go. You may not like what I'm going to say, but, since I may not see you again, I'm going to say it anyway. If things were different, if it were not for this infernal war, I'm sure I would fall in love with you."

She reddened to the roots of her hair, and she was near tears as she turned away.

"Will you shake hands as a friend?" he asked, extending his hand.

She could only think of getting away and hurrying home, but her heart would not let her be rude to a wounded man, so she extended her hand.

Before she knew what he was about, he took her hand

and pressed it to his lips. "Good-bye, Lucinda," he said sadly, looking up into her eyes.

"Good-bye, Martin," she said as she pulled her hand away. Then she turned and stumbled blindly from the stripping room.

The barn door was open, and a cooling breeze was sweeping through the driveway. It cooled her face, but it did not clear her mind. She could only think of getting away.

"Good-bye, Miss Lucinda. Yo' come back when yo' ken," Mandy called after her.

"I'll open the gap fo' yo', Miss Lucinda," Henry said, as he fell in step with her.

"Thank you, Henry," she managed, half choking with emotions too powerful and too painful for her to analyze or understand.

Henry opened the gap, and she passed through it and started silently and listlessly home.

Chapter 18

"*N*ancy, I'm going to Perryville today. Do you want to go with me?" Lewis asked as he sat down at the breakfast table the next morning.

"How are you going, now that you don't have the mare to pull the buggy?" she asked.

"I'm goin' to harness Ol' Jack to the buggy and drive him."

"Then you can go without me. I'm not about to risk my life riding behind that mule. You know he's not broke to the buggy."

"He's always been docile, and he'll be all right once he understands what I want him to do."

"I'll let you drive him until he gets that through his thick head. Besides, I'm not going to leave Lucinda alone again while the war's going on."

"I'm glad you're going to stay, Mama, even though I don't believe any soldiers will come," Lucinda said.

"I don't believe any soldiers will come either, but if they do, maybe the two of you can persuade them to leave without molesting the place," Lewis commented.

Lucinda's heart leaped as she wondered if she should go see Martin after her father was gone. Yesterday they had parted for good, she thought, but since then he had been much on her mind. She had been rude to him, had even rebuffed his offer of friendship. Perhaps she should tell him she was sorry. Since friendship was what he had asked, that was what he would have from her—for the present. After he was gone, she would try to put him out of her mind.

When Lewis came from the barn with the buggy hitched behind Ol' Jack, Lucinda and her mother watched from the doorway. Lewis had put the blind bridle on the mule so he wouldn't see anything on the way that would frighten him and cause him to shy around it. The mule was looking from side to side in spite of the blind bridle, and, because he was unaccustomed to the buggy harness and the buggy, he was stepping high.

Lewis was sitting calmly in the buggy seat and appeared to have the mule under control as he drove past the house and turned toward Mackville Pike.

"I hope troops don't stop Papa this time," Lucinda said.

"I don't think they will. Lewis and I saw the Confederates moving off toward Harrodsburg the day we came home. Later we saw Federal troops at a distance. Lewis thought they were trying to catch up with the Confederates."

"What about the soldiers that raided the farm?"

"I think they'll keep going. Next time they'll rob somebody else."

"If I'd known the trouble Martin could cause, I don't think I'd have bother to rescue him."

"I'm sure you would have, Cindy, regardless. Your heart is too tender for you not to have done what you could for him. Remember how hard you tried to save the baby rabbit your papa brought in from the field when you were a little girl?"

"That was different, Mama. The dog killed its mother, and it was helpless."

"And you wept for days when it died."

"But, Mama, it wasn't a Yankee rabbit," she laughed.

"I'm glad the war hasn't spoiled your sense of humor," Nancy remarked, laughing with her.

"I have to laugh to keep back the tears, Mama. They're awfully close to the surface these days."

"I know. When I think of your brothers being in the war, it's all I can do to keep from crying."

"Mama, I'd like to go see Martin today."

"Why do you want to see him?"

"I want to apologize. I was rude to him yesterday."

"What made you decide to do that?"

"I've had time to think, Mama, and it really wasn't Martin's fault."

"If you were rude, you should tell him you're sorry."

"I don't have any reason to go see him today. I'm sure he has enough food."

"Maybe you should take food to him today. When Lewis gets back, there's no telling when you'll get another chance."

"I believe Martin will leave soon, and I think he should."

"I think you're right. If word gets out about him, we won't have a friend left, unless you call the Taylors friends."

"I think we'd be hard up for friends if they were all we had," Lucinda retorted.

"I agree with you, but come, we had better get busy if you're going to take food to Martin before Lewis comes home," Nancy said as she led the way to the kitchen.

"After I apologize, I hope I never see him again."

"I think you're letting that soldier upset you more than you should," Nancy said, observing her closely.

"Everything is upsetting me these days, Mama. . . . the war, worry over Tad and David, the Yankee raid, and having that soldier on my hands."

"I think I'll bake him a pie," her mother said, smiling.

"I'm sure Mandy can bake a pie for him if he takes a fancy for one," Lucinda said sarcastically.

"I doubt that she has the ingredients."

"Mama, why are you doing this? I'm sure Martin can subsist on the simple food I've been taking him."

"As I told you yesterday, I'm sowing some good seed. Maybe someone will be nice to David or Tad."

Lucinda became thoughtful, but she did not answer.

In a little more than an hour, Lucinda started across the fields with another heavy basket of food for Martin. The day was warm for the time of the year, and, because of the recent rain, the grass was turning green. She was glad that there would be some late grass for the few calves they had left. She shifted the basket to her other arm and continued across the field.

When she came in sight of Mandy and Henry's cabin, she saw smoke rising from the kitchen flue. That meant that Mandy was at the cabin, cooking. She wondered if she had left Martin alone, or if Henry was staying with him.

She found herself trembling at the thought of seeing Martin. Yesterday he had said that, under different circumstances, he might have fallen in love with her. Perhaps she would have come to love him also, if they had met before the war. She shrugged and hurried on, wondering what she should say to Martin when she arrived. Since Mandy was at the house, she would stop and ask her to go with her to the stripping room.

Lucinda knocked on the cabin door, then tapped impatiently with her toe while she waited for Mandy to open it.

In a moment Mandy opened the door, and regarded Lucinda thoughtfully. "Law, Miss Lucinda, here yo' is with more food, and dat soldier has done took hisself off somewhar."

"You mean he's gone?" Lucinda gasped.

"I mean he's done gone, gone. After dark las' night, I kum to de house to cook fo' Henry, an' while I's here, he just got up and left."

"Oh, Mandy, I hope he was well enough to travel."

"Well ur not, he done gone. We done what we could fo' him. Now all we ken do is pray dat he makes out all right."

"I do pray he will, Mandy," she returned with a sinking feeling. "Thank you for all you have done, Mandy."

"I couldn't a done it if yo' hadn't a brung de food, Miss Lucinda."

"Speaking of food, I'm going to leave what's in the basket for you and Henry."

"Oh no, Miss Lucinda. Yo' don't have to feed us."

"Mandy, I'm not about to carry this heavy basket all the way back home. Please take it and empty it."

Mandy looked at her closely, then, concluding that she was serious, she took the basket into the cabin and emptied it.

"Thank yo', 'specially fo' de pie," she said when she came back.

"You're welcome, Mandy. I'm sorry Martin left so soon, but I'm glad we got through this without anyone finding out."

"Me too, Miss Lucinda, and Henry, he sho' is some kind o' glad de soldier's gone."

"You tell Henry that I thank him, Mandy."

"I will when he comes to de house. He's been all mornin' fixin' de strippin' room back like it was. He didn't want nobody to think we had made a place for somebody to sleep out dar."

"That's a good idea, Mandy. I have to say good-bye now," she ended.

"Good-bye, Miss Lucinda."

Lucinda turned and started home with bowed head and thoughtful heart. She was relieved that Martin was gone, though she feared he was not well enough to travel. She regretted the unkind words she had said to him, and she determined that she would apologize if ever she saw him again.

Her mother saw her when she reached the yard and went to the door to meet her. "You look depressed, Cindy. You walk like you've had lost your last friend."

"I'm not sure I have any friends, Mama."

"Now, what brought that on? You were in good spirits when you left."

"Martin is gone, Mama. He slipped away last night while Mandy was at the house, and I'm worried that he's not well enough to travel."

"Maybe it's the best that he's gone. You could have come to think too much of him," Nancy said.

"After all, he is a Yankee, Mama," she returned, wishing that she could stop blushing.

"When the war's over and enough time has passed, it won't matter as much as it does now that he is from the North. But there's more than that for you to consider. You don't know a thing about him or his family."

"I know Mama, and I've tried to put him out of my mind."

"I think you will, Cindy. You've always been a good, sensible girl."

Lucinda turned away and went aimlessly to the back door and out into the yard. Without thought she followed the path to the barn and went in. She closed the door behind her and leaned against it, trying to calm her emotions.

Soon she became aware of the atmosphere of the barn. She smelled the odors of hay and farm animals. Pigeons were cooing among the rafters. Pigs were grunting in their pen, and the cows were mooing forlornly back of the barn. But something seemed missing. Then she realized that it was the soft nickering of Katy and Ol' Joe. The fact that they were gone made her unutterably sad. She did not even have a horse to ride if she wanted to go somewhere, and they had only Ol' Jack to pull the buggy. Her father could buy more horses, but it was not likely that he would before the end of the war, for fear they also would be stolen.

"The Yankees are to blame for this. Oh, I hate them! I hate them! I hate Martin most of all!" she sobbed, clenching her fist and beating on the barn door until her fingers were sore and bruised. Then she cried uncontrollably.

A half hour later, with the worst of her grief spent, Lucinda dried her eyes and left the barn. She went to the springhouse, dipped her fingers in the clear, cold water and washed the tears from her eyes. She dried her face with the long tresses of her hair. Then she started back to the house, hoping that her mother would not be able to tell that she had been crying.

Chapter 19

*T*he following Wednesday morning Lucinda looked out the window and saw David riding a big gray horse along the lane to the house.

"Oh, Mama, David is here!" she cried as David dismounted at the front gate. Without waiting for an answer, she ran out to meet him. "Oh, David, what a surprise!" she greeted.

"Hi, Cindy. My, it's good to see you. You're as beautiful as ever." He gave her a brotherly hug.

She stepped back and looked up at him. "You're so tall and straight and so handsome in your officer's uniform. When did you get your promotion?" she asked as she fingered the stripes on his shoulder.

"Just last week. It wasn't easy but I finally made lieutenant," he replied, glancing at the stripes he had so carefully sewed on his uniform.

"David, I'm proud of you, even though you are fighting with the Yankees."

"David, I can't believe you're here," Nancy cried, coming out the door at that moment.

"Mama, look how handsome David is in his uniform. And look!" She pointed to his stripes.

"David, it's so good to see you," Nancy said.

"I'm not sure Papa will be glad to see you, David," Lucinda told him as they started to the house.

"Lucinda! Of course Lewis will be glad to see him," Nancy insisted. "We've all missed you, David."

"I thought Papa would be over my joining the Union Army by now," David said, looking disappointed.

"Lewis will be all right, now that you have come home, David," Nancy assured. "Come in and we'll make some coffee. I'll bet you're tired from traveling."

"Not too tired, Mama. I started three days ago. I only had to come from Bryantsville this morning."

"You're riding a strange horse," Lucinda observed. "Where's Charcoal?"

"I sold her right after I got in the medical corps."

"We haven't heard from you since the battle across the fields from here, and we've been worried to death about you," Nancy said. "Where were you at that time?" Lucinda asked.

"I was almost home during the Perryville Battle. I was on the Lebanon Pike with General Crittenden, but, there was no way I could let you know."

"I can't believe you were in that terrible battle, David. It's a wonder you weren't killed," Nancy moaned.

"I wasn't in much danger. Through some mix-up in orders we were never involved in the fighting."

"That's something to be thankful for, but I can't believe you were that near home and couldn't even send a message."

"Anyway, it's good to be home," he said as they entered the house.

"Why didn't you write that you were coming?" Nancy asked, pausing in the hall.

"I had no idea I could come home until we stopped the pursuit of General Bragg's army. We had been pursuing him since the Battle of Perryville. The pursuit was called off when we were almost to London. That's when I requested permission to come home."

"I'm excited to see you well and strong, David. I worry

about you all the time," Nancy told him.

"I wish you wouldn't worry, Mama. As a medic, I'm usually not in great danger."

"I can't help worrying, David."

"I'm going to run up to my room and leave my carpetbag. I'll be right back," he said as Lucinda and Nancy started to the kitchen. He ran up the stairs two at a time, and almost immediately he came bounding back down and joined them in the kitchen.

"Where's Papa?" he inquired as he pulled out a chair and sat down at the breakfast table.

"He's visiting some of the neighbors," Nancy responded.

"He's been going around to the other farms for the past several days," Lucinda added.

"Why is he doing that?" David asked with raised eyebrows.

Lucinda and Nancy exchanged quick glances.

"What's going on? Is there something I ought to know?" he demanded.

"We had just as well tell him, Mama. Sooner or later he'll find out anyway," Lucinda said, looking at Nancy for approval.

"Wait until the coffee is ready. We'll talk while we're drinking it," Nancy decided.

"It must not be too bad if we can talk about it over coffee. While we're waiting for the coffee to boil, I want to tell you about a wounded soldier I met in Richmond."

Lucinda's heart bounded as she wondered if it where possible that David had met Martin. It could have happened. Martin could have passed through Richmond on his way to rejoin General Buell's army. Yet it was not likely. There must be hundreds of wounded soldiers passing through the area.

"He was a Union soldier, I suppose?" she guessed.

"Why did you think that? There are as many wounded

Confederate soldiers as there are Federal soldiers."

"I thought you might not be on speaking terms with a Confederate soldier."

"It's a shame that people are so divided over the war. I don't even know who my friends are anymore," Nancy exclaimed.

"It's not that bad, Mama. We talk with men on the other side, long as we're not fighting," David told her.

"Well, what about the soldier you saw?" Lucinda asked.

"He was in a bad way. . . . looked like he belonged in a hospital instead of on the road. His wound was still oozing blood."

"Was he a Union soldier?" she insisted.

"Sure he was a Union soldier. I thought I told you."

"You didn't," she cried, turning pale. "What did he look like?"

"What do you care what he looked like, Cindy? He looked like a Union soldier. He was wearing a blue uniform and a slouch hat."

"Is that all you remember about him?"

"Well, let me think. He was tall, and that he had the bluest eyes I've ever seen."

Nancy cast a searching glance at Lucinda and saw that she was holding to the door for support.

"Where—where was—was the soldier going?" Lucinda questioned, stammering.

"Said he was trying to catch up with his division. Lucinda, why should you care where a wounded soldier was going?" David questioned. "I've never seen you take an interest in a man before, much less a Union soldier."

"I'm just curious," she replied, wishing she did not have to be evasive.

"The coffee ought to be ready," Nancy said, deliberately changing the subject. She kept her eyes on Lucinda as she went to the stove and pulled the pot away from the heat.

"I talked with the soldier, while the wagon he was riding in was stopped to change horses. He told me he was wounded at Perryville, and I told him that I was from Perryville."

"Is that all he said?" Lucinda asked as her right hand went to her heart.

"Not quite all. He was mighty curious for a sick man. Wanted to know if I had any brothers or sisters. Then he wanted to know their names."

"And after that?" Lucinda insisted waiting with bated breath.

"That's about all he said, except he asked for my address. Said he wanted to get in touch with me after the war."

Nancy looked at Lucinda knowingly, and David, following her gaze, looked at her also.

"Are you all right, Cindy?" he asked.

"Oh, sure," she managed, breathing a long sigh and thinking that Martin would soon catch up with his division, and they would put him in a hospital. Then, remembering how angry her father was over the Union soldier's raid, she hoped that Martin would leave Kentucky and not return until after the war was over. Perhaps then? Her heart beat strong with hope. Perhaps, after the war, Martin would return and get in touch with David.

Nancy got cups and saucers and put them on the table, and Lucinda went to the stove and got the coffeepot and poured the coffee.

"Remember, I like cream and sugar in my coffee," David said to Lucinda.

"Sure, I remember." She brought the cream and sugar to the table. Then she and her mother sat down at the table with David.

"Now you can tell me what has upset Papa," David said as he poured cream in his coffee. They both remained silent while he put in sugar and stirred his coffee.

"Lucinda, I've never known you to be so slow to talk," David said, looking at her.

"David, a few mornings ago some Union soldiers raided our farm."

"You don't mean it. What did they take?"

"They took Katy and Ol' Joe and all the meat we had. They even stripped the cornfield and drove off most of our calves."

"Didn't they leave vouchers for what they took so you would be paid?"

"They didn't leave anything but their tracks," Nancy interjected angrily.

"Supply wagons can't always replenish their supplies when they need to, so soldiers have to live off the land. Both sides do it. I don't know about Southern soldiers, but Union soldiers are under strict orders to give vouchers for what they take. When I get back to camp, I'll get someone to look into this."

"You can imagine how Lewis feels. He's fit to be tied."

"Maybe he'll be less upset if I can do something about it," David said.

"I doubt that anything will change Papa," Lucinda said, shaking her head slowly.

Just then they heard the front gate open and close.

"It must be Papa coming home," Lucinda breathed, and she ran to the front window and looked out. "It's him," she called, glancing at David.

"I hope Papa is not mad at me over what the soldiers did," David said as he and his mother arose from the table.

"He's been missing you and Tad both. Maybe seeing you will make him forget his anger for a little while."

Lucinda went to the door and waited for her father. "Papa, David is here," she said softly when he reached her. "He's in the kitchen with Mama."

"Just what I need, the mood I'm in," he said shortly, and he entered the living room and stalked toward the kitchen.

"Hi, Papa," David said, extending his hand.

"You're welcome under my roof, David, but that uniform ain't," Lewis responded coldly, folding his arms and refusing to take David's hand.

"I'm sorry, David," Nancy sobbed, looking first at him and then at Lewis.

Lucinda was amazed that her father had refused to shake hands with David, and that gave her additional reason to worry over what her father would do if he ever learned about Martin. *If he ever learns that Mama helped me prepare food for Martin, the roof will come right off the house,* she thought.

"Nancy may be sorry, but I'm not." Lewis said coldly.

"Then I'll get my things and leave, and I'll never come back. I'm sorry I came this time," David said angrily.

"Don't say that, David. I want you to come home as often as you can," Nancy said tearfully.

"I love you, David," Lucinda cried. Then she turned to her father. "Does he have to leave, Papa?" she asked brokenly.

"It ain't him; it's that uniform. I reckon I love David as much as you and your mama do, but I can't bide no Yankee under my roof."

"I only brought my carpetbag. I'll get it and leave," David said coldly.

He left the kitchen and ran up the stairs to his room. It was just as he had left it. The clothes he had left in his wardrobe were still there. Pictures he had placed on the walls were just as he had left them, and trinkets he had collected during his boyhood were still on his dresser. He turned slowly around and shrugged. Then he picked up his carpetbag and walked from the room and down the stairs.

Lewis had left the house while David was upstairs, but Nancy and Lucinda had remained in the kitchen, looking numbly at each other.

"I don't want you to leave, David," Nancy said brokenly.

"I don't want you to go either, David," Lucinda cried.

"I love both of you, and I love Papa, but my loyalty to the Union has come between us," David said, looking first at his mother then at Lucinda. "I'll say good-bye now, and I may never see either of you again," he ended with trembling lips.

"I'll pray for you every day and every night until you return, David," Nancy said brokenly.

"Thank you, Mama. I hope Papa will forgive me. Lucinda, I hope we meet again," David said as he turned to go.

They walked with him to the front door. There Lucinda kissed his cheek, but Nancy clung to him. "Don't go away like this, David," she pleaded.

"It's all I can do, Mama. Papa don't want me here." He walked out the door carrying his carpetbag and did not look back.

Nancy and Lucinda stood in the doorway and watched him cross the yard, let himself out the front gate, unhitch his horse, and swing into the saddle.

He turned and waved to them. Then he started the horse galloping along the lane.

Their eyes followed his broad shoulders until he disappeared on Mackville Pike. Then mother and daughter embraced, sobbing softly.

"Mama, have you thought what Papa will do if he finds out about Martin?" Lucinda asked as last.

"I have, and I've decided that we must never tell him. But we must keep on loving your father regardless of what he says or does."

"I wish David hadn't told us about seeing Martin. Now I won't be able to sleep for worrying about him," Lucinda said.

"Martin will be all right, Cindy. He'll soon catch up with his outfit, and they'll put him in a hospital."

"I hope you're right, Mama, and I'll pray that he'll get well."

"I wonder if he'll come here after the war," Nancy mused.

"I don't know, Mama. My heart wants him to come, but I almost hope he never does."

Chapter 20

"*I* wonder where Papa went," Lucinda said, still looking down the road the way David had gone.

"There's no telling, but I suppose he'll stay away until he's sure David is gone."

"The way things are, I wish I could walk out too, only I wouldn't want to come back."

"Lucinda! I don't believe you said that."

"I didn't mean it, Mama. I'd never leave home. I'm just frustrated, that's all."

"I know how you feel. Sometimes I feel the same way," Nancy said sadly. Then, after a pause, "I think I'll go in and get busy on the house. Maybe that will help me get things off my mind."

"I'll help, Mama," Lucinda offered. "Maybe that will relieve my mind too."

Both women went in and started working on the house with a vengeance, but the sound of hoofbeats soon drew Lucinda to the window.

"Who is it this time?" Nancy asked listlessly.

"It's Papa riding Ol' Jack out the lane. Maybe he's going to visit some more of the neighbors."

"I'm hurt the way your papa treated David, but I still feel sorry for him. I know he has reason to be upset."

"I agree, Mama, but there's nothing we can do about it."

"I know. We'll just have to try to get it off our minds."

Lucinda and her mother turned back to their cleaning and worked until time to start dinner. When dinner was ready, Lewis had not returned, so they sat down and ate alone. Then they returned to their cleaning.

Late in the afternoon, they started cooking supper. When it was almost ready, they heard Lewis ride the mule past the house on his way to the barn.

"That's Papa," Lucinda said.

"I'm glad he's back. I've worried all day that something would happen to him," Nancy said.

"Maybe he's settled down by this time," Lucinda observed.

"This much I know; he'll come in starved, so we had better hurry and get supper on the table."

They were putting the last of the supper on the table when Lewis came in.

"You're just in time for supper," Nancy said, turning to him.

"It's been awhile since I ate dinner, so I'm ready to eat."

"Where did you eat dinner?" Nancy asked.

"I ate with the Tates. It was almost dinnertime when I got to their place, and they insisted that I stay and eat."

"They're good neighbors," Nancy commented.

"What did you find out today, Papa?" Lucinda asked.

"Same thing. Several farms were raided, but we got hit worse than the rest. They stopped at Wider Jones' place, but when she told them she was a wider they left without taking anything."

"There must be some good in them if they let the wider be," Nancy observed.

"They're still Yankees, Nancy, and I'd sooner deal with rattlesnakes."

"Maybe they're not all that bad, Papa," Lucinda suggested.

"What are the other neighbors saying?" Nancy asked as she put a platter of fried chicken on the table.

"Squire Bottoms says the soldiers were supposed to leave a voucher for what they took, and the Federal Government is supposed to pay for it, though I suppose they won't pay till the war's over."

"But they didn't give us a voucher," Nancy said.

"The squire said for us to sign an affidavit, listing what they took, and he'll see that it's sent to the proper authorities. Still, I'm not sure we'll ever get anything. I think it will depend on who wins the war."

"It's anybody's guess who wins the war," Nancy responded.

"I don't dare say so outside the family, but I wish the South would win, even if we have to lose what the Yankees took," Lewis declared.

"Lewis! You could be sent to prison for saying that. I saw in the paper where men have been put in the federal prison at Nashville for saying less," Nancy warned.

"That's why I'm not talking outside the family."

"I got the rest of supper on the table," Lucinda said, for her mother had stopped where she was to talk to Lewis.

"I reckon we ought to be thankful we've still got something to eat," Lewis said, sighing heavily as he sat down at the table.

"I'll pour the coffee, Mama," Lucinda offered, and she turned back to the kitchen to get the coffeepot. She poured the coffee and returned the coffeepot to the range. Then she joined her parents at the table.

"Tomorrow, I'll go to Danville and get a lawyer to fix the affidavit. We'll sign it, and I'll take it to Squire Bottoms so he can send it in for us," Lewis said as he finished eating.

"I hope he can get something done," Nancy responded.

"Lewis, I'd like to go to church today," Nancy said

the next Sunday morning as they were eating breakfast.

"Me too, Papa," Lucinda spoke up. "It's been forever since we've been to church."

"I feel positively backslidden, staying out of church the way we have," Nancy added.

"There's been so much hard feelings, I think we're better off not goin'. The Taylors and a few more like them want to fight the war in the church," Lewis said half angrily.

"Maybe things have settled down by now, Papa," Lucinda suggested.

"Maybe Cindy is right. Let's go, Lewis," Nancy insisted.

"Well, I reckon we can go and see what happens," Lewis agreed reluctantly. "If Squire Bottoms is there, I'll ask him if he got our affidavit sent to Washington."

"I'm glad Ol' Jack is getting used to the buggy. Driving him will certainly beat walking," Nancy said.

"It's a good thing, since he's all we've got left to pull the buggy," Lucinda agreed.

"I'm glad the soldiers left him and Ol' Beck. I reckon they didn't think they were broke to ride," Lewis observed.

After breakfast Nancy and Lucinda made short work of setting the house in order while Lewis harnessed Ol' Jack to the buggy. He returned to the house and was dressed by the time the women were ready to go. Then they all went out and got in the buggy.

When they reached the church, they saw that there were only a few buggies at the hitching rail.

"Looks like there's not many people here," Lucinda observed.

"Most people are afraid to drive or ride their horses to church these days. . . . afraid they'll be stolen while they're there," Lewis explained.

"Maybe some people walked," Nancy suggested.

"We didn't see anybody walking on the road or in the fields," Lucinda exclaimed.

"I imagine the crowd will be mighty slim today," Lewis commented as he got out of the buggy and started hitching the mule.

"There's not even any young people on the porch," Lucinda commented when they started toward the church.

"The young men have all gone off to war, Lucinda. Maybe the girls have all already gone in," Nancy suggested.

When they reached the front door, Lewis opened it enough to peek looked in. Then he closed it again. "There ain't two dozen people here," he said. Then he opened the door for his wife and daughter to enter.

"The Petrees are not here. I suppose they've not started attending again," Lucinda whispered to her mother as they paused inside the door.

"I think you're right, but I see that nothing has stopped the Taylors from coming," her mother replied, rolling her eyes toward them.

"I noticed."

"Come on," Lewis whispered, and he led them down the center aisle to the pew where he and Nancy always sat. Lucinda sat down between them, remembering the happy conversations she used to have with the girls her age before services started. Today the church was almost silent, for not one person was talking to another.

At last Jackson Taylor arose and walked to the front of the church.

Lucinda felt her father tense, and she wondered what her mother was thinking. She glanced at Mrs. Taylor and Verna, wondering how they were reacting. Mrs. Taylor was looking smug, and Verna was looking at her father as if she were bursting with pride.

"Brother Western won't be here today—nor any other day soon," Jackson Taylor announced. "Federal authorities arrested him yesterday, and he's being sent to federal prison in Nashville for refusing to sign an oath of loyalty to the Union."

"I'll bet you're the one that got him arrested," Jim Broyles said hotly.

"I resent that, sir. If I wasn't a Christian, I'd challenge you to a duel," Jackson Taylor growled.

"Then I challenge you to a duel with bare fists. There won't be anything wrong with that kind of a fight. Come outside and I'll beat the devil out of you," Broyles countered.

"He's needed the devil beat out of him for a long time," Nate Fergerson mumbled loud enough for all to hear.

Jackson Taylor's face turned an even darker shade of red, than it usually was, and he rolled his tongue around in his mouth as if he were having trouble getting control of it.

"Sir, it's beneath my dignity to be involved in a brawl," he finally said, sounding like he was choking on his words.

"You're a yellow coward, that's why you won't fight," Jim Broyles hissed.

Lewis arose and stood tall and straight as he always did when he was angry.

Nancy caught his coattail and tried to pull him back to his seat. And Lucinda felt a lump in her throat that almost suffocated her.

"Church ain't no place for fightin'. So I'm goin' to take my wife and daughter and go home. And we won't be back," Lewis announced in a clear, strong voice that cut through the tension. Then he pulled Nancy to her feet, and Lucinda, proud that her father had dared speak his mind, stood up with them. Without another word, they left the church and went to their buggy.

Nancy and Lucinda got in the buggy while he was untying the mule. Then he got in beside them and started the mule toward home. For some minutes they rode in silence. Lucinda was the first to speak.

"I feel sorry for Mrs. Western and their little daughter, Emily," she said.

"I feel sorry for Brother Western too. He's a good man, and he ain't got no more reason for being in prison than I have," Lewis growled.

"I wonder if Jackson Taylor did have anything to do with him being arrested," Nancy said.

"It wouldn't surprise me in the least. Jackson Taylor ain't never been nothing but a troublemaker, like the Yankee that he is. There's no principle about any of them. To save my life, I can't understand why David joined the Yankee Army," Lewis expostulated.

Lucinda looked straight ahead, thinking that certainly David was not like other Yankees, and she doubted that Martin was either. One thing she knew, whether he was like other Yankees or not, he had so complicated her life that she wished she had never seen him. *Now that he is gone, I should forget him,* she thought.

"Regardless of who wins this war, the country won't never be the same again," Lewis said bitterly.

"Our neighborhood and our church won't ever be the same either," Nancy agreed.

Lucinda's eyes grew wide as she thought of the future and what it would bring to their community, their church and their family. And she wondered if she would ever see Martin again. If she did, it could lead to nothing, for her father would go wild at the thought of her having a Yankee for a beau. She shifted in the seat, trying to relax and wondering if any man that came back from the war would be one that she would consider marrying.

"Are you all right, Cindy?" Nancy asked after a long silence.

"Yes, Mama. I'm just worried, that's all."

"I guess we're all worried. We really need the help of

the good Lord in times like these. We ought to live close to Him and do a lot of praying, even if we can't go to church."

"It's goin' to be hard for me to do much prayin', long as I feel the way I do about them Yankees," Lewis said.

"Lewis, you need to pray about the way you treated David when he was home. After all, he is your son," Nancy told him frankly.

"I'm going to pray for you, Papa—and for David and for Tad—for you too, Mama," Lucinda cut in, trying to forestall bitter words between her parents.

"Lucinda is right. We all need to pray for each other," Nancy agreed.

Lewis made no reply, and he became very busy with the reins, as if he thought the mule was about to run away.

Chapter 21

By the end of the year few still believed that the war would be a short one, and the early months of the new year offered even less hope. For the struggle continued with both the Army of the North and the Army of the South destroying property and wounding and killing men. The bitterness on both sides continued to deepen. In Kentucky the bitterness was especially deep, for Kentucky had more families with men fighting on both sides than any other state.

As the months passed, newspapers continued to tell of battles in many places—often ill-conceived and bloody, with both sides sustaining heavy losses, and with both sides claiming victory.

The Perry family read the paper that came to their mailbox each Monday, slavishly searching for every scrap of news about the war. They especially watched for news of battles that were likely to involve David or Tad, though Lewis would never admit that he was concerned about what happened to David.

They read of battles in places they had never heard of, until the very reading of their names made them seem familiar. And they discussed the fighting in such places as Stone River, Charleston Harbor, Vicksburg, Fredericksburg, Chancellorsville, Jackson, Port Hudson, Tullahoma, and Gettysburg.

Lucinda continued to go to the mailbox each day, hoping to receive a letter from Tad or David. When a letter came from either or both of them, she would run joyfully home as if her feet had wings. But on days when no letters came, she would turn sadly away from the mailbox disappointed and walk slowly home.

Tad was still with the Army of Tennessee and what they read in the papers and in his letters gave them grave cause for concern. In September they read of the Battle of Chickamauga Creek, and that gave them fresh cause to worry, for according to Tad's last letter, that was where he was serving.

Before the soldiers had raided the farm, almost a year ago, when letters had come from David and Tad, Nancy had read them aloud, and afterward they had discussed what the letters contained. But after the raid, when Nancy read letters from David, Lewis pretended not to listen, and he refused to join in the discussion of what David had written.

One Monday morning in early October, Lucinda reached the mailbox and waited in a cold rain for the mailman to come. Finally, to her great relief, she saw his buggy coming slowly down the pike and stopping at almost every mailbox. She shivered from the cold and wished that he would hurry.

"Good morning, Miss Lucinda," the old mail carrier greeted when he finally stopped his buggy near her. Lucinda could not help thinking how old and decrepit the mail carrier was, and she remembered that he had been pressed into service after the regular mail carrier had gone off to war.

"Good morning, Mr. Preston," she responded. "Do you have any mail for me today?"

"I declare, I believe I do have a letter for you. Just a minute."

With gnarled and stiffened fingers, the old man

fumbled through the stack of mail under a waterproof covering in the floor of his buggy.

"Yeah, here it is. . . . a letter from your Confederate brother, I'd say. I'm not takin' sides, mind you." He winked at her and smiled. "It's his handwriting, I think, though it don't look exactly like it."

"I understand that you're not taking sides, Mr. Preston. May I have the letter please."

"Oh sure. Didn't mean to delay you. I know that, like you always do, you'll be a-runnin' home so your pappy and mammy can read the letter. I've got the Sunday paper for you too." He handed her the letter, then got the paper and held it out to her.

"Thank you, Mr. Preston," she said, as she glanced at the letter. The letter was from Tad, but, as Mr. Preston had observed, the address didn't look like his handwriting. It frightened her when she saw that his hand had trembled as he addressed the envelope. *Surely Tad must be wounded or ill,* she reasoned. She was tempted to open the letter, but she restrained herself and tucked both the letter and the paper under her raincoat and started running home with all possible speed.

"Mama—Papa," she shouted breathlessly as she reached the house.

Her mother opened the door at once, and Lucinda saw her father standing close behind her.

"I—got—a letter—from—Tad. Hurry—and—open it, Mama," she panted, handing her the letter as she entered.

Lucinda closed the door and leaned against it to make sure the latch had caught. Then she took off her raincoat and hat and followed her parents into the kitchen where they sat down at the breakfast table to read the letter.

Nancy looked at the letter for a long moment before she opened it. "I don't like this," she said. "Tad's handwriting looks awfully trembly."

"That's what I thought, Mama," Lucinda exclaimed.

With anxious fingers Nancy tore off the end of the envelope and pulled out a single sheet of paper and unfolded it.

Lucinda went around the table and looked over her mother's shoulder to see the letter. "The letter doesn't look like Tad's scrawl usually does either," she gasped as she scanned down the short page before her mother started reading. Then she crossed her arms over her aching heart, trying to stop the pain she felt.

Nancy started reading, and Lewis leaned forward to catch every word.

Dear Mama and Papa and Lucinda:

I'm too weak to write much. Was wounded in the battle of Chickamauga Creek, near Chattanooga. I lost a lot of blood. The doctor says I'm going to be all right, but I'm very discouraged. They had to take my left arm off at the shoulder.

The war is over for me, so I'll be coming home when they release me from the hospital. I reckon I won't be much help on the farm though, with only one arm, and that worries me.

Love to all,

Tad

"I can't believe it," Lucinda cried, looking at her mother. Her mother's face was ashen and she was biting her lip to keep back her tears. Lucinda looked at her father and saw he was slowly clenching and unclenching his fists. Then she leaned over and put her arms around her mother, and her mother closed her arms over hers and they wept together.

"Another score to chalk up to them Yankees," Lewis said bitterly. "I hope the Armies of the South kills the last one of them."

"Surely you don't mean that, Lewis," Nancy gasped.

"Yes I do. I mean every word of it."

Lucinda wondered what her father would say if he knew that she had saved the life of a Union soldier. *If her father ever saw Martin, would he want to kill him?* she wondered. With sudden revulsion she hated the war and everything that it was doing to them.

"I can't hate the North like you do, Lewis, but I think I would if David wasn't enlisted on that side," Nancy said at last.

"While this war lasts, I don't have a son named David," Lewis said sternly.

"Lewis, you don't mean that."

"Yes I do. I don't have a Yankee son."

Nancy looked at him for a long minute before she replied. "Anyway, we should be thinking of Tad now," she said at last. "I wish we could go and see him."

"Can we, Papa?" Lucinda pleaded. "We could go part of the way on the stagecoach and catch the train when we get to where it's running."

"Such a trip would be too dangerous, Cindy, even if we could get there. As you know, the railroads are often under attack. Half the time the trains can't run, and, when they do, they sometimes get caught in the midst of battles. We could be taken prisoners or killed if we attempted to make such a trip."

"Of course you're right, Lewis," Nancy agreed. "We'll just have to write to Tad and pray for him."

"I'm going up to my room," Lucinda said on a sudden impulse, and she ran up to her room and closed the door after her. Sobbing, she fell across her bed and wept until she had no more tears. She hardly knew whether she was weeping over what had happened to Tad or because she knew that, if ever her father saw Martin, he would hate him as he hated all Yankees. "The whole world is in a mess, and there's no hope it will ever be any better," she sobbed into the covers.

After a while her mind turned to a scene years ago when Tad had helped her put up a swing in the big maple tree in the side yard. In those days Tad was always doing things for her with both his strong arms. Now Tad only had one arm, and he would never be a whole man again.

"At least he still has his heart, and he can still love me as a sister, and I can still love him as a brother," she told herself. Then she arose and went to her dresser and redid her hair, just to have something to do. The face that looked back at her was from the mirror was tear-stained and sad. She grimaced at her reflection and said, "It really doesn't matter what I look like. Nothing will ever be right again. Tad will never be the same. Papa will never forgive David. I'll never have a sweetheart Papa will accept, and I'll never be happy again." A tear rolled down her cheek, and she stamped her foot in frustration.

After a long while she picked up the water pitcher from its table and poured water into the basin. She took a long time washing her face. Then she dried it on a coarse towel. Finally she left her room and walked slowly back down the stairs to rejoin her parents.

Chapter 22

*A*n infection slowed Tad's recovery, but in late December he was finally released from the hospital and told that he would be discharged from the army on Monday. Then he could go home, though travel in Kentucky would be difficult, because the railroad was again closed between Bowling Green and Lebanon Junction.

Tad decided he would travel by train as far as Bowling Green, then go the rest of the way on the stagecoach. So he wrote a letter home, telling his family that he would arrive in Perryville on the stagecoach, late in the afternoon of the Monday before Christmas.

The day Tad was mustered out of the army, he dressed at once in civilian clothes, packed his few belongings, and hurried to the depot in Chattanooga in time to catch the afternoon train for Nashville. There he would change trains for Bowling Green.

Several Union soldiers, who had been furloughed for Christmas, were waiting for the train when he arrived. He waited with them, glad that he was dressed in civilian clothes. They would know that he was a wounded soldier, but there was no way they could know that he had fought as their enemy.

He turned away, thinking how glad he was to be out of the army, and on his way home. He hoped his letter had reached his family so Papa would come to meet him in Perryville.

The stub of his left arm was almost healed, but the empty coat sleeve made him feel self-conscious. It also gave him a feeling that he was no longer a whole man, and it made him doubt that he would ever be able to earn a living, even on the farm.

When his train arrived, he boarded it and found that it was crowded with both civilians and Union soldiers. He pressed his way along the crowded aisle, carrying his carpetbag with his good arm. He passed men in high spirits, laughing and talking, happy to be going home. Some of them dropped their eyes or turned away when they saw his empty coat sleeve. Others gave him a cold stare, perhaps wondering if he had lost his arm fighting for the North or the South. He was hurt and angered, for he wanted neither their pity nor their hostility.

While he had convalesced in the hospital, he had thought he could wear that empty sleeve as a badge of honor. He had even fancied that the enemy would honor him for his courage. He had not faltered under fire, and he had given a good account of himself until he had been cut down by a musket ball. Now he was shocked by the way these more fortunate men had looked at him.

Near the end of the car, a civilian arose and offered him a seat. "You look like you need to sit down, soldier," he said.

The man who was seated by him also arose. "I'll go with you so we can finish our conversation," he said to his companion.

"I thank you both," Tad said as he slumped into the seat and placed his carpetbag on the floor beside him.

Soon he saw a man with one leg, coming along the aisle on crutches. Like him, he was dressed in civilian clothes. The man stopped when he reached him. "Mind if I set here?" he asked.

"Glad to have you. You goin' home?" Tad asked as

he moved over to make room for the man.

"No, I'm just goin'," he said as he sat down. "I ain't got no home. The house where I grew up was burned by bushwhackers, and my folks were all killed, except maybe my ma. You goin' home?"

"Yeah, I'm goin' home. I ain't seen my folks since last Christmas, so I'm glad to be goin'."

"What's your name?"

"Tad. Tad Perry."

"I'm Tom Stanton." He extended his hand.

Tad gripped the man's hand with his good right hand and looked into his blue, friendly eyes.

"You get that in the army?" he asked, looking at Tad's empty sleeve.

"Yeah. . . . got it at Chickamauga."

"Which side?" Tom asked in a lowered voice.

"The Confederacy," Tad whispered. "I take it you lost your leg in the war."

"Yeah. . . . same battle . . . same side," Tom whispered. "Where's your home?"

"Perryville, Kentucky."

"I know where that is! I fought there." He lowered his voice and added, "Polk's First Corps, Cheatham's Division. We fought them Yankees to a standstill."

"They say that was a rough battle. Where I got into it was at Chickamauga."

"Me too. I lost my leg there, but I found somethin' else."

"What can a man find in a battlefield?" Tad asked.

"I found the Lord, and that was the greatest thing that ever happened to me."

"You found the Lord on a battlefield?" Tad asked.

"I sure did. Layin' there with my leg hurtin' like fire burnin', and my blood runnin' out on the ground, I thought I was goin' to die. I knew I needed to pray, but I wasn't fit to pray. Then I remembered how Ma used to read the

Bible to me when I was growin' up. One verse she made me memorize came to my mind, and, in spite of my pain and all the noise around me, I repeated it aloud."

"What was the verse?"

"Call on the name of the Lord, and thou shalt be saved. I repeated those words over and over, and they seemed to sink into my heart. I thought of all the bad things I had ever done, and I was sorry. Then, though I was hurtin' like thunder and thinkin' I was dyin', I called on the Lord."

"Do you think the Lord heard you?"

"I know He did. Right there, with the cannons boomin', and the muskets rattlin', and the cannonballs and bullets whistlin' and screamin' through the air, peace came into my heart, and I knew that the Lord had saved me. My leg didn't stop hurtin', but I stopped worryin' about dyin'. Soon the medics came and took me back to the field hospital, and they took my leg off. I know the Lord was with me while they was doin' it."

"I'm glad you got saved, Tom. I was a Christian before I joined the army, but I got closer to the Lord after I was wounded."

Tom looked out the window at the passing scenery. "Pretty country out there," he said with a wave of his arm, "but I like the country around Perryville better. I had time to see some of it before the battle."

"You're lucky you got through that battle alive," Tad told him.

"I had a cousin who didn't. A lot of good men didn't come out of that one alive, I've been told."

The train slowed, then stopped at a station. More soldiers came aboard. Then the engine started puffing, the wheels started shuttering and skidding on the rails, and the train started on. The men who were already on the train resumed what they were doing, some drinking, some looking out the windows, and others gambling for small stakes.

"You have a family?" Tom asked.

"My mama and papa are living, and I have a brother named, David and a sister named Lucinda. We have a farm near where the battle was fought."

"What is you brother like? . . . and your sister?"

"My brother is taller than I am, and he's better educated. He was goin' to be a doctor before the war. Now he's somewhere in the medical corps, if he's still livin'."

"Our side?" Tom asked in a whisper.

"I wish you hadn't asked. He joined up with the Yankees," Tad whispered back.

A shadow crossed Tom's face, then he smiled wanly. "I hear that sort of thing happened a lot in Kentucky. I'm from Tennessee, and it happened there too. You didn't tell me about your sister."

"Lucinda? You ain't never seen a girl like her."

"What do you mean, I ain't never seen a girl like her?"

"Oh, I don't know. It's hard to put in words. She's high-spirited and pretty and fun to be around. She keeps everybody on their toes, and she keeps things organized and goin'." He paused, embarrassed. "I'm sorry. I didn't mean to carry on like that."

"Your sister must be some girl."

"She is. There ain't nobody like Lucinda."

"You have me curious. What does she look like?"

"Never tried to describe her. Let's see now, she's a tiny little thing, but she's built like a woman ought to be. She's got fair skin. She's got blue eyes and she's got the prettiest red hair you'll ever see, though she'll argue till the sun goes down that her hair is gold."

"She sounds like the kind of girl I would liked to have met before I lost my leg." He patted the stump where his leg had been cut off.

"I've been thinkin' about girls too. . . . especially

since I lost my arm, so I reckon I know what you mean. It wouldn't have done you any good to meet Lucinda though. She ain't never took a second look at any man, though she did have a childhood sweetheart once. Puppy love, Mama called it."

"Well, it doesn't matter. Since I've lost my leg, I don't expect any woman to want me anyway, but you shouldn't have to worry. I saw a woman a few days back with a soldier who'd lost both arms."

"Maybe she married him before he lost his arms."

"Could be. Anyway it's not the same. A man can do a lot with one arm, but a man without a leg—" He broke off abruptly and turned away.

"They'll get you an artificial leg, won't they?"

"The doctors say they will, and they say I'll learn to get around on it, but it won't be the same. I'll still be a cripple."

Tad wished there was something he could say to cheer Tom. "Where you goin'?" he asked to keep the conversation going.

"Don't know. Goin' off . . . somewhere. Anywhere to get away from where there's fightin'."

"Don't you know anyone you can visit?"

"Not really. The friends I made in school are all in the army somewhere."

"Why don't you go home with me, Tom? Before the war my folks were used to havin' two men in the house, so they'll be glad to have you."

"Won't your brother come home for Christmas?"

"I'm sure he won't. He's been home once since I left, and Lucinda wrote that Papa ordered him out of the house." He lowered his voice. "Papa can't bide no Yankees. He don't even claim my brother as a son any more."

"Too bad."

"The way Papa feels about David is about to kill Mama. We've always been a close family."

"I can't get over my family bein' gone."

"I want you to go home with me, Tom. It ain't right for a man to be alone at Christmastime."

"Won't my bein' there make extra bother for your mother and sister?"

"They'll love havin' you. I think your bein' there will keep them from missin' David so much."

"Then I'll go with you, but I'll have to leave soon after Christmas. I have to go back in the hospital so they can fit my artificial leg."

"How come you got on this train if you didn't know where you was goin'?"

"I thought I'd go to Kentucky and see that bluegrass country again."

"Then you can go with me. The train doesn't go past Bowling Green, so from there I'm goin' to catch the stage-coach to Perryville. Papa is goin' to meet me at Perry-ville with the buggy."

"If you're sure I won't be a burden to your folks, I'll go with you, Tad."

"I'm glad Tom. Havin' you along will make the trip more enjoyable."

In Nashville they had a layover of an hour. Then they boarded the train for Bowling Green. The train was slow, and it made frequent stops, so it was dark when they reached Bowling Green.

"Let's find the inn where the stage office is located and get somethin' to eat," Tad suggested as they got off the train.

"Sounds good to me, and, after that, I'll be ready for the bed," Tom responded.

"Me too," Tad agreed. "We'll need to go to bed early. We'll have to catch the stagecoach at five o'clock in the morning."

The trip by stage the next day was slow and tiring, and the sun was almost down when they came in sight of

Perryville.

"It will be dark before we get home," Tad said.

"You sure your father will meet us?"

"I'm sure. I asked him to meet me in my last letter."

The stagecoach clattered to a stop in front of the stage office. Tad looked out the window, and, in the fading light he saw his father standing on the street, looking expectantly at the coach. With a shock he realized that his father had aged perceptibly since he had last seen him.

"Hi, Papa," he called through the window at the top of his voice.

"Hello, Tad. Glad you're home," his father shouted back.

"I'll be there in a minute, Papa."

The other passengers, a man and two women, were getting out of the stage. When they were safely on the ground, Tad and Tom got out, as Lewis came to meet them.

"It's good to see you, Tad, but I'm sorry you lost that arm," Lewis said, looking at Tad's empty sleeve.

"At least I'm alive, Papa." He shrugged and turned to Tom. "Papa, this is Tom Stanton. He lost a leg in the war. I met him on the train and invited him to come home with me for Christmas."

Lewis took a good look at Tom, including his crutches and his empty pant leg, then he extended his hand. "It's good to meet you, Tom. I'm glad Tad brought you. My wife and daughter will be pleased to pieces to have company for Christmas."

"I'm pleased to meet you, Mr. Perry," Tom returned.

"We'd better get goin'. Be dark before we get home. You both got your bags?"

"Yes, Papa." He held up his bag with his good arm and motioned toward Tom's bag with his head.

"I hitched Ol' Jack around back. Broke him to pull the buggy after the Yankees took our horses," Lewis said.

"That's what Lucinda wrote."

"Yankees raided our place awhile back," Lewis explained to Tom.

"I'm sorry," Tom responded. "From what I hear, there's been a lot of that sort of thing on both sides."

"I can't believe our Southern boys are thieves," Lewis answered sharply.

Tad pulled Tom's sleeve and shook his head to warn him to drop the subject.

"Look at all the colors in the sky, with only the rim of the sun showing," Tom commented.

"It'll be dark before long," Lewis responded.

"How's Mama?" Tad asked.

"Same as always. She works too hard and worries too much."

"And Lucinda?"

"You know Cindy. She never runs down. She's more serious than she used to be though."

"We'll put our bags in the back," Tad said when they reached the buggy. They stashed their bags in the boot of the buggy, and Tad steadied Tom while he made the difficult climb to the buggy seat with the aid of his crutches. Then he got in beside him.

Lewis got in on the other side and picked up the reins. The mule at once turned the buggy around and started toward home in a canter.

"Ol' Jack is anxious to get to the feed trough," Lewis commented.

"He's no more anxious to get home than I am. I want to see Mama and Lucinda," Tad exclaimed.

"It won't take long if Jack keeps up this gait."

"I remember this country," Tom remarked as he watched the last rays of the sun burn and flicker through the trees.

"He fought at Perryville, Papa," Tad explained.

"He was fightin' for the South, I hope," Lewis said

apprehensively.

"I fought at Perryville in Polk's First Corps. We won too, though there's them that say we didn't."

"One of my neighbors said it looked to him like both sides lost. I helped him bury the dead Confederate soldiers, and we saw where the Union Army had buried theirs beside a fence on Springfield Pike."

"Tom lost a cousin in the battle, Papa."

"Too bad. Nobody's goin' to come out ahead in this war, lest it be the slaves."

Jack slowed to a walk as the last vestige of the sun disappeared behind a ridge and the shadows deepened in the valleys.

Lewis took the buggy whip from its socket and hit the mule on the rump. Jack jumped and spurted ahead for a short distance, then he slowed again.

"I reckon he's tired, but we'll soon be home, and I'll feed him," Lewis said.

"You still got to do the chores when we get home, Papa?" Tad asked.

"I'm sure Lucinda has already done the chores. About now she's helpin' Nancy finish supper. They ought to have it ready by the time we get home."

"I'm glad," Tad said. "We didn't eat much on the way. I'm sure Tom is hungry too."

"I could do with a bite, but I don't want to be no trouble to the womenfolks," Tom said.

"You'll won't be no trouble. They'll be glad to have somebody to cook for," Lewis told him.

When they reached the lane that led to the house, the mule turned from the pike of his own accord.

"It's not far now," Tad said, looking ahead in an effort to see the house. They passed a tree that was blocking the view, and he saw the bulk of the house against the darkening sky. Then he saw the slender form of Lucinda race past the lamp that was shining through the window.

"That was Lucinda, and that's about as still as you'll ever see her," he told Tom, laughing.

"I sure am anxious to meet that girl. Wish I had met her before I lost my leg."

Tad was not sure whether Tom was talking to him or to himself.

"You might as well rest your mind on that subject. As I told you, Lucinda ain't never took a fancy to any man. Whether you've got one leg or two won't make a whit of difference to her," Tad told him.

"Just the same, I'm lookin' forward to meetin' her."

Lewis pulled back on the reins and shouted, "Whoa, whoa," to the mule as they neared the gate, but Jack took the bit in his teeth, ducked his head, put his ears forward, and continued to the barn without slacking his pace.

"I was goin' to let you boys out at the house, but Ol' Jack kinda took things in his teeth. So I reckon you'll have to ride to the barn with me," Lewis chuckled.

Just then the front door of the house flew open, and Lucinda ran out on the porch.

Tad heard the door close and looked back. Lucinda was shadowed against the light that was coming from the big front window. She had left the door open, and he saw his mother standing in the doorway.

"Where do you all think you're going?" Lucinda screamed, waving her arms wildly.

"Jack won't stop," Tad shouted back.

Just then the mule did stop with his nose almost touching the barn door.

"I'll be back in a minute, Mama," Lucinda called over her shoulder as she charged down the steps and started running toward the barn.

"That's Lucinda, coming," Tad explained to Tom.

"She sure can run."

The mule started pawing the barn door with his front hooves.

"I'll open the door, Papa, before that mule tears it down," Tad laughed, getting out of the buggy.

"I'll have to back him up a bit, 'fore you can," Lewis chuckled. He pulled on the reins, forcing the mule back in spite of the grip he had on the bit.

Lucinda arrived just as Tad pulled the barn door open.

"Oh, Tad, Tad, you're home," she cried, throwing her arms around him.

"Cindy, it sure is good to see you." Tad hugged her with his one arm.

"You don't know how I've missed you, Tad," she said purposely avoiding any mention of his missing arm.

Lewis pulled on the reins with all his strength to keep the mule from charging forward again and running over Lucinda and Tad.

"Cindy I want you to meet the soldier I brought home with me," Tad said. "His name is Tom Stanton."

Lucinda turned and looked toward the buggy just as Tom was attempting to get out on his crutches. At that instant Ol' Jack lunged forward in spite of all Lewis could do, and Tom fell back to the buggy seat.

Lucinda jumped aside, pulling Tad after her, and the buggy swept pass them. The mule did not stop until he was in front of his stall.

"It's good to meet you, Miss Lucinda," Tom called back to her, recovering as much of his shattered dignity as he could.

"It's good to meet you, Mr. Stanton, I think. I haven't seen you yet," Lucinda laughed.

"Just a minute, Tom, and I'll help you get out of the buggy," Tad offered.

"I think this mule will stand still now that he's got his way," Lewis said.

Tom again started to get out of the buggy just as Tad reached him.

"Tom lost a leg in the war," Tad explained to Lucinda as he helped Tom get out of the buggy.

"What a shame . . . you losing an arm and him a leg," Lucinda exclaimed.

"Could have been worse. A lot of soldiers ain't livin'," Tad responded.

"I'd a heap druther be without a limb than to be dead," Tom agreed with a wry smile.

"Hush, you all," Lucinda insisted. "That's morbid talk. I'm sorry I mentioned it."

"You all go on to the house. I'll be in soon as I take the harness off this mule," Lewis told them.

"Want me to help, Papa?" Lucinda asked. "I'm sure Tad and Mr. Stanton can find their way to the house."

"Go on with them, Cindy. Most likely Nancy's got somethin' more for you to do."

"Let's go then, you two," Lucinda said, gesturing with both arms for them to precede her.

When they reached the front steps, Lucinda ran past them and up the steps two at a time. Then she bounded across the porch to the front door and pushed it opened.

"Looks like you've mastered walking on your crutches, Mr. Stanton," she said as she looked back and watched him climb the steps.

"I can't keep up with you, you're way out in front of me," Tom laughed.

"Lucinda is always out in front and behind and everywhere else," Tad commented dryly.

"You stop talking about me, big brother; he'll think I'm awful," she retorted.

"Seems to me that you're a girl with a lot of energy," Tom soothed.

Lucinda motioned them through the door. "Tad's here, Mama," she announced, "and he brought a soldier with him. His name is Tom Stanton."

"Oh, Tad! How good to have you home. I have really worried about you, especially since you lost your arm,"

Nancy exclaimed as she came from the kitchen to meet them. "It's good to meet you, Mr. Stanton," she said, turning to him. "I'm sorry you got wounded," she added when she saw his crutches.

"It's good to meet you, Mrs. Perry. I hope I'm not intruding," Tom said.

"Not at all. We're glad to have you." She smiled at him briefly then hurried back to the kitchen.

"Lucinda, I need your help," she called over her shoulder.

"Coming, Mama," Lucinda sang out as she started to the kitchen. When she entered she saw that her mother's face was flushed and that her hands were trembling.

"I've never seen you so flustered, Mama. Let me take over, and you go visit with Tad and his guest."

"Thank you, Cindy," Nancy said. As she turned to go Tad and Tom came into the kitchen.

"Mama, it's good to be home," Tad said.

"I'm thankful that I met Tad on the train, and he invited me to come home with him," Tom exclaimed.

"Tom doesn't have a family, so I invited him home with me for Christmas," Tad explained.

"Tom, I'm glad you've come," Nancy said, turning to him.

"I can't tell you how good it is to be with your family at Christmastime, especially since my family is gone."

"Your being here makes it almost like David was home. Only don't mention David in my husband's presence."

"This war has upset a lot of people."

"That's true, Mr. Stanton. Even our church is split up because of it, and our pastor has been sent to prison," Lucinda told him.

"It never would have happened if the Yankees had stayed up north and minded their own business," Tad said angrily.

Lucinda cast a worried glance at her mother. "Tad, why don't you change the subject," she said when she saw that her mother was near tears.

"That's a good idea, Lucinda," Nancy said. "While you're home, Tad, let's forget that there's a war so we can have a good Christmas," she suggested.

"I'm sorry, Mama. I didn't mean to upset you," Tad said.

"I hear Papa coming in from the barn, and I have supper almost ready," Lucinda announced loud enough to claim their attention.

"Then I'll set the table while you take up the supper, Lucinda," Nancy said as she started to the dining room.

"Papa, supper's ready. We'll have it on the table by the time you men wash your hands," Lucinda called as Lewis came in.

"I'm goin' to put some logs on the fire in the parlor before I wash up. The weather has turned cooler since the sun went down, and I want the parlor to be warm by the time we finish eatin'."

"Do you think it's going to snow, Papa?" Lucinda asked.

"I don't know, but the wind has picked up and there's clouds gatherin' in the west."

"Oh, I hope it snows. It will be so nice to have a white Christmas."

"I'm with you, Cindy," Tom said.

"I'd just as soon it didn't. It takes more feed for the stock when there's a snow, and we didn't put up too much feed this year," Lewis commented.

"I know, Lewis, but I reckon the young folks would like to see some snow," Nancy answered.

"While you're seein' to the fire, Papa, me and Tom will wash up," Tad said.

Soon they all gathered around the big table in the dining room to a supper of fried ham and gravy, veg-

etables, and hot biscuits. The aroma of hot food filled the
room. Two freshly-baked cream pies were residing on
the top of the buffet. A lighted lamp was on the table,
and another was on top of the china cabinet. The lamps
filled the room with a yellow glow, illuminating the faces
of those around the table, and enhancing Nancy's best
china and crystal and flatware.

"It's been a long time since I ate at a table like this,
and I don't mind sayin' that I'm hungry," Tom commented.

"Food ain't too plentiful in these times, but what
we've got is wholesome. I hope you will enjoy it," Nancy
responded, smiling as she had not smiled in months.

"Tad, will you say grace?" Nancy requested.

"Of course, Mama. Gettin' wounded has brought me
closer to the Lord than I used to be." He bowed his head
and thanked the Lord for the food and for the privilege of
being home.

"I'll wait on the table, Mama," Lucinda offered. She
arose and went to the buffet and picked up the platter of
ham and a bowl of gravy and carried them to the table.
"Have some ham and gravy, Mr. Stanton," she said.

"Let's get somethin' straight, Miss Lucinda. Please
call me Tom," he said as he took ham from the platter.

"Then you call me Lucinda."

He looked up and their eyes met. "All right, Lucinda."
His eyes held hers.

"The rest of you can pass this around," she said as
she turned away to bring more food.

She did not look directly at Tom again, but she was
aware that his eyes were following her as she served the
food. That both pleased and troubled her.

"That was a delicious supper, Mrs. Perry and Lucinda," Tom said as he finished his second piece of pie.

"You have to give Mama the credit. I only helped
her," Lucinda said modestly.

"Thank you, Tom," Nancy said, smiling happily. "Now why don't you men go to the parlor where you can sit by the fire while you talk? Lucinda and I will come in after we finish in the kitchen," Nancy said as they were getting up from the table.

"Tom seems like a nice young man, but it troubles me that he has no family," Nancy said when the men were gone. "I wonder what happened to them."

"Something caused by the war, most likely," Lucinda guessed as she started gathering up the dishes.

"He seems to be taking a liking to you, Lucinda. You had better watch it." Her mother paused at her task and looked straight at her.

"I don't know that he has, Mama."

"His eyes never left you while we were eating."

"I did notice that, and it made me uncomfortable," Lucinda admitted as she started to the kitchen with a load of dishes.

"I'd be on my guard if I were you," Nancy warned. "We don't know anything about him or his background."

"I know, Mama. The only good thing we know about him is that he lost a leg fighting for the Confederate cause. I really feel sorry for him."

"That doesn't necessarily make him good husband material."

"Mother! Who's looking for a husband? Not me, I'm sure."

"I know you're not, Lucinda, and I'm glad. There'll be time enough for that after the war is over."

"For the time being, Mama, let's forget it and finish the dishes so we can go in and visit with Tad."

"And Tad's guest?"

"Yes, Mama, with Tad's guest. We are supposed to make him welcome," Lucinda answered, smiling coyly to herself.

Chapter 23

*T*hat night after supper the Perrys and their guest sat long in the parlor talking. Tad wanted to know all that happened since he had gone into the army, and Lucinda and Nancy and Lewis were just as anxious to know all that had befallen him. So they asked him in detail about places he had been and battles in which he had fought.

Much of the time Tom sat listening and furtively watching Lucinda. He rarely participated in the conversation unless a question was directed to him. Finally Lucinda persisted until she got him to talk about his family and where he had grown up.

"My parents married late in life, so they were well along in years by the time my sister, Mildred, and I were grown-up," he finally told her.

"Was your sister younger than you?" she asked.

"Older. She was three years older than me. She and my mother were both in poor health when I joined the army. I guess my enlisting was the wrong thing to do, but all the young men in my community were signing up, so I did too."

"I felt the same way when I joined the army," Tad interjected.

"If I had known what was goin' to happen to my family after I was gone, I would have stayed at home as long as I could. I had been gone less than a year when a neighbor wrote me that bushwhackers had burned my homeplace and killed my father and my sister."

"What about your mother?" Lucinda asked.

"I'm not sure, but she may have escaped. A neighbor wrote that she had gone to the spring before the raid, so the bushwhackers may not have found her. I'm goin' to try to find her after the doctors release me."

"You see, Lewis, some other people have had it worse than we have," Nancy said.

"I reckon you're right, but I still ain't forgettin' what them Yankees did to us," Lewis muttered.

"I don't hold no hard feelings. I just hope I can find my ma," Tom said.

The clock in the hall started striking just then, and they all fell silent, counting the number of times it struck.

"It's twelve o'clock, and that's way past my bedtime. Think I'll turn in," Lewis said when the clock stopped striking. "You young people can sit up and talk long as you want to."

"I think we should all go to bed. Tad and Tom must be tired after traveling all day," Nancy said, rolling her eyes at Lucinda.

"Mama is right. There'll be plenty of time for us to visit tomorrow," Lucinda agreed, faking a yawn.

Lewis went to the front door and looked out. "It's gettin' colder, and there's the feel of snow in the air," he announced.

"Oh, I hope we have a really big snow, but I don't want it to come until tomorrow afternoon. I want to go to Perryville in the morning and do some last minute Christmas shopping," Lucinda said.

"I'd like to go along, if there's room in the buggy. But I suppose there won't be," Tom hastened to add. "Do you have a horse I can ride?"

"I've not replaced the horses the Yankees stole yet. I figured they'd just steal them too if I did. But you and

Tad can both go to town in the buggy with Lucinda—
that is if Tad wants to go," Lewis said.

"Sure, I'd like to go," Tad responded.

"Then we'll go," Lucinda said brightly.

"Good night, everybody. . . . think I'll turn in, if you're
ready," Tad said to Tom.

"I'm ready," Tom responded. Tad arose and led the
way upstairs.

"Mama, I hope I can get away from Tom in Perryville. I want to buy some presents we can give him for
Christmas," Lucinda told her mother after Tad and Tom
were gone.

"Ask Tad to take Tom to a different store while you're
shopping. I imagine Tom will want to do some shopping
alone also. That's probably why he wanted to go."

"I hope that's all he has in mind, since you think he is
attracted to me."

"Why wouldn't he be, Lucinda. You're an attractive
girl."

"Mama! Don't even think like that," she retorted.

The next morning the clouds were gray and low, and
it looked as if snow might start falling any minute.

"We'll have to hurr' if we're going to Perryville and
back before it snows," Tad said as they sat down to breakfast.

"It will surprise you how fast I can get ready, Tad,"
Lucinda responded, looking at him with her eyes filled
with excitement.

"I'll bet you can't get ready any quicker than I can
hitch the mule to the buggy, even though I just have one
arm," Tad challenged.

"We'll see about that, Tad," Lucinda exclaimed, nib-
bling at her food. Then she excused herself and ran upstairs to dress. In a short while she came gaily back down,
ready to go. She arrived at the front door just as Tad and
Tom drove up to the gate in the buggy. She called good-

bye to her parents and went out to join them.

"I know Tom helped you, Tad," she taunted.

"Whether he did or not, I still beat you to the front gate."

She made a face at him and hurried to the buggy and got in beside him.

Nancy watched from the window as they drove away. Then she started clearing the dishes from the breakfast table.

"Tad, you take Tom with you. I want to do some shopping by myself," Lucinda said as they were getting out of the buggy in Perryville.

"Lucinda, there ain't many stores in Perryville, but we'll go to the hardware store while you shop at the general store. You hurry! We'll come there after a bit," Tad told her.

"After I finish at the general store, I will probably go by the hardware. Then I might go by the grocery store. Where should we meet if we miss each other?" Lucinda asked.

"Let's meet back at the buggy, say, at eleven."

"I'll be here on time," she sang out as she started toward the store.

"We'll be here too," Tom called after her.

Snow was just beginning to fall when they met back at the buggy to start home.

"I'm glad it's snowing," Lucinda exclaimed as she watched the big flakes floating gently to the ground.

"If it keeps this up, it will soon cover the ground," Tad observed as they stowed their purchases in the crowded space in the boot of the buggy and in the space under the seat.

"I hope we have a big snow," Lucinda said as they were getting in the buggy.

"We probably will. It's cold enough for the snow to

stick, and there's no wind to drift it," Tom said.

"The ground is almost covered with snow already," Tad said a few minutes after they started home.

"Look how it's collecting on the cedar trees," Lucinda exulted.

"It makes them look like Christmas trees," Tom declared.

"I hope it keeps snowing so we can go sleigh riding tomorrow. We'll have loads of fun," Lucinda exclaimed. Then she saw the expression on Tom's face and realized that he could not go sleigh riding on his crutches.

Tad saw Tom's look of dismay also. "We could hitch Ol' Jack and Ol' Beck to the sled and have them pull us around the farm," he suggested.

"That sounds like it would be fun," Tom said, brightening and looking at Lucinda for approval.

"Then, that's what we'll do," Lucinda said.

Snow was still falling when Tad stopped the mule near the front gate at home.

"I think Lucinda is goin' to get the big snow she wants," Tom said, looking up at the lead-gray sky.

"I think you're right, Tom. Now, Cindy, if you'll get out, I'll take the mule to the barn and unharness him and put him in his stall."

"There's a couple of packages I want to get out of the buggy. You and Tom can bring the rest when you come," Lucinda said as she was getting out.

The snow fell gently the rest of the day, and it was still snowing when they went to bed that night.

The next morning Lucinda was the first to get out of bed and look outside. Excited, she saw that the ground was well covered with snow. She dressed quickly and started down the stairs singing, "Oh, it snowed, it snowed; we're going to have a white Christmas."

"Lucinda, you'll wake up everybody in the house making all that racket," Tad called from the head of the stairs just as she reached the downstairs hall.

"Go wash the sleep out of your eyes, Tad," she ordered, throwing him a kiss.

"I'll be down in a minute," he called over his shoulder as he turned toward his room.

When he came down a few minutes later, Lucinda was taking the ashes out of the range.

"I'll do that, Cindy," he offered.

"It would be better if you'd get the fires going in the grates in the parlor and dining room. I can handle this."

"Anything you say, Cindy."

"Is Tom awake yet?"

"He wasn't when I came down. Mama and Papa must still be sleepin' too. I never knew them to sleep past daylight before."

"They're both tired all the time these days. Besides, we were up past midnight."

"I don't see how the three of you have been doing all the work on this farm, Lucinda."

"It does keep us going, and, besides the hard work, Mama and Papa worry a lot. Papa has been especially worried since the soldiers raided the farm, and, because of their raid, he has a lot of bitterness."

"I can't help how Papa feels, but, now that I'm home, I'm goin' to help Papa all I can."

"Tad, it sure is good to have you home."

"Well, I'd better make myself useful," he said, and he started getting kindling from the wood box.

Lucinda was starting breakfast when she heard Tom come down the stairs on his crutches and stop in the parlor. Then she heard him talking with Tad. Moments later her mother came down and greeted Tad and Tom as she passed the open parlor on her way to the kitchen.

"I'm sorry I don't have breakfast ready, Mama," Lucinda said as her mother entered.

"I'm sorry I overslept, Cindy. I don't know why I'm

so tired these days. Lewis overslept, too, but he's up now. He'll be down shortly."

After breakfast, Tad volunteered to help Lewis with the chores. Tom wanted to go to the barn with them, but Tad discouraged him for fear he would fall on his crutches because of the snow.

Tom was relieved, for he thought this would give him an opportunity to get better acquainted with Lucinda. But to his dismay she stayed in the kitchen with her mother, and he was obliged to sit alone in the parlor. He soon left his place by the fire and went to the bookcase and selected a book of poems by Longfellow. Then he sat down by the fire and started reading.

"It's nice outside, but the wind makes it seem colder than it is," Tad announced when he and Lewis came in from the barn a half hour later.

"I see that the sun is shining," Lucinda exclaimed, looking out the window.

"Yes, and the sky is blue except for a few high, thin, white clouds," Tad responded.

"Those are cirrus clouds, Tad," Lucinda told him.

"They are, are they, Cindy? How did you know that?"

"I read it in a book, that's how."

"Anyway, it will be a good day to go ridin' on the sled, if you're still of a mind to go."

"I hope she is," Tom said, coming from the parlor to join them.

"Of course I'm of a mind to go. I'll help Mama get dinner, and we'll go after we eat. I can't think of a better way to spend Christmas Eve."

"That will be a good time to go," Lewis said. "This mornin' I'll work in the barn, and after dinner, while you all are gone, I'll keep Nancy company."

After an early dinner Lewis and Tad went to the barn and harnessed the mules to the sled, and Tom went upstairs and dressed for the outside. He came back wearing a boot and warm sweater and his army coat and slouch hat.

Lucinda dressed in her warmest clothes and put on her rubber shoes. Then she went to the front door and looked out.

Tad was just stopping the mules at the front gate.

"Just a minute, Tad," she called. "I'm going to pack some coffee and some cookies to take with us."

"Good idea, Cindy," he called back.

Minutes later Lucinda came from the kitchen carrying a basket, and Tom arose from his chair in the parlor to go out with her.

"Can you walk in the snow on your crutches?" Lucinda asked as they started out.

"If I can't, I'll be found trying. I have to do with these until they get my artificial leg. They say I'll be able to walk after that."

"I'm glad, but for now, I'll walk beside you so I can steady you if you slip in the snow."

"And I'd probably bring us both down. I'm glad you're goin' to walk with me, though."

"Tom, you hold the mules while I go in and get the buggy robe and some blankets," Tad said as he and Lucinda reached the sled.

"I'm glad you brought those bales of hay for us to sit on," Lucinda said as she climbed on the sled and sat down on one of them.

"Tom, I see you're wearing your army coat. Good idea!"

"I'm glad I brought it in my carpetbag. It feels good in this wind."

"I brought mine too. Think I'll get it. Be back in a minute."

Tad started hurrying to the house. Minutes later, he returned wearing his army coat and hat and carrying two blankets. He handed them to Lucinda.

She unfolded a blanket and handed it to Tom. Then she unfolded the other one and handed it to Tad. "Excuse me for taking the heavy robe, but my legs are freezing already," she said as she spread the buggy robe over her lap.

"We probably won't need the blankets, since we're wearin' our army coats. They are plenty warm."

"Aren't you all afraid some Union soldier will see you and start shooting?"

"It's not likely that there'll be any soldiers out here," Tad assured her.

"We can take them off if we see any soldiers," Tom told her.

"We have slept out on the ground so much that we are used to the cold. So we wouldn't be too cold without them," Tad said as he picked up the reins.

"Jack, Beck, get up," he called and slapped the mules with the reins and turned them down the lane toward Mackville Pike.

The mules dug their hoofs in the soft snow and started forward. The sled runners cut through the snow and screeched and crunched over the loose gravel. The cold wind bit at their cheeks, but the ride was so exhilarating that even Lucinda soon forgot the cold.

"You're not going out on the main road are you, Tad?" she asked as they neared the end of the lane.

"No. I'm goin' to drive along the fence that runs by the road to the end of the field. Then I'll turn up the hill."

"I remember this country well, but I didn't have time to enjoy it when I was here before," Tom reminisced. "We were right busy huntin' water holes in dry stream beds and fightin' off Yankees."

"Look!" Lucinda interrupted. "I do believe that's Mr. and Mrs. Taylor and Verna coming up the road in their buggy. Stay close to the fence, Tad, so I can see if it's them."

"I never knew you to be that anxious to see the Taylors," Tad laughed.

"The last time we were at church Mr. Taylor had a regular temper fit, and we all got up and left. I want to see if they'll speak to us."

"People ought not to be like that at church, even if there is a war goin' on," Tom commented.

"Tad, stop by the fence until they pass," Lucinda directed.

"Whatever you say, Cindy," Tad said as he pulled the mules to a stop.

The mules shook their heads and pawed the snow. Then they stretched their necks and brayed to the approaching horse.

The Taylors turned their heads away when they saw the young people on the sled, and Jackson Taylor took the buggy whip from its holder and struck the mare on her rump to make her go faster.

"Hello, everybody," Lucinda called, waving her hand as they drew near.

The Taylors drove past in stony silence, without acknowledging their presence by so much as the nod of a head. After they had passed, Mr. Taylor turned and looked back at them until the buggy rounded a curve out of sight.

"Well! What do you make of that, Tad?" Lucinda asked, letting her breath out in a great sigh of disgust.

"Looks like they're holdin' a grudge. I've never seen Mr. Taylor look at anybody that hard before."

"Maybe he was tryin' to figure out who I was," Tom suggested.

"Let's forget we saw them," Tad suggested as he started the mules forward and turned them toward the meadow behind the house. The gate to the meadow was open, so he drove through it and up the hill to the highest point on the farm. There he stopped the mules.

"Tom, when I was a boy, I used to trap down there along that creek in the wintertime," Tad said, pointing toward Hope's Creek.

"That must have been fun. I never did anything like that when I was growin' up. My folks lived in town when I was a boy. They bought a little farm, and we moved to it about the time I was grown."

"I used to go with Tad to set his traps, and sometimes, when he was helping Papa, he'd ask me to run his trap line for him. Remember, Tad, the day you had a coon in one of your traps, and I ran all the way back to the barn where you were helping Papa to tell you. That coon was growling and carrying on, and I didn't know what to do with him."

"And Papa had to let me go get the coon out of the trap."

"Lucinda, I can't imagine you tramping around in the woods like that," Tom said.

"There's a lot you don't know about my sister, Tom. She used to do about everything my brother and I did."

"I'm sure I have a lot to learn about Lucinda, and I want to learn all there is to know." He turned toward Lucinda, and their eyes met.

She blushed and turned away, wishing that he would not look at her so directly, yet pleased by his attention.

"Tad, drive to the back pasture where we keep the calves," Lucinda suggested. "I'll open the gate for you."

"All right, Cindy, if you say so."

When they reached the gate, she jumped off the sled and opened it. Tad drove through, and she closed the gate, and ran and got back on the sled.

"If I go straight down the hill, the sled will run over the mules," Tad said, as he turned the mules so they would angle around the hillside. Even so, the trace chains grew slack and clanked, and the mules had to step lively to keep ahead of the sled.

"Look at that big hawk," Lucinda exclaimed, pointing up. "Looks like he's hanging in the sky."

"I reckon he's lookin' for a rabbit for his dinner," Tad suggested.

They reached the bottom of the hill and Tad stopped the mules in a sheltered place among some cedar trees. "Cindy, I think some of that coffee would help drive the chill from our bones about now," he said.

"That's a good idea, Tad." She brought a basket out from beneath the corner of the buggy rug where she had placed it to keep it warm. Then she brought out a quart jar of coffee, wrapped in a heavy towel. "I hope the coffee stayed hot," she said as she unwrapped the jar. "You men can hold the cups," she added, handing each of them a cup.

She poured the coffee, and was pleased that it was still steaming hot.

"That's great coffee. I don't see how you kept it hot in this weather," Tom said.

"It was boiling when I put it in the jar, and you saw how I had it wrapped."

"You're an unusual girl, sufficient for all things," Tom mused.

She blushed and turned away. "Have some cookies," she said, holding the basket toward him with her face still averted.

"I envy you and Tad, growin' up in a place like this," Tom said as he munched the cookies.

"We like it here."

"Tad, have some cookies." She passed the basket to him.

"Tom, what are you goin' to do after this war's over?" Tad asked as he took some cookies from the basket.

"Don't know for sure. I'd like to serve the Lord in some manner. Since I got saved on the battlefield, I've wanted to do something useful with my life."

"I didn't know you got saved on the battlefield," Lucinda gasped, looking hard at him and seeing him in a new light.

"You are a Christian, Lucinda?" His inflection indicated a question.

"Oh, yes. I was converted when I was a little girl. Since the war though, I haven't been as close to the Lord as I used to be."

"You ought to do something about that, Lucinda."

"There's some of the calves comin' out of the bushes down by the creek," Tad interrupted. "I reckon they've been hidin' from the wind."

"Think about it, Lucinda," Tom said before he turned to Tad.

"That's all the calves we had left after the Yankee raid," Lucinda said.

"Too bad they took your calves, but surely the government will pay for them, if there is a government in Washington when this war's over."

"I doubt that we'll ever get anything for them," Tad said.

"I'm getting cold. Let's go to the house," Lucinda suggested.

"I'm ready," Tad said as he dumped the rest of his coffee in the snow. Then he put the cup in the basket, picked up the reins, and started the mules toward home.

"I've really enjoyed this, Tad. Thank you for bringing us," Lucinda said as they got under way.

Chapter 24

*L*ucinda awoke with the dawn on Christmas morning and arose and dressed quietly and quickly, determined that she would be the first one downstairs. When she reached the foot of the stairs, she went immediately to the parlor and, despite the chill in the room, stood before the Christmas tree, admiring it and thinking.

There had never been a Christmas like this one, with Tad wounded and David forbidden to come home. There were no presents under the tree for David. She and her mother had mailed his presents weeks ago. No doubt he had already opened them. She thought of the inexpensive gifts she had bought for Tom so he could not feel left out.

She sighed gently as her thoughts turned to Martin. She wondered where he was and what he was doing this Christmas morning. She had not bought him a present. Even if she had been so bold, she would not have known where to send it. She had heard nothing of him since David had told of seeing him in Richmond, and it was not likely that she would ever hear of him again. *Her episode with him was just an interlude in her life. It would always be a pleasant memory,* she decided.

Soon she heard the stairs creaking and turned and saw Tad coming down in his stocking feet.

"Hi, Tad," she greeted softly.

"Hello, Cindy. I thought I heard you up. Everybody

else is up. They will all be down in a few minutes," he said as he reached the foot of the stairs. "I think I'll go start a fire in the range."

"You had better start the fires in the rest of the house after you do that. It feels like the outdoors in here."

"All right, Cindy, I will."

"I'll start breakfast, Tad. Papa will want to eat before he feeds the stock and milks the cows," she replied, following him to the kitchen.

"When will we open the presents, Cindy?"

"After Papa gets through at the barn. You know he'll not want us to open them before that."

"Lucinda, what do you think of Tom?" Tad asked as he started taking the ashes from the firebox of the range.

"Why do you ask that, Tad?"

"I think he might be taking a fancy to you, and I was just wondering."

"I hope he's not, Tad. I hardly know him, and I know nothing about his family. What do you know about him?"

"Not much. He grew up in Tennessee, but, as he told us, his home and family are gone."

"He seems cheerful for someone who is alone in the world. . . . and him crippled besides."

"Maybe bein' right with God keeps him in good spirits." He went to the wood box and got kindling to start the fire.

"I'd better hurry breakfast so it will be ready when they come down," Lucinda said, and she went to the kitchen cabinet and started collecting the ingredients for biscuits.

"After breakfast, I'll help Papa do the chores so it won't take so long," Tad said.

"I'll hurry with the dishes, and, when you and Papa get back, we'll be ready to open the presents," she told Tad as he left to make fires in the other rooms.

By the time Lewis and Nancy and Tom came downstairs, the house was growing warm, and the smells of boiling coffee and frying ham were filling the air.

"Get ready for breakfast," Lucinda called. "I'm going to put it on the table in a minute."

Moments later they all sat down at the table and enjoyed the food, the conversation, and the good cheer of a Christmas morning breakfast. For a brief time they put thoughts of the war out of their minds. Even Lewis warmed to the occasion.

After breakfast Tad went to the barn with Lewis, and they hurriedly did the chores. Tom excused himself for fear that he might slip and fall in the snow. He went and sat in the parlor and read while they were gone. Nancy and Lucinda, both eager to open the presents, cleared the table and washed the dishes. They finished just as Lewis and Tad returned to the house. Shortly they all gathered in the parlor to open the presents.

Lewis and Nancy sat on the sofa, and Tom sat down in the horsehair chair. Tad knelt by the tree and brought out the presents one at a time and handed them to Lucinda. She sang out the name on each present, then gave it to the recipient with much aplomb, meanwhile laying her presents aside. When she had handed out the last present, she sat down and took her presents in her lap. They all took turns opening their presents, and each one was opened with exclamations of surprise and pleasure and with proper words of gratitude. Tom was near tears as he opened the small gifts the family had given him.

"I can't tell you how much I appreciate being here and being treated like a member of the family," he said at last.

"I'm glad you came home with me, Tom," Tad said, and he slapped him on the shoulder.

"We hope you'll always feel that this is your second home," Nancy told him.

"I didn't put this on the tree," Tom said, taking a

small package from his pocket and handing it to Lucinda. "It's not something new, but I want you to have it."

"Oh, thank you, Tom," she said, surprised and a bit apprehensive. She tore away the wrapping and opened a small box. "Oh, this is beautiful, but I can't accept it," she cried when she saw the tiny gold watch with a chain to be worn around the neck.

"Why can't you accept it?" Tom asked, looking hurt.

"It's too beautiful and too expensive. Tom, you hardly know me. You shouldn't be giving me such an expensive gift."

"It was my Ma's watch. When I went off to war, she asked me to carry it as a reminder that she'd be prayin' for me. Now Ma's gone, and I want you to have her watch. It should be worn by a beautiful lady, and I don't know a more beautiful lady to give it to."

Lucinda was greatly touched, yet she did not feel that she could accept Tom's gift. *If she refused, it would hurt his feelings,* she realized.

"I thank you from my heart for your thought, Tom, and I'll tell you what I am willing to do. For all you know, your mother may still be alive, and the day may come when you'll be reunited with her. I can't take her watch as a gift, but I'll be more than pleased to keep it for you until you find her."

"Thank you, Lucinda. I want you to keep Ma's watch, and I want you to wear it. If ever she is found alive, you can give it back to her, but if I don't ever find her the watch is yours. I want you to have it as a remembrance of this Christmas."

"I thank you, Tom. I will care for the watch as your own mother would," she said, clasping the watch in her hand.

"I appreciate the gifts from all of you. Think I'll take them upstairs and put them away," Lewis said as he arose from the sofa.

"Mama, I'll pick up the wrapping paper and string," Lucinda said as she started picking up the clutter.

Just then the sound of a sharp command, followed by the hoofbeats of several horses, caused them all to turn suddenly toward the front of the house.

"Now who can that be?" Lewis demanded, dropping his presents on the steps and hurrying to the door. He pulled the door open a crack and looked out. For a long minute he stood immobile. Then he slowly closed the door. "It's some more blamed Yankee soldiers," he stated coldly. "I'm goin' upstairs and get my gun."

"Lewis, that's the last thing in the world you need to do," Nancy screamed.

"Whatever happens, you don't need your gun, Papa," Tad said firmly, and he stepped between Lewis and the stairway.

"I'll go out and meet them!" Lucinda announced. "Surely they will show respect for a woman."

Tom tried to jump up and stop her, but he dropped one of his crutches, and before he could recover it, hatless and coatless Lucinda ran out on the porch. Then, standing tall and straight like her father did when he was angry, she looked defiantly at the soldiers.

The sergeant, riding in front of his men, reined in his horse at the front gate. "Mornin', ma'am," he greeted as if he were making a social call.

"What do you want?" she asked coldly.

"Ma'am, you don't appear very civil. I reckon you must be a Rebel sympathizer, like we was told," he said curtly.

"I have a brother in the Union Army," she retorted, lifting her chin a bit higher. "Does that mean anything to you?"

"Ma'am, I didn't expect to have to deal with a woman. Ain't your husband at home?"

"Maybe he's out harassing women like you and your

men are doing." Her words cut the sergeant, and she knew she had angered him.

The other men spurred their horses, and they closed around the sergeant's horse, pushing him against the yard gate. The gate splintered with a crash, and the broken pieces fell into the yard.

"Who's going to pay for that gate? The Federal Government never did pay for the horses and calves some of your soldiers stole, so I suppose the government won't pay for the gate either," she challenged.

"Ma'am, if you was a man, I'd horsewhip you," the sergeant snorted.

"Let's go in and get them Rebel soldiers and get going, Sergeant," one of the men insisted.

"What soldiers?" she demanded, looking at them disdainfully.

"We were told that your family is harboring two Rebel soldiers, ma'am. Now are you going to send them out, or do we have to come in and get them?"

"I suppose you'll break the front door down like you did the gate," she countered.

"That won't be necessary, Lucinda," Tom's voice cut in from the doorway. Then he came out on his crutches and stood beside her. She admired Tom's courage, but she feared what would happen to him.

"He's lost a leg, Sarge," one of the men gasped, "and he's not in uniform. He must have been mustered out."

"We don't need no more wounded men to take care of," another man said.

"Reckon you're right," agreed the sergeant. "Where's the other one?" He looked straight at Tom.

Just then Tad came out. "I'm right here, Sergeant," he said. "I only have one arm, but you can put it in chains if you want to." He walked down the steps and started across the yard toward the sergeant, holding out his arm.

"Sarge, I don't have no stomach for this. I've seen

too many men get their arms and legs cut off, and I've heard them scream while the doctors was doing it. Let's get out of here," one of the soldiers said.

"We'll go," the sergeant decided, looking around at his men.

"Good day, Ma'am." He lifted the brim of his hat to her. "I'm sorry to have troubled you."

His men moved their horses back, and the sergeant turned his horse about and led the way back toward Mackville Pike.

Just then Lewis came out on the porch with his musket in his hands. Nancy was hanging onto his arm.

"Put that gun away, Papa," Tad said firmly. "You ought to know you can't take on that many men single-handed."

"I know why they came," Lucinda said coldly. "Remember how Jackson Taylor looked at us the day we were riding on the sled. He saw Tad and Tom, and they were wearing Confederate Army coats. So he went straight to the Yankees and told them that we were harboring Southern soldiers."

"It's like him to do that. Them Taylors are Yankees through and through, and they won't never be nothin' but Yankees," Lewis said bitterly.

"Lewis, please don't hold a grudge like that," Nancy pleaded.

"Before this war, I considered myself a good Christian, but if grudge holdin' makes me a sinner, then I reckon that's what I am," Lewis said.

"Don't be like that, Papa. It's Christmas day, and we're supposed to be thinkin' about the Prince of Peace," Tad reminded him.

"I don't see how you can talk about peace, long as this war is goin' on," Lewis countered coldly.

Tad noticed that Lewis' face was white and that he was trembling. "Come on, Papa," he said, and he and

Nancy took him by both arms and led him into the house. Lucinda and Tom followed close behind them.

"I'm proud of you, Lucinda," Tom said when they were inside. "I never thought I'd see a woman stand up to an army officer like you did."

"It was nothing, Tom. I just went out there and got rid of them to keep Papa from getting himself killed," she replied.

"That's not the way I see it, and I won't never forget what you did," Tom declared.

Chapter 25

*T*he following Monday the Perrys and Tom arose before daylight so he could catch the early stagecoach to Tennessee to get his artificial leg fitted.

While it was yet dark, Lewis and Tad went to the barn, by the light of a lantern, to feed Ol' Jack and harness him to the buggy.

"I'm glad I don't have to go back with Tom," Tad said as they were working in the barn.

"I'm glad too, Tad. The Lord only knows how I've missed you since you've been gone."

"I'm goin' to help all I can with the work, Papa. I'm sure I can still make a good hand, even without my left arm."

"I'm sure you can too, Tad. I've been watchin' the way you handle yourself without that arm, and you're goin' to be all right."

They soon brought the buggy out to the gate and hitched the mule. They went in for breakfast just as Tom came downstairs ready to go.

After they finished eating, the men arose to go.

"Good-bye, Mrs. Perry and Lucinda. I have enjoyed every minute of my visit," Tom said.

"It was good to have you, Tom," Nancy said, smiling.

"I'm glad Tad invited you, Tom," Lucinda added coyly.

"I'm sorry to hurry, but I don't want to miss my stage," Tom said.

Lewis and Tad were already going to the door, and he picked up his carpetbag and followed them out.

Nancy and Lucinda went to the door and watched them go out to the buggy and get in.

"What are you goin' to do after the doctors release you, Tom?" Tad asked as they started on their way.

"I think I'll go back to the homeplace. The house is gone, but the land is still there. I may put up some kind of a shack on the place. Then I'm goin' to try to find Ma, or at least find out what happened to her."

"You will come back and visit us?" Lewis asked.

"Wild horses can't keep me away, Mr. Perry."

"I'll keep in touch with him, Papa, and I'll see that he keeps his promise," Tad said.

It was not yet daylight when Lewis stopped the mule in front of the stage office in Perryville.

"You go in with Tom, and I'll go hitch Ol' Jack," Lewis offered.

"All right, Papa." Tad got out and held Tom's arm to steady him as he got out of the buggy. Tom got his bag and they hurried in so he could pay his fare and be assured of a seat on the stage.

Shortly after Lewis came in, the stagecoach clattered to a stop in front of the office, and the passengers started boarding.

"Good-bye," Tom said, extending his hand first to Lewis and then to Tad. He turned to the stagecoach, and Tad helped him climb aboard.

"Thank your mother and Lucinda again for me," Tom called through the window as he settled into his seat.

"We will, and you hurry back," Tad called back.

Seconds later the stage driver picked up his reins, and, with shouting and the cracking of his long whip, started the four-horse team along the macadamized road that led out of town.

Lewis and Tad watched the stage disappear in the gray light of dawn. Then they went to the buggy and started home.

The next week Lucinda received a letter from Tom, thanking her profusely for the small gift she had given him for Christmas and for the welcome she and the other members of the family had accorded him. "Tell Tad I will always be thankful that we met," he wrote.

That part of the letter did not trouble her, but the rest of it did, and she read that part through a second time, open-mouthed with a mixture of pleasure and dismay.

> *Lucinda, there was something I wanted to say to you while I was there, but I didn't have the courage. It doesn't seem quite as hard to say it in a letter, so here goes.*
>
> *When Tad first told me about you, I asked him to describe you to me. Judging from his description, I decided you were the kind of girl I would like to have for a sweetheart. The minute I saw you, I knew you were the only girl for me. So it's up to you. Could you ever be interested in a man like me? The doctors say I will be able to get around just fine on my artificial leg, once I get the hang of it. So what do you say?*
>
> *If you write to me right away, I should get your letter before the doctors release me. After they do, it may be awhile before I have a permanent address. I've decided to try to find Ma before I do anything else. Do write to me, please.*
>
> *Yours affectionately,*
>
> *Tom*

After she finished reading Tom's letter, Lucinda sat for a long while, looking out the window in a deep study, hardly aware that her hand was fondling the watch he had given her.

"Would I be interested in having Tom for a beau?" she asked herself aloud. Honestly she did not know. She had enjoyed his company, and had even been fascinated by his attention while he was visiting them. Her heart had gone out to him because he had lost his leg and because he was alone in the world, but that was not enough to build a relationship upon.

His handicap did not trouble her greatly, but what she felt for Martin did. Martin was always in the back of her mind, even though she was certain she could never have a future with him.

Finally she put the letter back in the envelope and carried it to her bedroom and put it away in the little chest with her keepsake things. She would read it again in a day or two. Then she would answer it, though she had no idea what she would write to Tom.

While she was still debating what she should write to Tom, a second letter came from him. The doctors had released him sooner than he had expected, and he was getting around on his new leg just fine. If she had not already answered his letter, would she please wait until she heard from him again. He was leaving at once to go to his homeplace and inquire about his mother. If there were clues that suggested that she might still be alive, he would go looking for her. He would write again when he stopped long enough for her to get a letter back to him.

After reading Tom's second letter, Lucinda grew misty-eyed, sighed, then put it away beside Tom's first letter.

In the days that followed, letters continued to come from Tom, more or less regularly. They were always warm and affectionate, but always he wrote that he was still on the move . . . looking for his mother.

Tad was glad that the war was over for him, though he was still concerned about what the outcome would be. He did not feel that he had failed in any way. He had given his best for the Confederacy, and he would gladly have given his life. He had indeed given an arm. Now it was up to men who were able-bodied to carry on the war.

The outcome of the war now seemed uncertain to him, but he had come to believe that a higher power would determine that outcome. So he was content to go on with his life and leave the outcome of the war and the future of the country in the hands of God.

He soon came to believe that his arm had healed better than the spirits of his parents. His father was still bitter, and that bitterness made him solemn and morose. His mother was not bitter, but she was sick with grief. Neither his father nor his mother ever appeared to have a happy moment.

Lucinda was a mystery to him. She was still strong and high spirited, but much of her old gaiety was missing. She often appeared to have something on her mind. He could not guess what it was, and he knew that she was not about to take him into her confidence. He knew that Tom was writing to her, for he always included a message to him. Lucinda always delivered Tom's message. Tad could not imagine how Tom's letters could trouble her. Surely it must be something else.

Often he thought about David. David no longer wrote to them, and that made him wonder if he would ever come home. His father never spoke of David, and his mother never spoke of him in his father's presence. Even Lucinda had little to say about David. It was as if he was no longer a member of the family.

Tad knew that he was changed also. The war had done more to him than taking his arm. The noise of battle, the blood, the suffering, and the death he had witnessed had affected him in a way that was hard to understand.

Maybe if I had a sweetheart that would lift my spirits, he thought. But he did not know any girl that appealed to him. Besides, he would probably never find a girl who would want a man with only one arm.

He wondered that Lucinda had never had a beau unless Tom could qualify for that role. He knew that she had not answered any of Tom's letters. "Tom has no certain address," she had told him when he asked why she had not. Lucinda had never shared the contents of any of Tom's letters with any member of the family, but that was in character for Lucinda. She would only tell them what she wanted them to know, and that would be in her own time.

Early in the spring Lewis and Tad started breaking ground in the fields they planned to plant. Lewis plowed the first day, but on the second day Tad persuaded him to let him plow. It was difficult at first, managing the mules and guiding the plow with one hand, but he learned to manage it, and after a few days, when his arm had grown stronger, he was able to plow with little difficulty. He learned to do the other work on the farm as well, and Lewis declared that he would rather have Tad with only one arm than any other man he had ever worked who had two arms.

Lewis and Nancy and Tad passed the spring and summer doing the usual chores and raising larger than usual crops in the hope of recouping some of what the Yankees had carried away.

Once each week Lucinda hitched Ol' Jack to the buggy and drove the three miles to Pastor Western's home to visit with his wife, Martha Mae, and his daughter, Dora. Always she loaded the buggy with vegetables from the garden and with eggs and milk. After the chickens were large enough to fry, she took them a frying chicken each time she went.

They always appeared most grateful, and Mrs. Western always told her that she did not see how they could get by if it were not for help from them and a few other church members who had remained loyal.

Lucinda always returned from the Westerns' feeling hurt and angry over of what had happened to them.

One day the last of September, after the summer rush on the farm had passed, Lucinda did not feel pressured to hurry back from her weekly visit to the Westerns', so she decided to drive the back road that passed near the cabin where Mandy and Henry lived. She had not seen them since the day after Martin left, and she felt that she should go by and thank them again for all they had done for him.

Mandy was standing in the yard, shading her eyes and looking toward the road when Lucinda stopped the buggy and got out.

Mandy smiled and waved. Then she turned to Henry who had just come to stand behind her.

"Look, Henry. Oh my soul, I do believe dat's Miss Lucinda gettin' out o' dat buggy. Go open de gap in de fence an hitch dat mule fo' her."

"She be young and spry, an' I reckon she be able to hitch one mule and open dat little ol' gap in de fence," Henry declared.

"Henry, yo' is de laziest black man I ever did see," Mandy grumbled. "I'll go do it myself."

"Hold on, ol' woman. Big as yo' is, she'll have it done fo' yo' get turned around." He started toward Lucinda mumbling to himself.

"Law, Miss Lucinda, I sho' is glad to see yo', long as yo' don't bring no Yankee soldier fo' me and Mandy to take keer ob," he said aloud when he reached her. "Let me take keer o' dat mule," he continued as he opened the gap.

"Thank you, Henry. I don't have much time, so I'll run and visit with Mandy."

"Miss Lucinda, I's plum proud to see yo'," Mandy said as Lucinda drew near.

"And I'm glad to see you, Mandy. I'll never be able to thank you enough for all you did for Martin."

"He warn't no more your 'sponsibility than he was mine. He got hurt fightin' to free us colored folks, didn't he?"

"Yes, but I'm the one that got you involved."

"Now yo' ken tell Miss Lucinda what yo' got on your mind," Henry said as he returned from hitching the mule.

"I's been wantin' to see yo', Miss Lucinda, special since dat soldier wrote me dat letter," Mandy said.

"What soldier? What letter, Mandy?" Lucinda demanded breathlessly.

"De letter de mailman done brought yesterday, dat's de one. Best I ken make out, de soldier I done took keer ob wrote it."

"Martin? You mean Martin wrote to you? What did he say?"

"Don't zactly know, Miss Lucinda. I can't read too much, nohow. 'Sides, dar warn't no name on de letter."

"Then get the letter, Mandy, and I'll read it—if you don't mind."

"Dat's what she's been wantin' to see yo' fo', Miss Lucinda. She wants yo' to read dat letter fo' her."

"Hurry and get the letter, Mandy," Lucinda insisted.

"Yes ma'am. I'll get it." Mandy went into her cabin walking much faster than usual, and in a minute she came back, holding the letter up for Lucinda to see.

Lucinda took the letter from her hand before she could descend the two steps to the ground.

"I've been wondering if he got back to his outfit. Now that he has written to you, I will find out," she exclaimed. "Do you want me to read the letter aloud, Mandy?"

"Sho' I want yo' to read it out loud. I read 'nough to know he wrote to me and Henry boof.''

Lucinda felt a tremor of delight as she took the letter from the envelope and unfolded it. The letter was written in a firm, masculine hand, and the well-formed letters reassured her. Surely it had not been written by a sick or dying man. She glanced at the bottom of the page and saw that sure enough it had not been signed. That puzzled her, but she started reading the letter anyway.

Dear Mr. and Mrs. Jones:

I am sorry to be so long writing to you, but I have had little chance to mail a letter since I got able to write. I didn't go far the day I left your house. Just a few miles from there, I saw a house that was flying an American flag and went to it. The people who lived there took me in and got a doctor for me.

I stayed with them for two days, then left to try to catch up with my outfit. I got a ride to Richmond in a wagon. Then I bought a ticket on a stagecoach and rode to London. There I caught a Union supply wagon to the Union encampment, and the doctors put me in the hospital.

Now I am out and feeling well. If it hadn't been for you and Henry, and Miss Lucinda, I know I would have died. I will always be grateful to both of you and to her. When you see Miss Lucinda, tell her that I will always be thankful that she found me. Tell her also that I met her brother in Richmond. I promised to visit him after the war is over, but you can tell her that she is the one I really want to see.

Thank you

Lucinda was almost suffocating with excitement when she finished reading the letter. She wondered why her heart was beating so wildly, and she hoped that Mandy and Henry did not notice that she was blushing.

"Dat is one polite young man," Henry said.

"Now, Henry, ain't yo' glad we took keer o' him?" Mandy demanded.

"I's glad he's better, but I ain't zackly glad we took keer o' him. De Rebels still might kill us if dey finds out."

"They're not going to find out, Henry," Lucinda assured him. "I thank you and Mandy a thousand times for what you did for Martin. Just think, we saved a man's life."

"I reckon dat is something," Henry mused.

"I have to go now, but I'll stop by and see you again one day soon," Lucinda promised as she returned the letter to Mandy. "Keep this letter in a safe place, Mandy, where no one else will ever see it," she said.

"I sho' will, Miss Lucinda. Now yo' take keer, yo' hear."

"And you and Henry take care of yourselves."

"Henry, yo' go open de gap an' unhitch dat mule fo' Miss Lucinda," Mandy ordered.

"Never mind, Henry. I can do it myself," Lucinda called over her shoulder.

On the way home Lucinda wondered why Martin had taken the chance of writing to Mandy and Henry. Was she not afraid that someone would intercept his letter? Then she remembered that there had been nothing in the letter to indicate whither he was a Confederate or a Union soldier. And he had not signed his name. She smiled, realizing that he had found a discreet way to let her know that he was all right and that he planned to see her after the war.

She would like to see him again, out of curiosity if

nothing else, she thought, but what if he and Tom both came to see her at the same time?

"Well," she sighed, with a shrug, "if that happens, I'll just have to let things take their course. Only, I will listen to my heart. Yes, I will listen very carefully to my heart," she affirmed with a vigorous nod of her head. With that she took the buggy whip from its holder and whacked the mule lightly on his back to hurry him.

Chapter 26

*T*hrough the spring and summer of 1864 the Perrys continued to keep up with news of the war. When they read of Federal victories, they tended to discount them, and, when they read of Confederate victories, they were all encouraged—except Nancy. She was too worried about David to care about Confederate victories.

"It looks like we might whip them Yankees yet," Lewis exulted one day, when they had read of a Confederate victory.

"Could be you are right, Papa," Tad smiled, rubbing his chin and nodding assent.

Another day, when the paper told of a major Confederate loss, Lewis threw the paper aside and left the house in a huff, and Tad followed close behind him. After they had gone, Lucinda hurried through the house, looking for something to do that would take her mind off the war, and her mother went to the kitchen and started cooking dinner.

Finally Lewis had to admit that the tide of battle had turned against the South, and he started going about as if in a dream. Tad did his best to accept the inevitable and to believe that the will of God was being worked out. Lucinda, though outwardly calm, was distressed over the war and worried about David and Martin. Nancy was near the breaking point from worry over the war and over

David.

Near the end of July, Atlanta was under siege. In November Atlanta fell and everything in the city was burned except private homes and churches. That news filled Lewis with cold anger, and Tad, working beside him, feared that his anger and bitterness would undermine his health.

Finally Nancy decided that it would be better if Lewis did not have the paper to read. She suggested that they drop their subscription, but he would not hear of it.

"How do you think we're going to know what's happening without the paper?" he stormed.

So she dropped the subject.

Nancy and Lucinda both stopped reading the paper, but Lewis and Tad continued to read it. They kept up with General Sherman's march across Georgia, both of them angered, yet fascinated as they read of reported looting, of atrocities, of the rape of women and of home owners being murdered by soldiers who had come to take their property. Tad was saddened, and Lewis grew increasingly angry and bitter. At last, as Tad had feared, Lewis' health began to fail.

Lucinda and Nancy also noticed that Lewis' health was failing, and they worried and discussed what should be done for him. It was not easy to get him to a doctor, so they finally concluded that all they could do was pray for him and take as much of the work off him as possible. Tad tried especially hard to spare him by doing more and more of the work. Finally, with his father's permission, he hired Henry to help during the busiest times.

At last Nancy prevailed upon Lewis to go to Dr. Edwards in Perryville. Unhappily he went, and, when the doctor could find nothing wrong with him, he chided Nancy for insisting that he bother the doctor when he was only tired from overwork.

Dr. Edwards gave Lewis a tonic and told him to take

more rest. Lewis complied to a degree, but his health continued to fail. Finally he had to admit that he was ill, and he agreed to see Dr. Edwards again. The doctor still could find no cause for Lewis' illness, but he prescribed a round of calomel and another tonic.

"Maybe this will make you feel better," he told Lewis.

"I hope it does. It's got so I can't hardly put one foot in front of the other," Lewis replied.

The calomel only made Lewis' stomach hurt, and the new tonic did nothing for his listlessness. In late November he took to his bed.

"I don't know what is to be done for Lewis," Nancy said as she and Tad sat down at the dinner table one day while Lucinda was still putting the food on the table.

"For one thing, I think we should move his bedroom downstairs, Mama," Lucinda suggested as she brought a plate of hot biscuits to the table. "It's going to wear you out running up and down stairs every time he calls you. You're not well yourself, you know."

"That's a good idea, Cindy," Tad agreed. "If Papa is willing for us to move his bed, I'll help switch the furniture in the bedrooms the first thing after dinner. I know he won't give up his bed."

"It would be easier to wait on him down here, and your papa would be close to what's going on. Maybe that would keep him from worrying so much," Nancy sighed.

"It's strange that Dr. Edwards can't find out what's wrong with him," Lucinda lamented as she sat down at the table with Tad and her mother.

"I think most of it is caused by all the bitterness he's harboring," Tad observed.

"You may be right, Tad, but I don't know what we can do about it," Nancy said wearily. "Tad, offer thanks so we can eat," she continued after a pause.

After Lewis was moved downstairs, Nancy started

spending most of her time between his bedroom and the kitchen, carrying water to him, seeing that he took his medicine on time, and helping Lucinda cook dishes that she hoped would tempt his appetite.

Each evening, after the work was done for the day, Tad and Lucinda joined their mother at Lewis' bedside. And each evening all of them noticed that he appeared more gaunt than he had the day before.

One night in early December, as they all sat by Lewis' bedside, he suddenly raised on his elbow and let his eyes roam around the room and rest briefly on each of them.

"You know, I'm beginning to wonder if I'm goin' to get well," he said in a hoarse, weak voice, as his eyes came to rest on Tad.

"Sure you will, Papa," Tad assured him. "The end of the year is almost here, and after the beginning of the new year spring won't be far away. You'll feel better when warm weather comes."

"I don't think I'll live to see another spring, Tad."

"Sure you will, Papa. I won't know how to plan the spring planting without you. You at least have to get well enough to sit in the shade and tell me what to do."

Nancy sighed heavily, and tears rolled down Lucinda's cheeks.

"How long is it till Christmas?" Lewis asked, turning his eyes to Nancy.

"Less than a month, Lewis. Why do you ask?"

"I've been thinkin'. This might be my last Christmas, and I don't want it to pass me by."

"What can we do to make it a good Christmas for you, Papa?" Lucinda asked as she moved her chair closer to his bed.

"I reckon most of it is up to me, Cindy." He took her hand and held it as he had when she was a little girl. Then he turned and looked long and hard at Nancy.

"Nancy, I want you to write to David and ask him to

come home for Christmas," he said in a hoarse whisper.

"Oh I will, Lewis. I will, and I'll let Lucinda take the letter out to the box in the morning."

"Thank you, Lord," she whispered, looking reverently upward.

"Oh, Papa!" Lucinda cried, and she dropped on her knees by his bed and put her arms around him.

"I'm glad you've forgiven David, Papa," Tad said, moving to him and placing his hand on his shoulder.

That night, after Lewis had fallen asleep, Nancy wrote the letter to David, and Tad and Lucinda each wrote a page to be included with it. The next morning Lucinda took the letter to the mailbox and waited in the cold for old Mr. Preston to come. When he finally came he had no mail for Lucinda, but that did not trouble her, for her heart was warm because of the letter she was mailing to David.

"Mr. Preston, I want to put this letter in your hand," she told him. "Will you make sure and put it in the mail at the post office?"

"I do that with all the mail, Miss Lucinda," he said, pretending to look hurt.

"I didn't mean that you don't, Mr. Preston. I just want to make double sure that my brother gets this letter."

Lewis seemed more cheerful after the letter was mailed to David. He started eating better, and he soon appeared to be gaining a little strength.

A few days later Tad went to Perryville to buy groceries for the family, and he came home with the good news that Brother Western had been released from prison and was expected home by Christmas.

"I know his wife and daughter will be beside themselves," Nancy remarked, beaming.

"They were really discouraged the last time I went to take them some eggs and milk. This is the best news they could possibly have," Lucinda enjoined.

"I wish I was able to go to church the first Sunday he's back in the pulpit," Lewis mused.

"Papa, you hurry and get well, and we'll all go," Tad promised.

"I'm sure there's still hard feelings in the church, and there's no telling what Jackson Taylor might do. I reckon it's just as well if we don't go back till the war's over," Lewis decided. Then he turned his face to the wall and fell silent.

A letter from David came the week before Christmas. Lucinda wanted to open it at once, but instead she hurried home to share it with the other members of the family.

"Mama," she shouted as she entered the front door, "I have a letter from David!"

Her mother was in the bedroom with Lewis, and she came immediately and met her in the hall.

"Hurry and open it, Mama," Lucinda exclaimed as she handed the letter to her.

Nancy took the letter and held it at arm's length to see it better. "I don't like the looks of his handwriting. I wonder if he's sick?" she exclaimed as she tore open the envelope.

"Mama, aren't you going to share David's letter with Papa and Tad?" Lucinda querried.

"I have to see if David is all right first. You go to the back door and call Tad. He's doing something at the barn."

"I'll wait and see what's in David's letter first," she said, stepping behind her mother so she could look over her shoulder at the letter.

"I need better light," Nancy said, and she walked to the window and held the letter to the light.

Lucinda followed and looked over her shoulder and scanned down the page. "Oh Mama, David's sick," she sobbed.

"That's what I was afraid of. Here take the letter and read it to me."

Lucinda took the single sheet of paper the letter was written on and read it just loud enough for her mother to hear.

Dear Mama and all,

Your letter brought tears to my eyes and an ache to my heart. Tell Papa I thank him for asking me to come home. I wish I could, but I'm not able to make the trip. The doctors say I have consumption.

"Oh, no," Nancy sobbed. "My poor boy. I'll never see him again."

"Mama, people do get over consumption sometimes— if they learn that they have it in time," Lucinda said, trying to reassure her mother.

"Usually they don't, Cindy, but read the rest of his letter."

"All right, Mama." She turned again to the letter and continued reading.

I will be thinking of all of you at Christmas, and I'll be praying for the day when I'll be well enough to come home.

Tell Papa I'm sorry he is ill. With Love to all, especially to Papa.

David

Nancy looked at Lucinda for a long minute before she spoke. "This may be the death of Lewis, but we'll have to tell him," she said at last.

"Yes, Mama. We'll have to tell him. Let's go and tell him now. Then I'll read David's letter to him."

Just then Tad came in from the barn, and, seeing that his mother and Lucinda were upset, he hurried to them.

"David is sick," Lucinda mouthed in a soft whisper, rolling her eyes toward her father's room.

"Is he bad?" Tad asked in a whisper.

"Consumption!" Nancy answered in a sharp whisper.

Lucinda handed Tad the letter, and he read it slowly.

"We'll have to tell Papa," he said when he finished reading.

"Let's go to his room, and you can tell him now," Nancy told him.

Together they walked to Lewis' room and gathered around his bed. "Papa, I have some bad news," Tad said.

Lewis turned searching eyes upon him.

"Papa, David is sick," Tad continued.

"I'm sorry to hear that. Is he well enough to come home for Christmas?"

"He said in his letter that he wouldn't be."

"Read the letter to me," Lewis requested with burning eyes shifting from one to the other.

"All right, Papa," Lucinda answered, and she moved close to his bed and read the letter to him.

Lewis was silent for several minutes after Lucinda finished reading the letter, and a great sadness seemed to possess him.

"If only I could recall the day I drove him from this house," he finally said brokenly.

"You can't help that now, Lewis. Just be glad that David still loves you," Nancy consoled.

"I want you to write and tell him that we want him to come home the minute he gets able to travel. Tell him that this is his home for as long as he wants to stay," Lewis replied.

"Surely he'll get well. He has a great future as a doctor after the war's over," Lucinda remarked.

"We'll pray that he will. I have heard of cases . . ." Nancy's voice broke and she turned away.

"I have some work to do outside," Tad said, trying

hard to keep his voice from breaking. Then he went quietly out to his work.

After he was gone, Lewis turned his face to the wall and feigned sleep, and Nancy and Lucinda left his room and made themselves busy with housework.

One morning Lucinda awoke with the realization that Christmas was only days away.

Mama is too tired and worried to get excited about Christmas, and, since David is not coming home, Papa is too bitter to care whether we observe it or not, she thought. *So not a thing has been done. . . . no presents bought . . . no decorating done . . . not even plans for a Christmas dinner.*

"If we're going to observe Christmas this year, I'll have to take the responsibility for it," she said aloud as she got out of bed and started dressing.

Weeks ago Tad had expressed a desire to invite Tom to visit them again this Christmas, but they had no idea how to get in touch with him. His last letter, received a few days ago, had said that he was still trying to find his mother. He had learned that she had a distant relative in Alabama, and he was going there to ask if they had any word concerning what had happened to her. Traveling in the South was difficult because of the war, so he had no idea when or how he would find his mother's relative.

"Even if there's nobody but me and Tad and Mama and Papa, I'm not going to let Christmas pass without observing it," she muttered grimly. "It's just not normal for people to forget about Christmas, even when there is a war."

She wished that she could invite Martin to come for Christmas, but that wish was too outrageous to even consider. Sick as he was, her father would still go through the roof if a Yankee soldier showed up at their house for Christmas. Besides, she had heard nothing of Martin since

Henry and Mandy had received that one letter from him. That was weeks ago, and it was possible that Martin was no longer alive. She had checked back with them several times to see if they had heard from him again, but they had not. She remembered his mother's address in Ohio, but she did not dare write to her for fear Papa would find out.

She thought of broaching the subject of Christmas to her mother when they met in the kitchen to cook breakfast, but decided to wait until they were eating breakfast.

When breakfast was ready, Lucinda carried it to Lewis' room and placed it on the small table Tad had brought in soon after they had moved Lewis downstairs. Tad came to help her, and they moved the table against Lewis' bed so he could eat with them. Nancy came to join them, and they all sat down around the table.

"Christmas is almost here," Lucinda announced as they started eating. "I'm going out today and get us a tree."

Tad looked up and smiled, obviously pleased. "I'll get the tree for you, Cindy," he volunteered.

"Thank you, Tad. Do it today, and we'll decorate it tonight."

Lewis and Nancy exchanged glances, but neither of them spoke.

"I reckon we'll be having Christmas without company this year, but we still ought to make it a good one," Tad commented.

"Sure we will, Tad. There's no rule that says we have to have company for Christmas."

"I don't feel much like cooking this year. Guess I just don't have the spirit," Nancy finally said.

"I'll do the cooking, Mama. You just sit back and enjoy it," Lucinda told her.

"Oh, I suppose I'll help when it comes down to it," Nancy sighed.

"What about you, Papa? Aren't you going to get in the spirit for Christmas?" Tad asked.

"Since David can't come home, I reckon I've lost what spirit I had, but I won't spoil it for the rest of you," Lewis answered, showing no emotion.

That afternoon Tad went to the banks of Hope's Creek and cut a cedar tree that was tall enough to reach the ceiling in the parlor. After supper he set it up in the parlor while Lucinda and her mother were doing the dishes. Then Lucinda joined him, and they set to work decorating the tree with the ornaments she had brought from the attic that afternoon.

The next day Tad and Lucinda went to Danville to shop for themselves, and to buy the few presents Nancy had written on a list that she wanted. They returned home late in the afternoon.

That night after supper, Lucinda started singing Christmas carols while she did the dishes. After she finished in the kitchen, she started wrapping the presents, piddling at the task, to make it seem like there were more presents than there were.

In the coming days, Lucinda filled the house with the aroma of cooking food, and, while she worked, she sang and laughed and chattered, trying to make the old house seem less empty and quiet than it was.

Gradually Nancy entered into the spirit of the occasion, and even Lewis started looking less glum than he had since he had learned of David's illness.

On Christmas day, Lucinda got out of bed in high spirits, and, while she was cooking breakfast, she laughed and sang and cried. Finally Nancy joined her in singing a verse of a carol. Then she wiped a tear from her eye.

"Cindy, you're all right," Tad said, slapping her on the shoulder.

Lewis was cheerful during breakfast, and he agreed to allow Tad to get him up in a chair so he and Lucinda could carry him into the parlor to sit by the fire while they opened their presents.

The high point of the day for Lucinda was when they were seated at the dining table, loaded with steaming food, and Tad prayed as she had never heard him pray before.

She listened with rapt attention as he thanked God for the food, for his family, and for the one good arm he still had. Then Tad prayed for the war to end and that there would be a time of healing in the nation. He ended by thanking God that Papa had forgiven David.

"I didn't know you could pray like that, Tad," she said with tear-moist eyes.

"I can't usually pray like I want to, Cindy, but that prayer came out just the way I feel."

Lucinda saw that her father's eyes were downcast, and she thought she saw a trace of tears in his eyes. "You see, Papa, we are having a good Christmas, with just the family here," she said.

"I'm glad. It may be the last one I'll ever see. Thank you for planning it, Lucinda. . . . you too Tad and Nancy," Lewis said, smiling and wiping the tears from his eyes.

Chapter 27

*T*he next afternoon Lucinda heard a trotting horse on the lane and looked out the window to see who was coming. To her glad surprise she saw Tom riding on a black mare.

"It's Tom," she cried loud enough for all to hear. Then, without taking time to get her wraps, she ran out to meet him.

"Tom, it's good to see you," she cried as he rode up to the front gate.

"Lucinda, imagine you running out here in the cold without your wraps!" he exclaimed, smiling broadly at her.

"When I saw you, I was so excited I didn't stop to get them."

Just then Tad came to the door. "Good to see you, old man," he called as he hurried out to join Lucinda who had already reached the gate.

"I couldn't let Christmas pass without seeing you folks," Tom said as he swung down from the mare.

Lucinda watched, amazed and pleased as he led the mare to the nearest post to hitch her, walking on his artificial leg with only a slight limp.

"Sorry you missed Christmas dinner. We had it yesterday," Tad told him.

"I'll bet we can find something for supper," Lucinda

countered, smiling.

"Didn't you bring your bags? You are going to stay a while?" Tad asked as he opened the gate for Tom.

"Only one small bag. It's tied on behind the saddle. All these months traveling as I looked for Ma, I've learned to travel light."

"You didn't ride that mare all the way from Tennessee?" Tad asked.

"I rented her in Perryville. I rode the stagecoach that far."

"Then get your bag and come on in."

Tom quickly loosed the bag from the saddle and came to join Tad and Lucinda.

"I see you have a new gate since the Yankee soldiers broke the old one," Tom laughed.

"Yeah, I built a new one," Tad responded.

"Tom, come in out of the cold," Nancy called from the doorway. "Tad and Cindy will stand there talking half the day if you don't."

"Mrs. Perry, I can't tell you how good it is to see you. I'll be there in a minute," Tom returned. He paused to shake hands with Tad, then turned to Lucinda. "You're as beautiful as ever, Lucinda," he said.

Blushing happily, Lucinda smiled up at him. "I'm glad you've come, Tom. We have not had any company at all this Christmas," she hastened to add for fear she had appeared overly pleased to see him.

"I was afraid you would be angry with me for being such a poor correspondent these last few months, but I see that you're not," he observed as he touched her arm and turned her toward the house.

"You have not been a poor correspondent. Your letters have come regularly, but I could not answer them, because you didn't stay in one place long enough," she said in one breath.

"I wanted so much to hear from you, but I knew you

could not write to me while I was traveling from place to place."

"Did you find your mother?" she asked.

"I found where she was buried."

"I'm sorry."

"Well, at least I know she's not somewhere trying to get by on her own. Let's go inside before you catch a cold," Tom urged when she paused.

"I'm sorry we kept you waiting with the door open," Tom said, turning to Nancy who was still standing in the doorway.

"You are about to freeze me," Nancy teased with a twinkle in her eyes that Lucinda had not seen in weeks.

They went in then and closed the door, and Tom bowed over Nancy's hand and kissed it. "Where's Mr. Perry?" he asked.

"Lewis is in bed sick. We'll take you in to see him soon. He'll be pleased beyond words to see you."

"I hope Mr. Perry is not seriously ill. You people are like family to me," Tom remarked.

"The doctor can't find anything wrong with him, but he's taken to his bed," Lucinda told him.

"Let's go to the parlor where we can sit down and talk," Tad suggested. "We'll take you in to see Papa after we tell him you're here."

"I'll run up and take by bag first. Am I to stay in the same room I did before?"

"Sure thing. Sorry I didn't tell you. I'll go up with you and see that everything is in order. Later I'll start a fire in the room."

Tad led the way, and Tom followed him upstairs.

"It's hard to tell that he has an artificial leg," Nancy whispered to Lucinda.

"I'm glad he has it. It would be a shame if he had to be on crutches the rest of his life," Lucinda whispered back.

"Where was your mother buried, Tom?" Lucinda asked when he and Tad came back downstairs.

"Would you believe it? I found her unmarked grave in the cemetery at the village church near home."

"After you had gone all over the country looking for her!" Tom exclaimed.

"That's the way it happened. An old man, who lives by himself in a house near our place, found her body after she was killed. He's a kind of recluse, so he buried her without telling anyone he had found her. He was gone somewhere when I first went home looking for Ma."

"How strange," Lucinda remarked.

"It was strange, but that's the way it happened. When I returned a short time ago, he was back, and he led me to Ma's grave."

"That must have been a shock to you," Lucinda exclaimed.

"It was hard to give up hope, but I know Ma was a Christian, and it's a comfort to know that she is with the Lord."

"The day you gave me her watch, you told me that she promised to pray for you," Lucinda responded.

"Yes, and I know she did as long as she lived. I notice that you're not wearing the watch. Don't you like it?"

"Oh, yes, Tom, I love it, but I put it away and kept it safe for your mother in case you ever found her."

"Now it is yours, and I want you to wear it," he said firmly.

"Won't you take it back and keep it in remembrance of your mother?"

"I told you that it was made for a beautiful lady to wear, so I want you to wear it."

"Then I'll go upstairs and put it on right now," Lucinda said. She arose and hurried up to her room. Moments later she came gaily back down the stairs with the gold chain around her neck, and the watch dangling from it. She paused by the grandfather clock in the hall and wound the watch and set it before she returned to the parlor.

"It looks beautiful on you. I hope you will always wear it," Tom said.

"I'll keep it as a sacred trust, but if ever there is a woman in your family you want to have it, I'll return it to you."

"There is no woman in my family," he said, looking hurt.

"You may have a wife someday."

"If I do, I hope she will be wearing that watch when I propose to her."

"Then, I'll give it to the first girl I see you courting," she bantered to cover her embarrassment.

"Lucinda, we had better start supper. I'm sure Tom must be hungry after all his traveling," her mother said to rescue her.

"You're right Mama," Lucinda answered, and she arose to go with her to the kitchen.

"I'll take Tom to visit with Papa while you're cooking supper," Tad said.

"That's a good idea, Tad," Nancy responded.

"I know that will please Papa," Lucinda added.

"I think Tom really has fallen for you," Nancy whispered to Lucinda when they reached the kitchen. "What are you going to do about him?"

"I don't know Mama. I don't want to hurt Tom, but I can't get Martin off my mind."

"I think you're going to have to tell Tom something."

Lucinda started punching up the fire that had remained in the range from cooking dinner. She put in more wood before she answered.

"I really can't make a decision about Tom," she finally said as she straightened from her task.

"Then you had better think about it," Nancy said.

They started working on supper, warming up left-overs from their Christmas dinner and frying some ham to give the meal the appearance and smell of a fresh-cooked meal.

"I'm sure Tom won't mind eating in the kitchen, so I'll let him eat here with you and Tad. I'll eat with Lewis in his bedroom," Nancy said when supper was almost ready.

"I think Tad and Tom are still in Papa's room, so I'll go tell them to get ready for supper," Lucinda responded.

Soon Tad and Tom sat down with Lucinda at the breakfast table in the kitchen.

"Tom, what are you going to do now that you know your mother is gone?" Tad asked as they started eating.

"Tad, I'm going into the ministry. I have felt that God is calling me ever since I got saved."

"How will you go about getting into the ministry?" Tad asked.

"First, I'm going back to school. I'm going to enroll in a Bible school a pastor in Knoxville has in his church."

Lucinda looked at him in wide-eyed surprise. *Tom in the ministry? She could scarcely believe it. Well, that settled one thing. She just could not see herself as a minister's wife.*

During the rest of Tom's visit, he continued to pursue Lucinda. Finally she had to admit that he really was serious about courting her, but she gave him little encouragement. He was an attractive man, and, to her surprise, she found herself growing fond of him, but she told herself that she was not falling in love with him. Never would she marry a minister. Besides, she could not forget Martin. Surely, someday, she would see him again if he were yet alive.

Early on Monday morning, following New Year's Day, Tom saddled the mare and brought her out and hitched her to the yard gate. Then he went in and ate breakfast in the kitchen with Tad and Lucinda. After breakfast he told Lewis good-bye, and went up and got his bag.

Nancy went with him to the front door and wished him a safe journey, and Tad and Lucinda went out to the gate to see him off.

Chapter 28

*T*he night following Tom's departure, the Perrys ate supper in Lewis' room as usual. After supper, Lucinda went to the kitchen to wash the dishes, and Tad went outside to finish some chores. Nancy remained by Lewis' bedside and answered David's letter. When she finished, she read it to Lewis for his approval.

"That's just what I wanted to tell him," he said. "I want him to know that I have forgiven him and that I want him to come home when he gets able and stay as long as he wants to."

"I'll send the letter to the mailbox by Lucinda in the morning, Lewis."

"I can't tell you what a load sendin' that letter will take off my mind."

"And I can't tell you how glad I am that you have forgiven David."

In the days that followed Lewis became more cheerful, and Dr. Edwards, who now came to see him twice each week, thought his health was improving. Lewis soon started sitting up a short while each day, looking out the window, and often expressing the wish that spring would come.

One morning early in February, Lewis went to the parlor and sat for a time before the fire in the overstuffed chair. Nancy brought a quilt and tucked it around him, lest he catch cold, then sat down near him to keep him company.

He sat where he was, looking into the glowing embers until the clock in the hall was striking eleven o'clock. "Think I'll go back to bed," he said then, turning to Nancy.

"Cindy has dinner almost ready," Nancy told him. "Would you like to eat here by the fire before you go back to bed? If you would, we'll bring the table in from your bedroom so we can eat with you."

"I'd like that," he said.

"Then, I'll go tell Cindy, and I'll call Tad to come in from the barn and help me move the table."

Shortly Tad came in, and he and Lucinda brought the table from Lewis' bedroom and put it by his chair. Lucinda and Nancy brought the food in and put it on the table, and they all sat down with Lewis to eat.

Lewis ate better than he had in weeks, but when he finished, he asked Tad to help him back to bed.

The next day a letter came from David, written at his request by a friend. In the letter, David said that he was almost helpless, and that he no longer believed he was going to get well. He expressed his love for all of them and wished that he could see them. "Tell Papa I love him and that I hold no ill will because of what happened. I understand how he felt," he had his friend to write in closing.

"Oh, oh, my poor boy! How I wish I could see him," Nancy sobbed.

"I wish Papa was well enough for us to go see him," Lucinda exclaimed.

"It's a comfort to know that he holds no hard feelings," Lewis said, as tears rolled down his cheeks. "I wish I could tell him face to face how sorry I am for runnin' him away from home."

"You told him that in the letter, Lewis. We also told David that you are ill, so he knows we can't come to see him," Nancy said, trying to comfort him, though she was struggling to keep back her own tears.

"Cindy, go find Tad and tell him what's in David's letter," Lewis said gently.

After learning that David would probably not live, Lewis seemed calm enough, but the family feared that his dreaded bitterness would return. Through the remaining weeks of February and March, they watched him closely and were relieved to see that his bitterness did not return and that his health continued to improve.

The first week in April, on an exceptionally warm day, Lewis was well enough to sit on the front porch, wrapped in a heavy blanket, and watch Tad work in the field beside the barn. He took pleasure in watching him follow the mules and the turning plow around the field, and it pleased him to see the green grass turn under and the black, fertile, soil turn up.

He noticed that the trees in the yard and in the fence rows were turning green, and he watched a yellowhammer, hammering with his bill at the top of a fence post at the edge of the side yard.

"Looks like he'd drive himself batty before he makes a hole big enough for a nest," he remarked, pointing to the red-headed bird, when Nancy and Lucinda came out to keep him company.

"You'd think he'd give himself a headache or break his bill hammering like that," Lucinda remarked.

"I didn't used to take notice of things like that," Lewis mused, smiling wanly.

"Maybe you have more time to notice things, now that you're not busy," Nancy suggested.

"Maybe so. I've been lookin' at them pretty flowers blooming along the fence. I must have seen them a thousand times, but I never noticed them before."

"Buttercups, they call them," Nancy told him.

"Some people call them daffodils, Mama," Lucinda

remarked.

"Well, they're pretty, and they tell me that spring is almost here. Never thought I'd live to see it," Lewis continued.

"I hope you'll still notice things like that after you get well, Papa," Lucinda told him.

"I think I will, Cindy, whether I get well or not. I've been thinkin', God still makes things beautiful in spite of the war. Man is destroyin' all creation, but God is making things grow."

"I never heard you talk like that before, Lewis," Nancy remarked.

"Reckon I never took time to think about it before."

The following Monday morning Lucinda went to the mailbox to get the paper and any mail that might come for them. When she returned, Lewis was still in bed, but he was awake. And when she burst through the front door shouting at the top of her voice, he almost jumped from the bed.

"Mama, Papa, the war's over! The war is over!" she shouted. "I read it when I got the paper out of the box." She ran through the house to Lewis' room, waving the *Louisville Journal* over her head.

Nancy was already out of the chair beside Lewis' bed, and they were both looking at her intensely.

"The paper says that General Lee surrendered to General Grant at Appomattox, Virginia yesterday. Isn't that the grandest news?" Lucinda cried.

"Praise God it's over," Nancy said. "Now if only David could come home, I think I could be happy again."

"I wish he could," Lewis agreed.

"Just think, Papa!" Lucinda cried, jumping up and down, "the war is really over."

"It will take more than the war endin' to put this country back together," Lewis said solemnly.

Just then Tad came in from the outside. "I heard Cindy

shoutin'. What's all the ruckus about?" he asked.

"The war's over, Tad. It says so in the paper," Lucinda exclaimed, holding up the paper for him to see.

"There's no way the government can ever make up to the South for all the crimes they've committed," Lewis said with anger in his voice.

"Papa, remember what President Lincoln said in his inaugural speech. *With malice toward none, with charity for all*," Tad reminded him.

"High soundin' words. That's all they are," Lewis muttered. His hand went to his head, and he fell back on his pillow.

"Papa, are you all right?" Tad asked, stepping up to the bed and placing his hand on his head.

"Sure I'm all right. This will pass in a minute,"

"I'm going after the doctor, Papa," Tad told him.

"No, Tad, I'm all right, just weak that's all."

"I think you should see Dr. Edwards again, Papa," Nancy declared.

"If nothing else will do you, I'll go see him the first of the week," Lewis agreed.

"Everybody sit down and I'll read you what the paper says about the end of the war," Lucinda spoke up.

Nancy sank to her chair, but Tad remained standing, leaning against the wall. Lucinda stood at the foot of Lewis' bed and scanned down the page. Then she started reading aloud.

She read of telegraph keys clattering with the news that Confederate President, Jefferson Davis, and his cabinet had departed from Richmond on Sunday, April second. That news had set off celebrations in Washington City, and soon the walls and windows all over the city were shaken from massive cannonading. On Tuesday night candles had been set blazing all over the city, and all the federal buildings had been illuminated. For the first time in history, the capitol building had been ablaze from top to bottom with gas lights, forming letters two stories high that blazed out the words from Scripture:

THIS IS THE LORD'S DOING, IT IS MARVELOUS IN OUR EYES

"I'm not sure that God had anything to do with the way this war ended," Lewis interrupted bitterly.

"I think you're wrong, Papa. I fought for the Confederacy, but since I've been home I've come to believe that the outcome of the war would be settled in Heaven instead of on earth," Tad soliloquized.

"I don't see how you can think that, Tad," Lewis countered.

"Maybe God wants this country to still be one nation, Papa."

"It will take a heap of healin' before this will be one nation again, Tad."

"Papa, if you and Tad don't mind, let's listen while Lucinda reads us the rest of what the paper says," Nancy suggested.

"Well, let's see. There's too much to read all at once, but it says here that when news reached Washington City one week later that the war had really ended, the celebration started all over again."

"I'll bet there wasn't much celebration in the South," Tad interrupted.

"I reckon the slaves are celebratin'," Lewis muttered disconsolately.

"Read us the rest of it, Cindy," Nancy said, hoping to end the discussion. So Lucinda read on, and the others listened, hardly able to believe that the war had really ended.

While the Perrys were still rejoicing over the end of the war, they learned that President Lincoln had been assassinated.

"How dreadful!" Nancy exclaimed. "I didn't always agree with the things the President did, but I think he was a good man, and I think he did the best he could."

"I despised him for gettin' us in the war, but I didn't want him killed," Lewis remarked.

"What's done is done. The country will just have to go on from here," Lucinda said.

"I still believe that God will take care of the country," Tad declared.

"Seems to me that the war was a terrible blunder," Lewis continued with a hint of the old bitterness. "The war has ruined the South. It will take a hundred years for it to recover. The North will have to pay too. A generation of its young men have been killed or maimed. I don't see what either side got out of it. I know our family has been made to suffer. Tad is without an arm. He won't never grow another one, and David is dying."

"What's done is done, and we'll just have to pick up the pieces and go on," Tad suggested.

"Lewis, try to put it out of your mind," Nancy soothed, taking his hand.

"I'll try, Nancy, but it ain't easy," Lewis replied.

In the coming days, Tad remained hopeful for the future, but Lucinda was uncertain. For the first time in her life, she was given to changing moods. At times she looked forward to the future. At other times she was depressed and felt that there was no future for her, or for the country.

Nancy was relieved that the war was over, but a great sadness had settled upon her. Lewis was a broken man. He was suffering and growing weaker again. David, still not able to write, had a friend write that he believed the end was near for him.

The night after David's letter came, as Nancy sat by Lewis's bed, he raised his hand to claim her attention.

"I may not live as long as David does, so I have something I want to tell you," he began. "If I go first, when David dies, I want him brought home for burial."

"Lewis, you both may live for years to come," Nancy responded, pretending a cheerfulness she did not feel.

"Nancy, you know that it's not likely that David or me either one will live to see the harvest this fall."

"Lewis, that is morbid."

"No, it's not. We all have to go sometime. I'm prepared, and I hope that David is. What was it he said in his last letter?"

"He said that he was at peace with God and man, but that does not mean that he's going to die," Nancy said, placing her hand on her husband's arm.

"It does mean that he is ready though." Lewis was silent for a few moments as if lost in thought. "I've always liked the family burying ground in the corner by the orchard. It's peaceful out there under the trees, and it's high enough on the hill for the wind to sigh through the leaves. And I like the way the mockingbirds come and perch in top of that dead oak tree in the corner and sing."

"I never knew you felt that way, Lewis."

"Well I do, and that's where I want to be buried. Then, when your time comes, I want you buried beside me. And in the future, I want Tad and Lucinda buried there with their families, if they have any."

"Lewis, I'm going to blow the lamp out and come to bed, and I don't want to hear any more talk like this," Nancy told him firmly.

"I'm sorry to trouble you, Nancy. I just wanted to make sure that you have David brought home when he dies, if I'm not able to see to it."

Without answering, Nancy blew out the flame of the lamp. Then she got into bed and crept up close to Lewis' back and put her arm around his shoulder. He stroked her hand gently, and soon fell asleep. But she lay awake most of the night, too troubled for sleep or tears.

Chapter 29

*T*he next morning Nancy awoke worried, and all morning she could not get what Lewis had said the night before off her mind. When Lucinda started to the mailbox, she watched with a heavy heart as she walked out the lane. "Good news never comes from that box anymore," she whispered to herself with a feeling of foreboding.

"I only have one letter for you this morning, Miss Lucinda," Mr. Preston said in a somber tone when he arrived.

While he fumbled for her letter, she searched his face and thought she detected pity in his eyes. When he handed her the letter, her heart skipped a beat, for she saw at once that it was from the War Department and knew instinctively that it could only contain bad news.

"Thank you, Mr. Preston," she said, struggling to control her voice, as she took the letter.

Without opening the letter, she started back to the house, walking slowly and feeling that her heart was beating a funeral dirge.

"Mama, Papa," she called when she entered the house, "there's a letter and I brought it for you to open."

Nancy came at once and met her in the hallway.

"I know it's bad news, Mama," she stated flatly.

"It must be about David. I've been feeling all morning that something has happened to him."

"It's from the War Department, Mama."

"I can't bear to open it," Nancy exclaimed as she took the letter.

"Maybe we should let Tad open it."

"If the letter is about David, your father will have to know."

"Tad will have to tell him. He can do more with Papa that anyone else."

"We'd better call Tad to come in from the field."

"He should be here. He saw me coming from the mailbox and waved to me that he was coming."

"Look out the kitchen window and see if he's almost here."

Lucinda went to the window and looked out. "He'll be here in a minute," she announced as she went to open the back door and wait for Tad.

"Tad, a letter came from the War Department," she said softly when he reached her. "I think it's about David. Mama wants you to open it, and, if it is bad news, she wants you to tell Papa."

"Why didn't you open the letter?" he asked.

"I didn't have the courage to open it. . . . Mama didn't either," she told him as Nancy came to join them.

"Let's see it, Mama," he said when he saw that she was clutching the letter in her hand as if it were something she had to control.

Nancy handed him the letter, and he tore open the envelope and removed a single sheet of paper and looked at it.

"David's gone," he said softly, turning to face his mother. "Let's go and tell Papa."

Tad led the way to his father's room, and Lucinda and Nancy following close behind him.

"We have bad news, Papa," Tad said as they entered his room.

"A letter came, Lewis," Nancy sobbed. "I—"

"Here's the letter, Papa." Tad held the letter up for Lewis to see.

"Get hold of yourself, Nancy," Lewis said as he took the envelope from Tad's hand. He looked at it quietly for a long moment. Then he took the letter out and looked at it as if he were having difficulty grasping its meaning. "David is dead," he finally said in a controlled voice.

"I'll never see my boy again," Nancy sobbed.

Lucinda threw her arms across her chest and hugged herself in her characteristic way. Her lips were parted, but she did not speak.

Tad saw how shaken she was and put his hand gently on her shoulder.

"We'll have them send his body home, and we'll bury him here, where he belongs," Lewis said.

"I'm glad you're going to do that, Lewis," Nancy said. "I'll feel better knowing that he's buried here."

"I'm going to write Tom. He'll want to know," Lucinda said.

When Tom received Lucinda's letter, he answered immediately, saying that he would come to the funeral if he knew when it would be. She shared the letter with her family, and they were all pleased that Tom wanted to be with them in their sorrow.

"We don't know when David's body will get here," Tad said thoughtfully.

"You're right, Tad. I'll write and tell Tom we appreciate him wanting to come, but that we don't know when David's body will get here. There won't be time for a letter to reach him between the time David's body arrives and the funeral," Lucinda responded.

Two weeks later, Mr. Sims, the undertaker from Perryville, went to the railroad station in Lebanon Junction with his hearse and got David's body. He brought it home and put it in the parlor near the front window. Brother

Western and his family and the Tates and the Crabtrees came and sat with the Perrys that night.

The Perrys were disappointed that none of the other neighbors came. "I know why nobody else came," Lucinda said to the family after their visitors had gone. "The people who were for the South didn't come because David was in the Union Army, and the others didn't come because Tad fought for the South."

"I'm surprised the Taylors didn't come. After all, Verna did used to be David's sweetheart," Tad said.

"The Taylors were ashamed to come, Tad," Lucinda declared with an edge of anger in her voice.

"I reckon people in this country won't never get over their hard feelings," Lewis said sadly.

"It will be a miracle if they do," Nancy agreed.

The next day Brother Western, Mr. Tate, Mr. Crabtree, Tad, and the undertaker and his helper carried David's body from the house in closed casket and placed it in the hearse that was drawn by two black horses. Then the undertaker climbed onto the seat and drove the team slowly toward the open grave in the family cemetery.

Lewis insisted that he was strong enough to walk to the grave, so he and Nancy and Lucinda followed on foot. Mrs. Tate, Nelly Crabtree, Mary and the Crabtree boys, John and Ned, walked with them.

When the undertaker reached the cemetery, he stopped the hearse by the grave. The pallbearers took the casket from the hearse, and set it down beside the open grave and stepped aside.

The wind was rustling the leaves on the maple tree that shaded the grave. A mockingbird was perched atop the snag of a big oak tree a short distance away, and his song was high and sweet.

Lewis and Nancy and Lucinda stopped by the casket, and Tad came to join them. Then Brother Western moved to the head of the casket.

"I'm sorry we don't have anyone to sing," he said and paused. In that instant Lucinda lifted her sweet, young voice and sang softly:

Jesus, lover of my soul,
Let me to They bosom fly,
While the nearer waters roll,
While the tempest still is high!

Hide me, O my Savior, hide,
Till the storm of life is past;
Safe into the haven guide,
O receive my soul at last!

Her voice fell silent, and the notes of the mocking-bird filled the void.

Brother Western cleared his throat, opened his Bible, and looked at the page as if he were trying to decide what to read. After a long pause, he read in a solemn voice:

Let not your heart be troubled. Ye believe in God, believe also in me. . . .

His voice droned on, but no one appeared to be listening. Nancy was weeping silently. Lewis was looking stern and solemn. Tad was looking sad, and the Tates and the Crabtrees appeared to be almost as sad as he was. Mary Crabtree, wiping tears from her cheeks with a tiny, embroidered handkerchief, came to stand beside Tad.

After Brother Western finished reading, he brought a brief message. Then he prayed for God to comfort the family in their grief and to bless the memory of David, who had lived a Christian life and had done his duty as he saw it.

After the prayer, Lucinda and her parents lingered, still looking sadly at the casket. Tad hugged them with his one arm. Mary, still weeping, also hugged them. "I'm so sorry," she said to Nancy.

"Thank you for coming, Mary." Nancy put her arms

around the girl and hugged her.

"You had better take Mama and Papa to the house," Tad told Lucinda.

"I agree, Tad." She took her parents by their arms and walked them slowly back to the house. Once Lucinda looked back and saw Tad and Mary standing close together, talking.

The men closed the grave. Then Brother Western shook hands all around.

"Brother Western, have people started comin' back to church since the war is over?" Tad asked as the pastor took his hand.

"Some have, Tad, but others are still afraid to come. There's still a few renegades in Kentucky. They're staying mostly in the mountains, but some people are still afraid of having their horses stolen if they come to church."

"We've talked about comin' back, but Papa is afraid there might be another ruckus like there was the last time we came."

"I don't think there will be, Tad. There's still hard feelings, but people are not as outspoken as they were during the war."

"Do you think people will ever get over their bitterness?"

"Not unless they get right with God. I've been praying that they will," Brother Western replied.

"Then I'll start prayin' that way too," Tad told him.

"I think we should all start praying that way," Mary said, still dabbing at her eyes with her handkerchief.

"I'm glad I can depend on you young people," Brother Western said, and he placed his hand on Tad's shoulder. "I think a lot of you and your folks, Tad. Martha Mae has told me that she couldn't have got by while I was in prison if it hadn't been for your family and one or two others."

"I'm glad we could help, Brother Western."

"How about me and my family driving over to visit with you folks one night the first of the week?" the pastor asked.

"We'll be glad to have you, Brother Western."

"Then look for us next Tuesday night."

"I'll tell my folks that you're coming," Tad replied.

"I want to see your families in church next Sunday," the pastor said, turning to Mr. Tate and Mr. Crabtree.

"We'll be there, Brother Western," Mr. Tate answered.

"So will we," Jim Crabtree, promised.

The pastor walked back to the yard with the others, mounted his horse, and started home.

The next day Lucinda wrote to Tom and told him about the funeral and where they had buried David. He wrote back that he was sorry he had not been able to come. His sympathy and prayers were with them, and he would come to see them soon.

Her tears stained Tom's letter as she read it. He really does love me, she thought, and I ought to be honest and tell him that I can never think of being the wife of a preacher.

"Anyway, I think I'm in love with Martin," she murmured under her breath, blushing that she had said it, even to herself.

Chapter 30

*P*astor Western continued to be burdened by conditions in his church and in the community. His burden caused him to search the Bible as never before, seeking answers, and it drove him to his knees to pray for wisdom and for power.

Martha Mae shared his concern, but she did not believe that anything could be done to remedy conditions. Yet she and Dora joined him in nightly prayer for the church and the people they knew.

There was no early evidence that their prayers were being answered, so Brother Western's burden deepened. He soon started riding his horse the two miles to the church each morning, arriving around five o'clock, and spending an hour in prayer before he returned home for breakfast. For weeks he prayed alone each morning. Then one morning Brother Petree met him at the church.

"I've been seeing your horse hitched at the church every morning for awhile, and I decided that you must be coming to pray, so I've come to pray with you," he announced.

"Glad to have you, Brother Petree," the pastor told him, gripping his hand warmly. "The Bible teaches that if two will agree on what to pray for, the Lord will answer. I've been praying for people to get over their hard feelings and come back to church, and I want you to pray with me for that to happen."

"I'll be glad to, Brother Western, and I believe that we also need to pray for a God-sent revival. That's what we need in this country."

A few days later Jim Crabtree and Sam Tate came to pray also, and soon after that other men started coming to the early morning prayer meetings from time to time.

Early in May Pastor Western attended a pastors' meeting in Danville. There he heard preachers talk about an evangelist named March Raney, who was having meetings of far-reaching consequences in the neighboring state of Tennessee.

A pastor who had attended one of Evangelist Raney's meetings told of hundreds of people attending and of scores going to the altar to confess their sins and get right with God. Among them were many hardened sinners.

The pastor also said that, as a result of the revival, people had sought their enemies and made peace with them. Old grudges had been put aside, and a time of healing had come to the entire region.

At once Pastor Western decided to invite Evangelist March Raney to come and hold meetings at his church. The next day he dispatched a letter to him, inviting him to come. To his great joy, the evangelist wrote back that he would come and start meetings in his church on the first Sunday in July.

Pastor Western announced the meeting the next Sunday, and the news spread through the community.

Lucinda and Tad were excited, and Nancy thought the meeting might be just the therapy Lewis needed, if only they could get him to attend. Finally, with some reluctance, he agreed to attend a few of the services.

"Papa is not the only one that needs to attend the revival," Lucinda said to her mother a few days before the meetings were to start. "I know I have drifted from the Lord since we've been out of church, and I want to get back close to Him like I used to be."

"I suppose we all have drifted except Tad. Since he's come back from the war, he's more spiritual than he used to be."

"I want to attend every night, and I'm going to try to talk Papa into going every night too," Lucinda said.

"That may not be easy. He still gets tired when he over does it."

"I know, but maybe Tad can get him to rest some during the day."

"We'll just have to wait and see."

"You will want to go every night, Mama, and you'll not want to leave Papa by himself."

"I'll try to help you and Tad talk him into going. Have you written to Tom and asked him to come while the meeting is going on? I think he would like to come if he can leave his classes."

"I've already written to him about it, Mama, and he wrote back that he plans to come and stay a few days."

"And of course that will give him a chance to see you."

"I didn't ask him to come for that reason, Mama. I don't want to encourage him, since he's going to be a preacher."

"Lucinda! I can't believe you said that, but you're right not to encourage him unless your heart tells you to."

"I've already promised myself that I'll listen to my heart, Mama."

On the Saturday before the meeting was to start, a visitor unexpectedly arrived at the Perry's front gate, riding up on horseback in the shadows of twilight.

Lucinda was upstairs in her room, so she did not hear the horse come down the lane, but Tad heard it and went to the front door to investigate.

"It's a man, but I can't see who it is," he said to his

mother as she joined him at the door.

"Hello, stranger," Tad called as the man dismounted and started hitching his horse.

"Good evening," the man returned. "Does David Perry live here?"

"He used to, but he's dead now," Tad returned.

"I'm sorry to hear that. I met David once during the war, and I promised to visit him after it was over. Was he killed in battle?" he asked as he started up the walk toward the house.

"Consumption took him away," Tad replied.

"I'm Martin Colver," the man said as he came up the porch steps.

"I'm Tad Perry, David's brother, and this is my mother."

"It's good to meet you, Tad and Mrs. Perry." Martin removed his hat and bowed to Nancy.

"Come in, and we'll have supper after a bit," Tad invited.

"Thank you for the invitation, but I don't want to intrude."

"I know who you are, Mr. Colver," Nancy interrupted. "Lucinda told me about you. You're welcome to have supper with us and to spend the night, but don't say anything about having been in the Union Army in the presence of my husband. He's still bitter because of the war."

"I understand, Mrs. Perry, and, under the circumstances, I think it would be better for me not to come in."

"Who is it, Mama?" Lucinda asked, coming down the stairs at that moment.

"Cindy, it's Martin Colver!"

"Oh, oh," Lucinda cried, throwing both arms across her chest as she always did when she was under stress or excited. She hurried to the door and saw Martin standing there in the shadows. His handsome face was dimly illuminated by the light from the lamp on the parlor mantle, but she could not see the color of his eyes, though she remembered how blue they were.

"What a surprise to see you, Martin," she greeted.

"You know this man, Cindy?" Tad asked in dismay, looking first at Lucinda then at Martin.

"We've met, but it's a long story," Martin answered for Lucinda. "I really should go. I'll spend the night at an inn in Perryville. Then, if it's all right, I'll come out and visit tomorrow."

Because she knew how upsetting the appearance of a former Union soldier could be to her father, Lucinda looked at her mother then at Tad for an answer. Nancy was the first to speak.

"Mr. Colver, we never turned a stranger from our door before the war, but . . . now . . . perhaps your suggestion is best. My husband has not been well, and being brought face to face with a man who fought in the Union Army might be upsetting to him."

"I'm going to be honest with you, Mrs. Perry and Tad. I really came to see Lucinda. I have never thanked her properly for what she did for me. Perhaps it would be best if I see her somewhere away from home," he suggested.

Tad looked sharply at Lucinda, then at his mother. "I don't think that's a good idea," he said decidedly.

"Just a minute, Tad," Lucinda cut in. "I really would like to talk with Mr. Colver." She placed her hand on Tad's arm.

"How did you come to know this man, Lucinda?" Tad demanded.

"I'll tell you about it later, Tad."

"I have an idea. Lucinda, why don't you invite Mr. Colver to attend church in the morning?" Nancy suggested. "He can talk with you there, and that will be entirely proper."

Tad looked at his mother as if he could not believe

what she had said.

"That's an excellent idea, Mama. Martin, will you come to church in the morning?" Lucinda asked, turning to him.

"Thank you for inviting me, Lucinda. I'm not much for going to church, but if I have to come to church to see you, I'll come. Where's the church located?"

"It's the big white church on the road to Perryville. You'll see it on your left, about a mile down the road, as you go. The service starts at eleven o'clock," Lucinda said all in one breath.

"Then I'll see you in the morning. It's good to have met you, Mrs. Perry and you, Tad. He turned and went back to his horse, mounted and rode away in the darkness.

With a troubled heart, Lucinda watched him go.

"Who was that on the horse?" Lewis asked when he came in from the barn a few minutes later.

"It was a young man looking for David. Tad told him that David is gone," Nancy responded.

"That's strange. . . . must be someone David met in the army. . . . a Union soldier, I reckon. That's just what I need, a Union soldier comin' to visit. You didn't ask him to stay for supper I see."

"I did, but he was of a mind to go. He said he was going to stay in Perryville tonight. Lucinda invited him to come to church in the morning, and he promised to come."

"I'd just as soon not have any Yankees comin' to church, but of course Jackson Taylor and his family will be there, so I reckon one more won't make much difference."

"The war is over, Lewis, and you shouldn't be too hard on the Yankees. After all we have a Yankee soldier buried in our cemetery."

"I reckon you're right, Nancy," Lewis replied, rubbing his chin and smiling sheepishly.

Nancy looked at him closely, scarcely believing that he had agreed with her.

The next morning, much to everyone's surprise, when they finished eating breakfast, Lewis sent Tad to the barn to hitch up the buggy.

"Hitch the new mare I bought at the horse sale in Danville last week to the buggy," he told him.

"Papa, I call the new mare Midnight."

"I reckon that's as good a name as any. While you're at the barn, I'm goin' to dress. You had better hurry, Nancy," he said turning to her.

"I will, Lewis. They say people are even coming from Perryville, so we'll have to go early so we can get a seat."

A short time later Tad came in. "I hitched Midnight out front," he called up the stairs. "I'll be ready in a minute," he continued as he started up the stairs.

"Lewis and I are ready," Nancy called back.

"The rest of you go in the buggy. I'm goin' to walk," Tad returned.

"I'll walk with Tad," Lucinda called as she came from her room.

"There's room for you in the buggy, and I'm sure Tad won't mind walking by himself," Nancy responded as she came from her room.

"I'd rather walk with Tad, Mama. We'll see you and Papa at church."

Minutes later Tad and Lucinda started, and they were half way out the lane when their parents passed them in the buggy.

"We'll save you a seat at church," Nancy called.

"All right, Mama," Lucinda called back.

"Midnight sure is steppin' high and movin' on," Tad observed.

"And look at the dust she's raising. I don't want to get dust all over my white dress and hat. Let's wait until it settles before we go on."

"We'd best cut through the fields. That way we'll avoid the dust on Mackville Pike. It's a good thing you're carryin' your good shoes."

"Isn't it," she laughed. "I'll change before we go in the church."

When they came in sight of the church, they saw that Lewis had hitched Midnight at the hitching rail, and he and Nancy had already gone in. More people were coming in buggies and on horseback and on foot. They were coming from both directions on Mackville Pike, and they were coming through the fields.

"There's goin' to be a big crowd at church today, and they're comin' early," Tad observed.

"Tad, I wonder if Martin is here."

"He may not be. There's a lot of strange horses at the hitching rail, but I don't see the one he was ridin' last night."

"I hope he comes. I really would like to see him."

"Cindy, you still haven't told me how you met him."

"I'll tell you, Tad, the first time we get a chance to talk."

"I don't feel easy about him, Cindy. From what I saw of him last night, he's a smooth talkin' Yankee."

"Wait until you get to know him before you make up your mind, Tad," she answered impatiently.

They walked in silence until they reached the church. All the while Lucinda was looking for Martin, hoping that he would be outside waiting for her. At last, with a slight sigh of disappointment, she decided that he had not come. Perhaps he will come later, she thought as she and Tad entered the church.

Chapter 31

When Lucinda and Tad entered the church, they found that it was already crowded. Lucinda's eyes swept the congregation before she started down the aisle to the seats Nancy had reserved for her and Tad, but she did not see Martin. *Surely he will come later, but I'll not be able to see him until after church,* she thought.

Nancy smiled a welcome as Lucinda and Tad reached the pew and sat down. "I've never seen this many people in this church before, and they're still coming," she whispered to Lucinda.

"I know, and just think how few attended during the war," Lucinda whispered back.

Lucinda noticed that there was a buzz of excitement in the congregation, and there was an unusual sense of expectancy. Looking around, she saw members of the congregation who were known enemies, and they appeared bewildered and overwhelmed by the number of new people who were crowded around them. She looked to the front of the church and saw that the choir was packed with people, and that Pastor Western and a man she had never seen before were seated in the pulpit chairs.

That must be Evangelist March Raney, she thought, observing the man closely. He was tall and gangly. He was not a handsome man, but there was something entrancing about him. She could not help wondering what it was. Then she noticed that his face appeared radiant, as if some inner light was shining through it. His dark eyes roved over the congregation. Then he smiled and his smile enhanced the radiance of his face. *He must be a godly man,* she concluded.

Time for the service to start drew near, and people were still arriving. They filled every seat, then stood crowded in the aisles and along the walls. Finally Pastor Western asked the small boys and girls to come and sit on the floor of the rostrum so more of the adults could sit in the pews.

Timidly some of the children started to the front, urged on by their parents. There followed a general surge of boys and girls to the platform, and soon every available space was filled, and the people who were standing near the vacated seats promptly filled them.

Pastor Western then spoke briefly, welcoming the people and introducing the evangelist. "Brother Raney leads the singing as well as doing the preaching in his meetings, so I'm going to turn the service over to him," he said in conclusion.

Brother Raney arose and walked to the pulpit and laid his Bible down. Then he picked up a hymnbook and announced the number of the opening song. The pianist played the refrain. Then March Raney started leading the choir and congregation in singing. There followed singing such as no one had ever heard at Bethel Church. The people were caught up in the singing, moved by it and swept by it. Lucinda and her mother and Tad joined in the singing. Even Lewis nodded his head in rhythm with the singing.

Such joy flooded Lucinda's heart that she forgot to wonder if Martin had come.

The song ended, and softly murmured "amens" and "hallelujahs" swept across the congregation. Many of the people were filled with joy, but others sat with anguished faces, evidently convicted because of their sins.

There was scarcely a break between March Raney's singing and his preaching, and there was no break at all in the emotional impact of the service. As he preached, the people were greatly moved. When he ended his sermon, he started the altar call, and at once people rushed to the front and fell around the altar, sobbing, and praying, and confessing their sins. There followed shouts of joy, and people arose with shining faces and confessed that they had made peace with God. Former enemies then fell into each other's arms and freely forgave each other.

Lucinda saw that her father was watching as if he could not believe what was happening. Her mother was praying silently, and Tad was smiling for joy.

The service finally ended at three o'clock in the afternoon, and people, shaking hands and sometimes hugging each other, left the church to go home and attend to their chores so they could return for the evening service.

The Perrys left the church together. When they were outside, Lucinda saw Martin standing by the road, watching the departing people.

"There's Martin," she exclaimed. "Surely he will see us."

"Who is that man?" Lewis asked, turning amazed eyes upon Lucinda.

"It's the man who came to the house last night, Lewis," Nancy answered for Lucinda.

"The Yankee? What's he hangin' around for?"

"He and Lucinda have met before, Lewis. Last night he said their meeting was a long story."

"I can't wait to hear it," Lewis muttered sarcastically.

"Let's go home Lewis," Nancy suggested. "I'm sure Tad and Lucinda will come shortly."

"I want to have a talk with that young lady when she gets home," Lewis said, and he turned reluctantly and went to the buggy with Nancy.

Martin waited impatiently for Tad and Lucinda to come.

"I'm sorry I missed you in all the crowd," Lucinda greeted.

"I didn't come until twelve o'clock. I thought church would be over by then. Do you realize how long I've been waiting?"

"I'm sorry," she exclaimed, taken aback by his attitude. "I didn't mean to discomfit you."

"Even if we'd known you were out here, we wouldn't have walked out of the service," Tad told him flatly.

"Do church services always last this long in the South?" Martin asked.

"They almost never do. This was the beginning of a revival, and the service was so wonderful we're just now getting out." Lucinda explained, hoping to soothe his bruised ego.

"Remind me never to attend a revival," he said bitterly.

"Then you'll not see Lucinda again," Tad said firmly.

With a visible effort Martin got control of his ruffled feelings. "I'm sorry," he said. "Surely the service won't last this long tonight. What time does it start?"

"It will start at the edge of dark, but we have no way of knowing when it will end," Tad answered for Lucinda.

"I'll come, but I'll leave before it's over if it lasts as long as it did this morning."

"I'll expect you not to embarrass me if you sit with me," Lucinda told him forthrightly.

"I suppose I can sit through one service, even if it does last half the night," he growled. Then he turned and walked abruptly to his horse that was hitched at the roadside and mounted and rode away in the direction of Perryville.

When Tad and Lucinda reached home, Lewis was walking the floor. "Come here, young lady. I want to talk to you," he said as they entered.

"All right, Papa," she responded, amazed at how calm she was in the face of her father's apparent anger. Surely the service this morning had given her some new inner strength.

"I want to know where you met that Yankee that's been hangin' around," Lewis demanded.

"I found him wounded on the battlefield while you and Mama were in Perryville, Papa."

"Did you? And then what happened?"

"I got Henry to move him to his barn, and Mandy nursed him until he was able to leave. Please don't tell anyone. I don't want to get Henry and Mandy in trouble."

"You should have thought of that before you got them involved. I can't believe that you saved the life of an enemy in time of war," he said incredulously.

"I'm not sorry I did it, Papa," she said with her head high and her eyes meeting his. "I couldn't just walk away and let a man die, no matter who he was."

Lewis turned away and started pacing the floor again. After several minutes he turned back to Lucinda. "Savin' his life was one thing, but havin' him hang around after you is another. I forbid you to go to church again as long as he's in the neighborhood," he told her, trying hard to keep the anger out of his voice.

"But, Papa. I don't want to miss the revival."

"You heard me, Lucinda, and that goes for me and your mama too. Tad is a man, so he can do what he wants to do, but the rest of us will stay away from the meetin' until that man leaves the country."

"Then I'll go Papa," Tad responded. "I need to be involved in the meetin'. I wish you would go with me, even if you don't want Mama and Lucinda to go."

"I'll go to church after that Yankee leaves.

Martin was waiting in front of the church when Tad rode up that night.

"Is Lucinda coming tonight?" he asked when Tad stopped the mare beside him.

"She'll not be comin' tonight. She is at home with our parents."

"I suppose they got enough of church this morning. Will Lucinda be coming tomorrow night?"

"I'm not sure."

"Then I'll be going."

"Since you're here, you might as well stay for the service. I'll tell Lucinda you came."

"I didn't come all the way from Ohio just to go to church," he growled.

"I wish you would," Tad insisted.

"No. I'm not going to play church with you." He turned on his heel and went to his horse.

Tad watched him go, then went into the church. Halfway through the service, he saw Martin enter the church and stand in the back. Later he looked that way and saw that he was gone.

The next night, Lewis still refused to go to church, but Tad prevailed upon him to let Nancy and Lucinda go. "I'll look after Cindy, Papa," he promised.

"Since you insist, Tad, I'll let them go, but I expect you to keep Cindy away from that Yankee."

"I promise that I won't let him talk to her alone, Papa. That is the best I can do."

Tad and Lucinda and Nancy arrived at church in the buggy, they found Martin waiting at the hitching rail. He waved to them as Tad drove up and stopped the mare.

"Good evening, Mrs. Perry and Lucinda, and Tad," he greeted, and he stepped forward and took Nancy's hand and helped her down from the buggy. Then he took Lucinda's hand as she alighted.

"May I sit with you tonight, Lucinda?" he asked, bowing over her hand.

"Will it be all right for me to sit with him, Tad? Papa did ask you to look after me."

"I don't see how Papa can object as long as you sit on the pew with me and Mama."

"That's kind of you, Tad," Martin answered curtly, and he offered Lucinda his arm.

She did not like Martin's attitude, but she allowed him to walk her to the church. He paused at the door and opened it, waiting for Tad and her mother to enter. Then he led Lucinda down the aisle and waited as she entered the pew and sat down beside her mother. He sat stiffly down beside her.

During the service, Lucinda watched Martin furtively and thought he seemed affected by the singing and the preaching.

He must not be a Christian, she decided, and she whispered a prayer that he would be saved.

During the invitation, many went forward, but Martin sat stiffly in the pew, looking bored.

After the service he walked Lucinda to the buggy, and Tad and Nancy followed.

"Good night. I'll see you again tomorrow night," he said as they reached the buggy.

"Then I'll look forward to seeing you," she responded.

"And you will sit with me again?"

"Of course." She smiled and let him help her into the buggy.

The next afternoon Tom arrived at the Perrys' house, riding a horse he had rented in Perryville after arriving by stagecoach.

Lucinda ran out to meet him, delighted that he had come, yet realizing that his arrival placed her in a quandary. Tom would expect to sit with her in church tonight, but she had promised to sit with Martin.

"Good afternoon, Lucinda," Tom greeted, smiling

pleasantly.

"Tom, it's good to see you," she returned, though she could not imagine how she could avoid hurting his feelings tonight.

"I'm glad I was able to come during the meetin'," Tom said as he dismounted.

"The meeting is wonderful, Tom. I know you'll enjoy it."

He hitched the horse, then started to the house with her. "I also wanted to see you," he said, smiling down at her.

"It's always good to have you come. You are like a member of the family," she managed.

"I hope someday I will be," he said, looking at her closely.

"Come on in, family member." She shrugged and walked with him to the house.

That night, after an early supper, while Lucinda was still debating what she should do, Tad and Tom persuaded Lewis to go to church. *That complicates matters even more,* she thought, wondering what her father would do when he saw her sitting with Martin.

"I don't want to break my word to Martin, but what will Papa do, and what will Tom think?" she asked herself.

While she was dressing for church she kept wondering what she was to do. Finally she decided that she would tell Martin her father did not want her to sit with a former Yankee soldier. She would also tell him that, if she disobeyed her father, he might not allow her to come to the revival again. Then she would sit with her parents. That would take care of Martin. Tom could think what he would.

That night at the supper table, Lucinda took charge of the arrangements for getting to church. "I'm going to ride in the buggy with Mama and Papa tonight. Tad, I hope you and Tom don't mind walking," she said.

"I don't mind if Tom don't," Tad answered.

"Sure, we'll walk, if we can leave early," Tom said.

Tad and Tom were waiting in front of the church when Lucinda and her parents arrived in the buggy. When Lewis stopped the buggy at the hitching rail, Martin came from the shadows. When Lucinda got out of the buggy, he unceremoniously took her arm and started walking her toward the church. Lucinda heard her father protesting and her mother doing her best to quiet him.

"Let's hurry," she whispered to Martin. But, when they reached the front of the church, she paused and went through her rehearsed speech, explaining why she could not sit with him in church.

He turned away angrily, muttering something she chose not to hear. Then, to her dismay, she saw that Tom was standing near enough to hear what she had said to Martin. In the corner of her eye she saw Martin go back to his horse. Chagrined, she waited for her parents, then went in and sat with them. She was not surprised that Tom sat with Tad in a pew behind her.

During the service, she joined in the singing and did her best to put Martin and Tom out of her mind. Then she listened attentively as the evangelist preached. The message moved her as she had never been moved before, and she forgot about her conflict over Martin and Tom. Instead, she thought about her own life, realizing that she was far from the Christian she should be. *I should do something about that,* she decided.

When the invitation was given, Lucinda went forward and knelt and promised the Lord that from that day forward she would live only for Him. As she prayed, she felt that the Lord was asking, "Are you willing to be the wife of a preacher if the opportunity should ever come?" She knew immediately that that had been an area of rebellion in her life. She knew also that what she felt for Martin was not true love, and she decided that at the first opportunity she would send him on his way.

"Lord, You will have to tell me what to do about Tom," she prayed. "I really want to know your will about him."

She arose from her knees with an almost suffocating joy in her heart.

Tom was the first to congratulate her, though he had no idea why she had gone forward. Tad was close behind Tom, and he embraced her warmly. Then Nancy and Lewis came to her. Nancy embraced her, and Lewis placed his hand fondly on her shoulder.

Later, as she left the church, Lucinda saw Martin standing by his horse at the roadside. He tied the horse and came toward her. "I see that church has finally let out," he sneered.

She thought she detected the smell of alcohol on his breath.

"Martin, I can't believe that you think that way. You talked about angels when I first knew you, and I concluded that you were a Christian."

"I was talking about angels on this earth. I don't believe there are any other kind."

"I'm sorry. I wish you were a Christian."

"Not a chance. I see I don't belong here, so I'll be leaving tomorrow. Since I won't see you again, I'll thank you now for saving my life, and when you see Mandy and Henry, thank them for me." He turned and walked stiffly away.

"I'm glad I did what I could for you," she called after him.

He did not answer, so she watched him go, then she turned toward Tom.

Tom smiled at her, and she felt as if her heart were standing on tiptoe and applauding for joy.

Chapter 32

*L*ucinda waited as Tom came to her. "I've been wondering who that man is and where you met him," he said, motioning the way Martin had gone.

"I found him on a battlefield and helped save his life. Now I'm glad he is gone."

"Me too. For awhile he had me worried. Want to walk home with me and Tad?"

"I'd love to. Wait until I tell Mama and Papa."

Just then Tad came from the church with Mary walking shyly at his side. "Lucinda, if you'll walk home with us, Mary's parents say that she can too," he said.

"I've already told Tom that I would."

"Good. I told Mary's parents that we'd bring her home on our way," he explained.

"Oh, Mary, I'm glad you're going to walk with us," Lucinda exclaimed, putting her arm around her.

"I appreciate Tad asking me," she said, smiling happily.

"Mama and Papa must be visiting with someone. I'll run in and tell them," Lucinda said.

"We'll walk in front," Tad told Lucinda when she returned. Then he and Mary led the way from the churchyard. Tom offered his arm to Lucinda. She placed her hand gently on his arm, and they fell in step behind Tad and Mary. Lucinda noticed that Tom was barely limping on his artificial leg and realized she had almost forgotten that he had lost a leg.

"Let's walk slow so they will get ahead," Tom said softly. "I want us to talk without them hearing."

"All right, Tom," she answered gently as they slowed their pace.

For a few minutes they walked in silence along the road that was illuminated by the light of a full moon. Lucinda watched Tad and Mary walking ahead of them, and noticed that their heads were bowed and that they appeared to be talking intimately.

The night suddenly darkened, and she looked up and saw that a small, white cloud had moved across the moon. The edges of the cloud were silvered by the moon. The cloud passed, and the full light of the moon again fell upon them.

Tom pulled her to a stop, and she looked up at him.

The moonlight bathed her face and cast silver highlights in the stubborn strands of her hair that would never stay tucked beneath her bonnet.

"You're so beautiful in the moonlight, you take my breath away," he whispered.

"Then, I guess I'm not pretty in the daytime," she teased.

"You're beautiful anytime, Cindy."

It was the first time he had called her Cindy, and she liked him calling her that.

"I suppose you say that to all the girls."

"Stop teasing me, Cindy. I'm dead serious. You are the only girl in my life. There will never be another one, but when I heard you telling Martin why you would not sit with him, I thought I didn't have a chance."

She paused and looked up at him with parted lips.

He looked back at her, stifling the desire to take her in his arms.

"Tom, I've finally come to my senses. I've decided

I'd like to be your sweetheart if you still want me to."

"You know I want you to, Cindy! I want you for a sweetheart more than anything in the world." He took her hand in his and held it. "Lucinda . . . "

Moonbeams were dancing in her eyes, and her lips were parted in a smile as she looked up at him.

"We've lost too much time already," Tom said huskily. "Cindy, will you marry me?"

"Oh, Tom, I didn't expect you to ask so soon, but I've already decided that I want to marry you. Only—"

"Only what, Cindy?" he asked when she paused.

"Only I can't . . . at least not right away."

"Cindy, why do you say that? What is to keep us from getting married now?"

"Tom—" She looked sadly up at him. "Tom, I can't leave Mama and Papa now, not until their health improves. Papa has been so sick for so long, and he's just lately started getting better. And Mama is far from well. . . . there's so much work . . . Mama and Tad can't possibly do it all."

"I understand, Cindy, but that's no reason why we can't be engaged. We'll get married later, after your parents are better."

"Let's wait, Tom. Papa worries a lot. If he knows that I have promised to marry you, he'll believe that I will soon leave home, and that could make him worse." She stood on tiptoes and kissed him lightly on the lips.

"You sweet, impulsive, unpredictable girl," he exclaimed. "Let me hold you, and I'll kiss you properly."

"Should I, Tom? We're not even engaged!"

"One kiss won't hurt you," he said, and he took her in his arms and held her gently and kissed her tenderly. Then he released her.

"Oh Tom, Tom, what is to become of us?" she sighed.

"I'll tell you what is going to become of us. When your father and your mother are better, we're going to get married, and you're going to come and live with me and share my life and my ministry."

"Oh, Tom, that sounds so wonderful, but I can't see that far ahead."

At that point they became aware that Tad and Mary had turned and were coming toward them.

"Tad and I have something to tell you," Mary cried joyfully as they drew near.

"Hurry and tell me," Lucinda cried, half hoping, half believing, yet half doubting that Tad had declared his love to Mary.

"Cindy, Tad has asked me to marry him," Mary declared joyfully.

"And she has agreed," Tad enjoined.

"Would you believe that I proposed to Cindy and she turned me down?" Tom asked sadly.

"But why, Cindy?" Mary cried. "Surely you love Tom. I saw the way you looked at him tonight."

"I do love him, Mary, but I can't leave Mama and Papa with all the work to do and them both sick."

"You silly girl! You can too. After Tad and I are married, he says we'll live at the homeplace for a year or two. So I'll do for your mama and papa just like I'd do for my own."

"But you will move away in time," Lucinda objected.

"Not far away, Cindy," Tad interrupted. "We'll build a house nearby on the farm."

"That's too much to expect of Mary," Lucinda objected.

"It is not. I'm young and strong, and I'll love helping with the work," Mary declared.

Mary turned suddenly to Tom. "Tom, Lucinda will marry you. I'll see that she does," she exclaimed.

Lucinda was opened-mouthed with surprise and chagrin when Tom turned to her.

"What do you say to that, Cindy?" he asked.

"I—I don't—don't have anything to say. She's already said it for me," she stammered.

"Is that supposed to mean yes?"

"Yes it is. She'll marry you the same day I marry Tad," Mary gushed.

"That means we'll have a double wedding," Tom agreed.

"Wait, you all," Lucinda cried, stamping her foot in mock anger. "Don't I have anything to say about my own wedding?"

"You had your chance and messed it up, so I'm deciding for you," Mary laughed.

"Now, wait just a minute, future sister-in-law. I can make my own arrangements, and I don't think I like you trying to do it for me." She laughed in spite of her pretended anger.

"Mary, if you don't mind, I'd like to have a word with Cindy," Tom said. "Cindy, are you going to marry me or not?"

"Yes, Tom. I'll marry you if Mama and Papa will agree to accept Mary as a daughter in my place."

"Then let's go home and ask them," Tom insisted.

"Let's stop by Mary's house first, like we promised," Tad responded. "Her family should be home by now, so I'll go in ask her parents if I can marry her. If they agree, we'll all go to our house together, and Mary and I will tell Mama and Papa the good news."

"Then I'll ask for Lucinda," Tom said happily.

"And I'll tell them how we plan to work things out," Mary offered.

"Lucinda and I will wait outside while you and Mary talk with her folks," Tom said when they reached the gate at Mary's house.

"It won't take long. My family will be glad to get rid of me," Mary bantered.

"We'll go in and see what happens," Tad teased.

"Tom, how will we live while you're in school," Lucinda asked when Tad and Mary had gone inside.

"I haven't had a chance to tell you, but I've been called to pastor a church near Knoxville. The salary is not large, but they have a parsonage we can live in, and the pay will be enough to buy necessities."

"But will you have to drop out of school after we marry?"

"I said the church was near Knoxville. I can pastor it and still go to school."

"Tom, I'm glad. I'll love sacrificing with you while you finish your education."

Just then Tad and Mary returned, smiling happily.

"I told you they'd be glad to get rid of me," Mary said. "Mama told me she's glad I'm marrying a man with one arm because he can't whip me very hard."

"I don't believe a word of that," Lucinda gasped.

"The part is true about them letting me marry her," Tad laughed. "Let's go home and tell Mama and Papa. Then Tom and Lucinda can talk with them."

Lucinda burst into the house ahead of the others when they got home. "Mama, Papa, Tad and Mary have something to tell you," she exclaimed.

"Cindy, if you don't mind, Tad will make our announcement," Mary cried as they all crowded through the door.

"What is all the commotion about?" Nancy asked as she and Lewis came into the hall.

"Mama and Papa, I have asked Mary to marry me, and she has agreed," Tad exclaimed.

"Oh, Tad, I'm glad. I'll love having Mary as a second daughter." She put her arm around the girl.

"I'm glad for you both. Tad will make you a good husband, Mary," Lewis said.

"I have always thought that Mary was a wonderful girl, but I don't know how I'm going to cope with her and Cindy both," Nancy laughed.

"You won't have to," Mary gushed, then paused. "Tom, you and Cindy better tell them," she ended, blushing profusely.

Tom stood up and looked first at Lewis and then at Nancy.

"Mr. and Mrs. Perry, this not easy for me, but I want to ask for your daughter's hand in marriage," he said.

Nancy looked startled, but Lewis looked relieved.

"I have asked her to marry me and she has accepted," Tom continued.

"And if you think you can't get along without Cindy, I'm young and strong, and I can work as hard as she can," Mary said.

"I wasn't thinking of that," Nancy defended.

"Tom, Lucinda is an unusual girl, but I've never met a man I'd rather for her to marry than you," Lewis told him.

"Cindy, are you sure you love Tom enough to marry him?" Nancy asked.

"Oh, yes, Mama. I'm sure. I know I can never marry any one else."

"Then I give you my blessings, my children," Nancy said.

Lewis arose and put his hand on Tom's shoulder. "Tom, I'm glad to welcome you to the family. I give you my daughter, Lucinda, but I warn you that she's a handful to handle."

"Papa! He'll think I'm awful," Lucinda cried. Then she kissed her father on the cheek.

Chapter 33

*T*hat night at church, Lewis proudly sat in the pew with his family and his daughter-in-law and son-in-law to be. Mary's family sat at the other end of the pew.

Lewis watched as people crowded into the church and filled every pew and every available standing place. He looked out the nearest window and saw people crowded around it, looking into the church. Many others were standing in the church yard, waiting in the gathering darkness for the service to start.

"I see Henry and Mandy out there, and they've brought some of their friends. I'm glad they've come," Lucinda exclaimed as she also looked out the window.

"There's more people in the churchyard than there is in here," Lewis said softly.

"Looks like we ought to move the meeting outside if the weather stays good," Tad whispered.

"Or to Squire Bottoms' barn. He's got the biggest barn in the county, and there's a good road to it. Think I'll mention it to the squire and Brother Western after the service."

The service soon began and continued with tremendous effect, as had the previous services. When Evangelist Raney gave the invitation, Lewis was one of the first to go forward and kneel at the rapidly filling altar. Nancy followed him down the aisle and knelt beside him.

"I'd go and kneel with Papa if there was room," Lucinda whispered to Tom.

"So would I," Tom mouthed in return.

Tad smiled happily, and Mary wept silently.

"I never realized that I could feel so happy and free," Lewis said to Nancy on the way home in the buggy after the service.

"I feel the same way, Lewis, and it's so good to know that other people are getting right with the Lord and that they are forgiving each other after all the hard feelings they've had. At last I feel like I have friends again."

"About everybody we know except the Taylors have gone to the altar since the meetin' started," Lewis said.

"I saw them leave tonight without speaking to anybody," Nancy replied. "I'd like to talk with them, but I'm almost afraid to."

"They're not easy people to talk to. Maybe Lucinda can talk to Verna, but I don't know. She's an odd sort of girl," Lewis said.

"I saw you talking to Squire Bottoms and Brother Western. What did they say about moving the meeting?"

"They're for it. Brother Western is goin' to talk with Brother Raney, and, if it's all right with him, Brother Western will make an announcement tomorrow night that we're goin' to move the meetin'."

Three nights later, after men had cleared the farm machinery from Squire Bottoms' barn and had built rough lumber benches for the people to sit on, they moved the meeting. The first night the crowd overflowed the barn, so they opened the wide, double doors so people could congregate outside and still see and hear.

In the following nights, the crowds grew even larger, with people coming from surrounding communities and from nearby towns. Many stayed and camped in the open fields and along the road. So, at Evangelist Raney's suggestion, they started having services in the barn and in the fields both day and night.

Evangelist Raney and Brother Western could not possibly minister to all who came, so Tom wrote a letter to his school and another one to his church, telling them that he would be late returning because of the revival. Then he started preaching under some trees at the edge of the field. And Tad, though he did not feel called to preach, started holding services under a tree in a different part of the field. Other ministers came to help, and soon meetings were being conducted in several places, with preachers standing on stumps and on rocks to preach so they could be seen above the heads of the people.

There were often tears of repentance and frequent shouts of joy, both by day and night, as people got right with God. There was no way to count all who came to the altars, but those involved in the meetings knew that they were experiencing a time of real revival. The revival brought the healing of old wounds and the ending of grudges that otherwise would have lasted a generation.

After several days, Lucinda remembered that she had not seen the Taylors since the revival had been moved from the church. She mentioned it to her family at breakfast the next morning.

"I'll ride over there before the early services start this mornin', and see if any of them are sick or if something else is wrong," Tad said.

"If you don't mind, I'll go with you," Tom offered.

"I'll be glad to have you, Tom. It may take both of us to do anything with the Taylors," Tad replied.

Tad and Tom left after breakfast to go visit the Taylors, and they soon returned with the news that the Taylors were gone.

"The house and the barn were both empty. They've moved away," Tad announced.

"And they moved away without forgiving the people they were holding grudges against," Nancy said, looking troubled.

"What a shame that they let the revival pass them by," Lucinda remarked.

"They never did fit in. Maybe they've gone back north where they belong," Lewis suggested.

"Lewis you shouldn't say that," Nancy reproved.

"We can pray for them," Tad suggested. "God can touch them up north as well as He can here."

Even though the revival was conducted after crops had been laid-by and before the beginning of harvest, the days and nights were still extremely busy. For, in addition to attending the meetings, the stock had to be fed, the cows milked, and the house kept in order. Tad and Mary and Tom and Lucinda did their part, but they still found time to plan for the future.

Tom decided that he should return to Knoxville to preach in his church. While he was there, he would ask the people of his church to help clean and furnish the parsonage. Then he would return to Kentucky to marry Lucinda. After they were married, they would return to Knoxville and he would resume his duties as pastor and continue with his studies in Bible school.

Lucinda did not want to be parted from Tom, even for a day, but she agreed for him to go, after making him to promise to return at the earliest possible moment.

"While you're gone, we'll work our fingers to the bone, getting everything ready for the wedding," Lucinda finally said.

"Tad and I will help her. We'll get everything ready for the prettiest double wedding this county's ever seen," Mary declared.

"Don't I have anything to say about my own wedding?" Lucinda teased.

"Of course you do," Mary scolded in mock anger. "I was just repeating what you told me last night."

They all laughed together.

At the end of the week, the revival closed so Evangelist Raney could go back to Tennessee to keep an appointment in another church. Tom was greatly pleased that he could travel to Tennessee on the stagecoach with him.

After his first Sunday in Knoxville, Tom wrote Lucinda that the people of his church were excited that he was getting married, and they were working hard to get the parsonage ready for his bride. He would have everything in order in time to return to Perryville on the stagecoach the last Tuesday afternoon in August.

When that day came for Tom to return, Tad went to Perryville in the buggy to meet Tom. He was waiting at the stagecoach office when Tom arrived.

"Cindy wants to see you so bad she's fit to be tied, but she didn't come to meet you because she and Mary are up to their ears with fixings and plannin' for the weddin'," he greeted as Tom emerged from the coach.

"Putting it mildly, I'm right anxious to see her," Tom returned. "How is everybody? Are Mr. and Mrs. Perry in good health?"

"Mama is doin' great, and you won't believe the change in Papa. He's like a new man."

"I'm glad. I never thought he'd be well again," Tom exclaimed.

"I think his sickness was caused by all the bitterness that was festerin' in him."

"Could be. How is Cindy takin' all the excitement?" Tom asked as he got his bag from the baggage handler.

"You know Cindy. She's higher than a kite," Tad replied as they started to the buggy.

"And how is Mary?"

"Tom, she's the sweetest woman that ever lived. I

can't thank the Lord enough for givin' her to me."

"I could debate the sweetness part with you, but I'm glad the Lord has given Mary to you."

Lucinda and Mary were standing at the gate when Tad and Tom arrived.

Tad stopped the buggy and wrapped the reins around the dashboard and tied them to hold the mare. Then he and Tom got out of the buggy and hurried to the gate to meet the girls.

"Lucinda!" Tom exclaimed, looking her over from head to toe. "You're always beautiful, always dressed pretty, and always smilin'. I don't know how you manage it."

"Oh, Tom! Tom! I thought you'd never get here."

Tom took her hands in his, then kissed her on the forehead. "I'll do better when we are alone," he told her. Then he turned to Mary.

"Mary it's good to see you lookin' so happy. You are as pretty as a flower. I can see that bein' engaged to Tad has been good for you."

"Tom, you flatterer," Mary responded.

"Are you coming in, Tom?" Nancy called from the doorway. "I'm dying to see you, and Lewis is too. He's upstairs changing from his work clothes, but he'll be down in a minute."

"I'll be there in a minute, my mother-to-be," Tom returned.

"Tom, we're going to have the biggest wedding ever," Lucinda said as they started to the house. "Brother Western announced it at church, so there's no telling who all will come."

"Now that people are no longer holding grudges, all our old friends will come," Mary contributed.

By noon the next day, the young people had the big front porch of the Perry home decorated with roses and greenery that the girls had gathered from the rosebushes and flower gardens of both their homes. Tad and Tom had fashioned an arch of wire and covered it with white roses and placed it on the porch in front of the entrance to the house, and the girls had placed potted red geraniums on both sides of each step leading up to the porch.

After lunch the girls went upstairs to dress for the wedding. Tad and Tom hurriedly carried every chair in the house to the front porch so the guests could be seated. Then they went to the downstairs bedroom to dress.

Jim and Nelly Crabtree soon arrived, expressing fear that it was going to rain. "On our way here, we saw dark clouds gathering in the west," she told Nancy.

"We'll just have to pray that it doesn't. Where are the boys?" Nancy asked as she led them to the parlor to be seated.

"They'll be here in a few minutes. They're walking through the fields," Nelly responded.

"I hear buggies coming down the lane, and Lewis is upstairs dressing. I'd better see if he can come and help hitch the horses as people arrive," Nancy exclaimed.

"I'll take care of that, so you don't need to bother Lewis," Jim Crabtree volunteered.

"Thank you, Jim. I know Lewis will appreciate it."

By the time Jim reached the yard gate, buggies and horseback riders were backed up on the lane to Mackville Pike.

It required more than half an hour for all the people to arrive, get out of the buggies and off the horses, and hitch the horses to the fence.

Nelly Crabtree came out on the porch to welcome old friends and neighbors as they arrived and to seat them until all the chairs were taken. After that, she apologetically told the guests they would have to stand. When there was no more room on the porch, people gathered under the big maple tree that was near the house.

Henry and Mandy walked across the fields. Arriving tired and short of breath, they paused back of the crowd that had gathered under the big maple.

Brother Western and his family arrived a few minutes before the wedding was to start, and he soon positioned himself before the arch of roses. Then Tom and Tad took their places beside him.

Mrs. Sanders started playing a love song on the piano that had been moved into the downstairs hall, and Lewis and Jim ascended the stairway to the upstairs hall. Moments later Lucinda and Mary, came from their dressing room to meet them. Lucinda placed her hand on her father's arm, and he started leading her slowly down the broad stairway. Mary, on her father's arm, followed close behind her. Those who were near the big front window looked in and watched.

At the foot of the stairs the fathers led their daughters across the hall to the front door and out on the porch. They stopped beneath the arch of roses, facing Brother Western. Then the fathers stepped aside, and Tom and Tad stepped into place beside Lucinda and Mary.

The girls were wearing white gowns and long white gloves. Lucinda's white veil covered her face and her red-gold hair, except for some frenzied strands that would not be controlled, and the knot, pinned at the back of her neck. She had pinned yellow roses on each side, behind her eyes. Mary had pinned red roses to her warm, brown hair. They contrasted beautifully with her white veil.

The men were both wearing dark blue suits, and they had red roses pinned to their lapels.

At that moment distant thunder rumbled in the west, and a sudden gust of wind swept the yard and wrestled in the branches of the trees.

"Oh no," Nancy moaned. "We'll have to move inside, and after all the work they've done on the porch."

Large, scattered drops of rain started pelting the roof

and the front steps and the edge of the porch. Those standing near the edge of the porch moved away from the rain, and the people under the tree moved closer to its trunk for shelter.

Then, as suddenly as it had started, the wind abated and the rain stopped falling. The sun broke through the clouds, and its rays bathed the yard and shined on the people.

Brother Western cast a look at the clouds, then he turned to the young couples and started the ceremony.

While the young couples were saying their vows, the clouds continued to move, and by the time the pastor pronounced Tom and Lucinda man and wife, then turned to Tad and Mary and pronounced them man and wife, heavy clouds had covered the sky from the battlefield to the horizon. Thunder continued to rumble for a moment, then fell silent. A moment later, as if projected on canvas, a rainbow appeared. It formed an arch across the cloud. The foot of the rainbow appeared to reach the ground, and the people started murmuring explanations of pleasure and amazement.

"Look," Tom exclaimed. "The rainbow means that judgment is passed. It's a good omen for our future, Cindy." He turned to her, and she looked at him with shining eyes.

"Surely the future is bright for our country and for us," Tad declared.

Tom put his arms around Lucinda, and they continued to look at the rainbow.

"The rainbow is the symbol of our future happiness," Lucinda breathed. Then Tom took her in his arms and kissed her.

"You can't get ahead of me, Tom," Tad said, and he put his arm around Mary and kissed her.

"We also claim the rainbow as our good omen," Mary said.

Mandy urged Henry from the shelter of the tree to the porch steps. "I prays dat all yo' young people will always be happy and dat your future will be bright and pretty like de rainbow," Mandy called to them.

Lucinda led Tom down the steps to where Henry and Mandy were standing.

"Mandy and Henry, I'm glad you came. I would have been greatly disappointed if you hadn't. Tom, these are good friends. They really stood by me when I needed them," she ended.

"I pray de good Lord will stand wid yo' boof and wid de other young people too," Henry said.

"Thank you Henry and Mandy," Tom said, and they went back to stand by Tad and Mary to receive the best wishes of other friends who were gathering around them.

Don't Miss These Great L. Walker Arnold Novels

L. Walker Arnold, a native of Kentucky, in the past few years has become a widely-read, greatly-loved inspirational author.

He has written seven novels in the past eight years. All of them have been well received by the reading public.

Hundreds of his readers order each of his new books long before they are off the press. Many have placed standing orders for every book he writes. Thousands have written to praise his books.

Mr. Arnold's readers write that they appreciate his ability to create strong characters, his unique powers of description, and the gripping, emotion-filled stories he writes.

Titles Listed in the Order Written

The Legend of Old Faithful, Hardcover	$14.99
Out of the Night, Hardcover	$15.99
Fathoms Deep, Hardcover	$13.99
Riverman, Softcover	$ 8.99
Riverman (Audio) read by author on cassette	$11.99
White Angel, Paperbound	$ 1.00
Sunshine Valley, Softcover	$ 8.99
Euroclydon, Softcover	$ 9.99
Lucinda of Perryville	$ 9.99

If L. Walker Arnold novels are not available at bookstores in your area, order from Arnold Publications.

Please include $2.00 postage and handling for one book, $3.00 for two books, $3.50 for three books, $4.00 for four books, and $4.50 for five books. We pay postage on orders over $50.00. Prices are subject to change without notice.

Arnold Publications
2440 Bethel Road
Nicholasville, KY 40356

Phone toll free 1-800-854-8571